Blood Of Fire

Book Two

of the

Blood Burden Series

Wenona Hulsey

ISBN: 0985730714

ISBN-13: 978-0-9857307-1-0

Dedication

To those who dare to live a dream.

"Obsessed by a fairy tale, we spend our lives
searching for a magic door and a lost kingdom of peace."

~Eugene O'Neill

ACKNOWLEDGMENTS

A day doesn't past that I'm not grateful for the support and love of my friends and family. My Dad, Step-Mom, Siblings, my children and husband all believed in me and without them I would have never made the leap into publishing.

A big thanks to Sarah Hicks and Rodney Shirley who have allowed me to pick their brains about everything police related throughout the Blood Burden Series. Thanks for helping me get my details correct. You've helped me more then you will ever know.

Also where would I be without my wonderful circle of author friend? Still stuck obsessing over chapter one! There are too many of you to name but my I.C. Author's know who they are. From beta reading, book covers, editing and most importantly, reminding me to laugh—You all are the best of the best.

I've been blessed with some of the most supportive readers a writer could ever ask for. I cherish each wonderful email and social network post that you all take the time to send me. Fans like you keep me moving forward so thank you.

The many adventures of

<u>The Blood Burden Series</u>

Blood Awakening-Novelette

A Warrior's Blood-Luke's Novelette

Burden of Blood-Novel

Blood of Fire-Novel

Chapter 1

Nicole stared out the airplane window while tapping her fingers on the arm-rest in a fast, steady rhythm. The other passengers were slowly filing in. Some struggled with carry-on luggage while others towed small, fussy children by the hand behind them. She glanced around, taking in the faces, and then leaned back into her seat to resume drumming. For the moment she was sure she hadn't been followed but that uneasy, on-edge feeling wouldn't stop tugging at her mind.

Her gaze settled on the early morning sky. She took in the vibrant oranges, soft pinks and deep purples coloring the horizon as the sun began its daily journey. Nicole was still amazed that no matter how bad things were in her life, or how downtrodden she felt, or how lost she was, that the world could continue on so beautifully, unscathed by her pain. Not that she really thought the world would stop for her, but it would be nice if the sky would pour down sheets of heavy rain hiding away the cheerful sun. It would be much more fitting to her current situation. Maybe then she would feel like Mother Earth was being sympathetic to her plight and could be her silent ally in the lonely world she had created for herself.

Her mind rolled back over the past few months as she wondered how things had gotten so out of control. One day she's the best cop her small Alabama town has ever seen then the next she's a fairy/warrior hybrid with her world completely upside down. All while falling in love with Luke, her partner in the police department, who also turned out to be an ancient warrior sent to protect and train her. In the end she had to turn her back on him and everyone she cared about; it was the only way to protect them. She had to keep Loch from using her loved ones in order to lure her to Ireland where he expected her to join him in some master scheme of his. Exactly what that was, well, she wasn't quite sure. Nor was she sure where she fit into his plans but she was positive it wasn't good for her or anyone else. Loch only cared about ridding the world of the fairy race and he didn't care who he had to step on or use. Not even Luke, his own flesh and blood, was held higher than Loch's obsession with putting the warriors on top.

The best solution she could see was to beat Loch at his own game by surprising him in Ireland and putting an end to him. The hardest part would be finding him; she didn't even know where to start looking for the ancient warrior who was planning to kill all of fae kind. Nicole also knew that if he found her first and she refused to help him that she would be killed. Her only option was to beat him at his own game.

The banging of the overhead luggage compartment above her seat snapped Nicole back into the moment. She turned her attention away from the rising sun and her depressing thoughts, as someone took the seat next to her.

"This must be your first time flying?"

Nicole found herself staring into the most beautiful pair of ice blue eyes she had ever seen in her life belonging to a face that was as equally heaven sent. The man that had just occupied the seat next to her had light blond hair that framed his face, reaching just below his broad jaw line in silky strands. Her gaze was drawn to an adorable dimple forming in his cheek as he gave her a one sided smile. "Yes," she finally stammered, "This is my first time." She lied thinking it was better for him to assume her anxiety was due to her fear of flying and not the fact that she was going into a viper filled snake pit blind and alone.

He laughed softly, "I figured so, since you seem determined to drum a hole in your armrest." He extended a hand towards her, "I'm Slade."

Nicole shook his hand and gave a small, nervous laugh before replying "Nicole." As she leaned back into her seat, she laced her fingers together to control her anxious energy. The last thing she wanted to do was draw attention to herself and acting as if she was about to have a nervous breakdown was a sure way to turn all eyes on her.

"So where are you heading?" Slade asked casually as he adjusted his seat.

She turned to look at him, this time paying more attention to all of him, and not just his cover model face. He was dressed in a dark suit that looked expensive, maybe Calvin Klein she surmised but then again she wasn't an expert on designer clothes. Underneath the tailored jacket was a perfectly pressed, white dress shirt and a black, silk tie. His shoes were gleaming like black onyx and his hands were smooth and looked too soft to belong to someone who did physical labor. His overall appearance was certainly alluring but something in his demeanor hinted at danger yet she couldn't pin down where the feeling was coming from.

"Ireland," she said giving him a weak smile as the memories of why she was traveling pushed to the front of her mind, "How about you?"

"Dublin, Ireland. I've been here on business for a while but Ireland is my home."

"Really? Your accent sounds American to me."

Slade shrugged, "I've been fortunate to travel all of my life. I've lived years in France, Germany, Africa and America but the place that always felt closest to my heart was Ireland. It's such a beautiful country with a rich history." He smiled at her showing dimples in both cheeks. "You'll love it there, I promise."

Nicole nodded as the pilot chimed in announcing the flight was about to depart. She quickly buckled herself in, hoping everyone would do the same so they could get off the ground. She knew there was a good chance Luke might try to stop her and she wasn't sure how long the prison of wind she had created would hold him.

Though her powers were great, she was still learning how to control them. She had actually been quite impressed with herself when she realized she was able to trap two powerful warriors and one fairy in her barrier of wind. But her pride in the discovery didn't ease the pain of leaving them there so she could fight this war alone. The memory of the hurt she saw in Luke's hazel eyes as she trapped him and then walked away was still in the forefront of her mind haunting her.

She turned her attention back out the window as she settled in for the long flight. The sight that met her eyes had her gasping. Luke stood at the edge of the runway, his dark blond hair disheveled and his black t-shirt torn from the night's battle, staring back at her. She wasn't sure how he managed to get so close without her sensing him. Maybe she had been too distracted to notice the pull she normally felt when a warrior was near. Her heart started to beat painfully fast as she stared into his stone set face. Dried blood was still streaked across his tanned cheek but the cut that was there was now healed. She wished all wounds healed so easily. She wanted to run to him and away from him at the same time. The very sight of him was ripping her apart.

The plane began down the runway, moving away from her love as he stood, watching her go. She leaned closer to the window, desperately reaching out to his mind, wanting to hear what was going on inside his head. She wanted to tell him this wasn't farewell forever but she couldn't reach his thoughts. She was being blocked from connecting with his mind. *Blocked or ignored*, she wondered. *Punished,* she thought, her heart began to break as realization set in. Luke didn't want her to hear him; he was saying goodbye in the most painful way he possibly could...silence.

She closed her eyes, hoping to trap the tears fighting to escape as the plane took to the sky, leaving Alabama and everyone she loved behind. For the first time in her life she was truly alone.

~**~**

Nicole ran water into her hands and splashed the cold liquid across her face, trying to clear away dirty film that was covering her skin from the long flight. She stared at her reflection in the mirror; the dingy florescent lights didn't help make the dark rings under her ghostly blue eyes look better as she dabbed her face dry with a paper towel. She didn't get much sleep on the flights because she kept trying to figure out what her next step should be but it was ultimately pointless. She still didn't have a clue where to begin. This was the first time she had ever been out of the south, let alone flying to a country that she scarcely knew anything about. Unless eating cereal with a little leprechaun on the box counts as research there was little locked away in her mind that could help her here.

After quickly combing her fingers through her tangled mass of long, brown curls, she walked back out to the bustling airport and made her way to a rack of tourist brochures. She picked up one and began searching the pages.

"I've got to find somewhere to sleep and something good to eat. I feel like a bum," she mumbled to herself as she scanned the pages. While searching for accommodations a scream rang out in the distance followed by the sound of gunshots. Her body tensed and her police officer instincts kicked in as she scanned the airport for the shooter among the swarm of running people. Just as she began to reach out with her mind to find her target, another gunshot rang out. Nicole found herself being pressed to the floor and covered by a hard, masculine body.

"Damn it woman, you're either very brave or very stupid," Slade whispered in her ear as he used his body to shield hers.

Nicole ignored the man hovering over her and tried again to use her powers. She reached out to the shooter's mind but there was nothing. Not a whisper returned to her, not an image of a thought or a twinge of the gunman's emotions even though she knew he was still out there. The crowd in the airport was in hysterics so someone had to be causing the violence. She frantically reached out her powers trying to touch anyone's mind, not just the gunman's. She didn't care who, she needed to hear a thought, any thought, so she would know her power was still working. Just a small taste to confirm nothing had changed since she left Alabama.

Panic filled her as a lump formed in her throat. Nothing returned to her. Not even the tainted thoughts she had heard for years when her powers first emerged. Her mind started to race back to the last time she had heard anything. She had tried and failed with Luke before her plane took to the sky but the last time it had worked was when she had wrapped her friends in a chamber of wind to keep them from following her. *Did I lose my powers?* She wondered as Slade moved off her and offered her his hand.

"Are you alright?" he asked softly.

Nicole nodded as she tried to push away the anxiety that was begging her to test more of her powers. "Yes, thank you. What happened?"

Slade shrugged, "I'm not sure but it looks like security has it under control now." He pointed toward a swarm of uniformed men escorting someone out a door.

"What a welcome to Ireland." Nicole laughed as she straightened her wrinkled shirt. "Guess I better get moving. Thanks again Slade, and it was nice meeting you," she offered him a handshake.

Slade took her outstretched hand and pulled it to his lips, kissing it softly before letting go. "I was wondering, since we are going the same way and all, if you would allow me to take you to your hotel?" Slade asked giving her a small, one sided smile as he took in her stunned face.

"Oh, that's very nice of you Slade but I couldn't ask you to do that."

"It's no trouble at all, I promise. So, where are you staying?"

Nicole bit her bottom lip as she debated on what to tell him. She was a bit embarrassed, she had nowhere to stay yet and she didn't know how to explain the sudden trip without it being obvious that she had left the United States in a hurry.

"Well, I'm a spontaneous kind of girl. I was hoping one of the hotels would jump off the brochure and I would take a taxi to it," She waved the pamphlet out in front of him to validate her story.

"Wow, I wish I could be a little more daring like that," he smiled, "But to be honest, I had some ulterior motives in offering to drive you to your hotel..."

Nicole's eyes got wide with shock and her cheeks flushed, "Really. Well, I'm afraid I must decline your offer." Pulling her backpack up from where it leaned against her legs, she slung it over her shoulder and turned to walk away.

"Oh God, no...That's not what I meant," Slade stammered as he stopped her escape by gently grabbing her elbow. "That came out completely wrong," he continued, "See, I was wondering if you had plans tonight?"

Nicole crossed her arms over her chest to make it clear that she wasn't up for any games. She wasn't *that* type of girl and she was by no means looking to play the dating game with Fabio's hotter brother. The nine plus hours of plane hopping, layovers, and the need for a hot shower wasn't helping her mood either.

"I'm expected at a cocktail party tonight and I was

hoping that you would come with me. I had a friend accompanying me but she just canceled," his eyes pleaded with her as he waited for her answer. "I can call ahead and have you a room booked at the hotel where I'm staying," he offered in hopes it would sweeten his proposal.

Nicole let her bag drop down to her elbow as she weighed her options: get lost in a city that she had never been in or go with the super hunky guy who could act as her guide and ultimately keep her from sleeping on a park bench somewhere... She sighed deeply as she slid her arms back through the straps of her backpack, "Whose party are we going to?"

Slade smiled broadly at her, "Let me get that for you." Mr. Handsome took the bag from her shoulders and placed his hand on her lower back to guide her towards the exit.

"Where's your luggage?" Nichole asked as they walked out the airport doors and among the swarm of travelers scrambling to hail a taxi. Chatter about the shooting was loud and frantic. Nicole overheard one woman saying it was an attempted robbery gone bad. She had to pull her attention from the chatter that her police side wanted to cling to and focus on the changes around her. She was taken aback by the softness of the air in her lungs. The thick humidity that Nicole had always known from Alabama's summers didn't exist here. It was pleasantly warm and felt more like spring. Nothing at all like the smothering August heat she had left back home.

"My driver has already put them in the car," he motioned towards a sleek, black limousine sitting next to the curb. The driver, a large muscular man who had a deeply lined, stone face, stood holding the door open.

Nicole's police training kicked into gear as she

studied the man's strong demeanor. "He looks military to me. A man doesn't get a cold look like that without seeing some hard things," she whispered to Slade as they walked towards the waiting car.

Slade nodded with a mix of surprise and admiration playing across his face, "You are a very observant woman, Nicole." He handed her bag off to the driver then offered her his hand so he could help her into the limo.

She took his hand politely and ducked inside the car. Slade sat across from her with a smirk on his face, "So tell me what you do for a living?" He put up his hand to stop her from answering. "Wait, let me guess. I'm pretty good at reading people too," he leaned back, rubbing his chin as he studied her face. "You are either government or law enforcement. I'm willing to bet money that you're a police officer."

She smiled softly as she thought of the best way to answer, "Let's just say that I don't know who or what I am anymore. I'm on a path of discovery in a far-away land," Nicole's smile broadened as she thought about the underlying truth behind her explanation.

"I change my answer...you're a hippie," he chuckled as the car began to move. "Fine, I'll give you the self-discovery answer but there has to be some truth to my guess. I mean, you did peg Claude in less than ten seconds. He's ex-military, of sorts, and one hell of a bodyguard."

"Of sorts?" Nicole's curiosity was thick in her voice, "Are we talking IRA?"

Slade smiled, "You're changing the subject. Fine," he shrugged, "I won't pry... I was just curious."

Nicole chuckled, "Okay, you're correct. I'm a police officer, well, *was* a police officer but things have changed and now I'm here." Nicole looked out the window at the passing buildings and changing scenery, it was all so different from her home town. All the buildings stood five stories tall with bricks in unusual shades of red, orange and yellow catching her eyes. Various statues dotted the open spaces; each one telling of its own moment in time with a frozen stare. After a few moments a sly grin crept across her lips, "So would you say Claude wears a large t-shirt?"

Slade's brow furrowed in confusion as he studied Nicole's face, "I guess so, why?"

"I'm thinking a Megadeth t-shirt would be the perfect gift for him," she smirked, "I hear they are the IRA's favorite band."

"You're as smart as you are beautiful," he winked as he complimented her. "I like that in a woman."

Nicole's smile fell from her face as she turned her attention back to the green hills in the distance. Her mind began to drift back to the day she and Luke had a similar conversation while sitting at her dad's kitchen table. Her heart ached to hear his voice again, to smell his woodsy scent and to feel his lips pressed against her skin. But she had released him of his oath. By doing this, she set him free of the tie that bound him as her warrior. Luke had given his word to her grandmother, Titania, Queen of the fae to protect her blood line with his life. Nicole was his to protect but she turned her back on him.

She knew the full ramifications of releasing Luke from his oath and leaving when she last saw him on the runway and he had blocked her from his mind. *But perhaps he wasn't blocking me*, Nicole argued with herself, after all she couldn't hear anyone's thoughts in the airport earlier either. *I can't blame him. I wouldn't want to be mixed up in this bull shit if someone had given me a way out*, she thought as she forced her bubbling emotions to ebb back to the recesses of her heart.

Chapter 2

Luke's arms covered in goose bumps as the sweat cooled his skin. A copper taste lingered in his mouth even though his split lip had healed moments after the impact of Ronald's punch. Everything had happened so fast but yet so slow at the same time. First he was squaring off with Ronald, then suddenly, the tables turned when Kat was shot. Seeing your best friend's life slowly draining away would be enough to make anyone turn hard but he never expected that to happen with Nicole.

Turning on his heels, Luke bounded back into the woods surrounding the airport. The image of Nicole's face staring out the airplane window was seared into his mind as he moved with inhuman speed, gracefully skirting trees and leaping ravines without as much of a thought. He had to return to Nicole's home quickly so he and Rhys could decide what to do now. *I can't let her face Loch alone*, he thought. He stopped in his tracks as his thoughts started to consume him. His body rippled with anger and forced him to start pacing; dead leaves crunching beneath his shoes with each step. "She's so damn stubborn," he growled. "It may get her killed this time and it's my fault for letting her go!" He punched a giant oak with all the power he had left in him. The tree splintered from the impact and a deep indent remained when he pulled his fist away. He let out a thunderous scream.

"Do you feel better now?"

Luke shook out his throbbing fist, but not from the pain, he was too angry to feel pain. He could tell he had broken most of the bones in his hand but he knew his warrior body was working to heal the damage by the tingling sensation that pulsed through him. After he was satisfied that the bones had realigned and he could move his fingers again he turned to face the voice, "Much. What are you doing here?"

Sage snorted and shook her head, causing her short, black bobbed hair to shift revealing her pointed ear. "Did you think I was going to let you handle all of this alone? Please..." She trailed on as she rolled her eyes.

"Sage, I'm not in the mood for your bull. You did your part and I'm grateful to you but now, you're just in my way."

"*Oh*, the 'big bad warrior' doesn't need the 'cute little fairy' anymore," she purred. "To...damn...bad," Sage poked Luke in the chest with a black fingernail as she said drew out each word. "You're not the only one with a stake in how this turns out, Luke."

Luke stared down at the petite fae adorned in a long black dress with silver corset and wearing a studded dog collar around her neck. She was as far away from the typical image of fairies you heard about in stories growing up as you could ever get. But in Luke's opinion she had proven herself loyal to Nicole and that's what mattered most. He let out a deep sigh and ran his hand through his disheveled hair, "Fine."

He started moving forward again but not before seeing Sage's bright red lips turn up into a cocky smile. She loves to win.

~*~**

"Where the *hell* is my daughter, Luke?" The shouting came from James, Nicole's father, as he broke loose from Kat's grasp and bounded off the front porch of his country home toward Luke with surprising speed. "Why did you let her leave? You know they want her dead and you just let her waltz away just as pretty as you please," the elderly man's body was shaking with anger but his eyes were wide with shock and worry.

"I'm sorry, James. Your daughter is too strong for her own good. She was already on a plane before we could break the barrier she trapped us in." Luke stopped in front of James ready for anything he could throw at him. He owed that much to her dad. He knew he had failed everyone, including himself.

"James, it's not his fault. We both know how Nicole is," Kat looped her arm into James' and began guiding him back toward his house. "She thinks this will protect us and she didn't give anyone a chance to talk her out of it."

"Don't worry, we're going ta get da princess back James." Rhys had appeared to stand beside Luke, still dirty and smelling of smoke from the night's battle. His face was hard and determined but without any sign of his normal, arrogant demeanor showing.

"And how do you plan on doing that?" James

turned to face Luke and Rhys, pulling his arm away from Kat. "Just how are you going to save her from a man who is more powerful then all of you combined," he spat, pointing his finger between Luke, Rhys and Sage. "You can't even save her from herself," his voice choked off into a whisper.

"I will make this right, I swear it." Luke looked at Sage and Rhys then started walking to the pasture behind the house.

"Where are you going?" asked Kat.

"To save Nicole," Sage rolled her eyes at having to answer such an obvious question.

Kat ran up to the group and fell into step, "Not without me."

Everyone stopped as Sage let out a loud groan. Luke and Rhys turned on Kat who was standing with her hand on her hip. "Bloody hell woman, we won't be baba sitting ya so get your arse back ta da house," said Rhys stepping in front of her and waving an arm in the direction of James' house.

Kat pulled her long black hair back behind her and in one smooth motion tied it into a loose bun at the base of her head then smiled, "Good thing I don't take orders from male chauvinistic pigs in skirts."

Sage let out a small laugh, "Oh, I like you." She looped her arm through Kat's and moved forward without the guys. Anyone who was game for giving a warrior a hard time instantly had Sage's respect.

Luke shook his head and reluctantly started moving forward again with Kat now part of the group.

"Ummm...Not to be the bearer of bad news or anything but the cars are parked in the driveway not the pasture. I'm not walking all the way to the airport."

"Stop ye whining. Ye wanted to tag along kitten."

"It's Kat not Kitten," snapped Kat.

"And this," Rhys swept a hand across the lower half of his body, "Tis a kilt not a skirt."

"Will you two lay off already? We're almost there." Luke turned into a thicket of trees when they reached the far side of the pasture. He ducked below the low hanging branches then disappeared into the trees.

Kat stood staring after Luke and Sage with a twist of disgust to her lips, "But there are ticks and snakes in there."

Rhys gave her a pat on the butt as he strolled past making her squeal and spin around while holding her rear. She glared at him with wide eyes as he turned back to look at her, "Ah Luv, ya can't let a wee bug keep ye from da Princess."

Luke was at his limit with the game he could see building between Rhys and Kat. Kat may not see it yet but Luke had seen this game play out in Rhys' favor many times before and it would only be a distraction for Rhys. Luke spun around to face the two who were glaring at each other as they crossed the tree line, "Listen, we aren't thinking clearly. We can't leave James unprotected."

Sage caught onto where Luke was going fast. "Nicole would be pissed at us if we let something happen to her dad." She stepped to Luke's side crossing her hands across her chest.

"How about if Sage and I go to Ireland and you and Rhys looked out for James? I think that would be the best protection for everyone." Luke placed his hand on Kat's shoulder as he talked. "Nicole would never forgive us if we just left him here alone."

Kat eyed Luke suspiciously, "Are you just trying to get rid of me?"

"No...I wouldn't do that," Luke lied. He didn't need Kat tagging along and distracting Rhys from the job. It was best to leave them both behind. It would be safest for everyone.

"My brother is right. I'll stay with you and James until I'm summoned." Rhys nodded toward Luke as he guided Kat back toward the pasture.

"What? Like I need you to protect me? I don't think so." Kat argued but didn't resist following Rhys out of the woods.

Luke got the feeling that Kat was relieved to not have to go. He didn't doubt that she loved Nicole and wanted to help but she had been through so much in the past two days. He was sure if it wasn't for Nicole's healing touch Kat would be curled up in a hospital right now if she had managed to hang on to a thin thread of life when she was shot. Luke turned his attention back to Sage, "Let's go."

Chapter 3

Nicole was in awe as she stepped out of the limo. The hotel was amazing, with its large towers and gleaming windows. It was just like a modern day castle had been set down in the middle of the Garden of Eden. Her eyes danced across the vision of an artist's dream as she took in all of the vibrant reds, blues, pinks and greens in the landscape. She recognized giant azalea bushes, white roses and royal blue iris's but there was still so many flowers and trees that were new to her.

"So glad to see you back, sir," said a tall, slim man in a blue suit as he motioned a young bell-hop towards the trunk. "Your room is ready, exactly as you asked."

"And have the spa appointments been arranged?" Slade asked.

"Yes sir, everything is in order."

"That's wonderful, thank you," Slade offered his arm to Nicole as they made their way into the hotel. She wrapped her hand into the crook of his arm and fell into step with him.

An elaborate chandelier glistened in the center of the lobby immediately drawing Nicole's eye's up into the dome shaped-ceiling high above. Each crystal shimmered like a diamond casting reflection's against the walls and down onto the floor. Slade led her past the lobby and down a long hallway. "This is a beautiful hotel." Nicole chatted as she let Slade guide her along.

"It is my favorite of all the hotels in Ireland. It has a kind of story-book quality to it like it was pulled from the history and fables of Ireland by someone who lived in those worlds hundreds of years ago."

Within minutes they were entering a room the size of an apartment filled with lush, tan carpet. A large, cream-colored leather sofa and chair were centered in the room and came with beautiful, ornately carved side tables and there was a matching desk in the corner. Slade walked to the far side of the room and opened two French doors revealing another room.

"This will be your room, Nicole." He pointed back across the room to another identical set of French doors, "That will be my room. Both have their own bathrooms so you won't have to deal with me in your space."

Nicole looked around uneasily as she twirled her finger around a curl, "I don't mind getting my own room, Slade. I mean, you barely know me. I can't just let you pay for all of this just so I have my privacy."

Slade smiled, "It's no problem at all, plus it will make things easier for when I pick you up later." He walked to the table near the door, picked up a paper and then turned back to Nicole. "Here. I hope you don't mind but I set up a few spa treatments to help you get over the long flight. I've some business to attend to but I'll be back in time to pick you up." He handed her the paper then walked back to the door.

Nicole glanced down at the list of treatments she would be receiving then back up at Slade's beaming face. "Ummm....Thank you, but I can't accept all of this Slade."

"You and your Alabama girl pride," he rolled his eyes. "This is my hotel so I'm free to use anything I want and since you're my guest you will receive the best," he winked at her as he backed out of the door. "Oh and if you need me just have me paged. I won't be far," he shut the door behind him.

Nicole sat down heavily into the oversized leather chair, "Great, this is getting me nowhere. I'm surrounded by luxury with Mr. Money bags when I should be figuring out what to do next." she sighed. *I need somewhere private to test my powers*, she thought. *I also need to find Loch but how? I don't know enough about him do I?* She rubbed her temples as she tried to make a mental list of what she did know: *He wanted me to come to Ireland, he is very damn old, and that most likely means he's powerful.*

She sat up straight in the chair as her mind worked toward a growing light of an idea. *Powerful means he has money. After all, he sent a jet to retrieve me from Alabama so that means he has lots of money and he must run in high class circles. Circles that could be at this cocktail party tonight*. She smiled as she looked at the list she had dropped onto the coffee table. "Guess having a massage, manicure, pedicure, and my hair and makeup done is all part of the job today."

~*~**

Nicole lay face down as the massage therapist kneaded the knots in her back. She had to admit this was a wonderful treat. She sat through the manicure and pedicure, which she did enjoy but having her legs, along with other places she didn't plan on anyone seeing, get waxed was a horrifying experience. There were many moments when she thought of punching the smug little woman who she suspected to be enjoying her whimpers each time she ripped another sticky strip off her skin. Nicole swore she saw the esthetician smirk with each "yip" out of her mouth.

She exhaled deeply as the woman's fingers worked their magic on her tight muscles. She began to relax, taking in the smell of lavender incense and the sound of water flowing from a small fountain in the corner of the room. She closed her eyes and let her mind drift without purpose. Within seconds a vision started to form. It was a haze at best but it was the first sign she had gotten from her silent powers since leaving home so she grabbed onto the image tightly.

Nicole tried to focus the vision but it remained fuzzy and dark, it reminded her of looking through a dirty window at dusk. She could see the silhouette of a man with his back to her. He was standing behind a desk with a cell phone pressed against his ear. His dark hair and broad frame didn't look familiar but the power that radiated from him did. She had felt a similar power the night her mind reading ability had surfaced, ultimately ending the evening with her in the hospital.

She pressed her power harder trying to hear the man's words. The energy warmed her veins as it pooled into her palms—a feeling she had thought was lost to her just hours ago. Jumbled words started to dance in her ears, like she was flipping the dial on a radio.

"Soon....this time...Don't lose her or you will regret it." The last block of words was enough that she knew he was talking about her. The shadow of the man in her vision had to be Loch. She tried to latch on to the graying image, wanting to know more; she needed more

time to look for clues to his location but the vision liquefied and Nicole found herself listening to the soothing trickle of water again.

"Damn it," she cursed punching the massage table. "Who was he talking to?"

"Oh, sorry Miss. I didn't mean to hurt you," The therapist whispered with wide eyes.

Nicole shook her head as she got off the table, "Sorry about that. Guess I Just have too much on my mind to relax." She looked down at her palms expecting them to be glowing with power but she only saw normal hands. Not even a tingle remained as proof that her energy had been there. She wrapped the sheet around her body then turned to the therapist to apologize for her interruption. The masseuse was busily cleaning up her supplies and humming; obviously happy to move on to her next client. Nicole reached out with her power, trying to hear the woman's thoughts but heard nothing. She sighed as she thought of the possibility that the vision was all just in her imagination.

An hour later after all her spa services were over, she made her way back to her room. She had kept her appointment for hair and makeup so she would be ready for the night without having to fight the long curls she hated to style. She let herself into the suite and started to make her way to her room when a knock sounded on the door shortly after it closed behind her. She was instantly on edge, and tried to push her powers outside the door to see if the visitor was friend or foe. Reluctantly, Nicole was forced to do it the old fashioned way and used the peephole when her magic failed once again.

"I have a delivery for Miss. Keenan," came a voice through the door.

Nicole could see a teen boy in a red bell hop uniform, holding a garment bag over his arm and a shoe box in his hand. She opened the door and smiled nervously, "I'm Miss. Keenan." Nicole took the bag and box with her brows crumpled together, "I wasn't expecting anything." The boy shrugged his shoulders and turned back down the hall. He didn't even hang around for a tip.

Nicole carried the bag inside and laid it across her bed before she raised the plastic covering. She gasped at the most beautiful, black satin cocktail dress she had ever seen. She held it up against her body, admiring the mermaid fit and the perfect princess cuts down the sides. A delicate strip of black chiffon lay across one shoulder, held into place by a large diamond broach. She didn't know a lot about dresses but she knew for sure this one cost more than a month's pay back at the police department. "Kat would die to wear this," she whispered as she stood in front of the full length mirror on the bathroom door. A bit of homesickness filled her heart as she thought of her best friend. This was the first time they had been this many miles apart since they met in middle school many, many years ago.

With a sigh, Nicole pushed the memories to the back of her mind. She was in Ireland to keep Kat safe, along with everyone else she loved. She wouldn't let Loch use Kat or her dad again to trap her. There was no going back until her job here was done so she continued preparing for the night to come. At the same time she prayed the gift that she had loathed for so many years had now not left her forever.

Laying the dress back across the bed she wondered why Slade was going through such trouble to for her. Was it that he thought she could be easily swayed by gifts and flaunting his elite status into being more than friends? She shook her head at the thought. He didn't strike her as a womanizer so she hoped his kindness was just the result of observing all her belongings were packed into a single backpack which couldn't possibly contain a dress appropriate for a cocktail party. Why else would he send her such a beautiful gift? Nicole was having a hard time profiling him, which was an action ingrained into her DNA thanks to her years of police work, and it was putting her on edge.

Shortly after she had finished the final touch ups on her lip-gloss she heard a soft knock on the closed French doors of her room. She slid on the strappy, black shoes from the box then opened the door to see Slade dressed in a black tuxedo with a crimson tie and gleaming diamond cufflinks. His hair lay in silky, blond strands framing his face and his light blue eyes were glowing with desire as he stared at her.

"You look stunning, Nicole." Slade smiled taking a step back to get the full view of the long dress. "I knew it was a beautiful dress but now I can see that it was made to be wrapped around you."

Nicole could feel her cheeks heating from his smoldering stare, "Thank you, Slade. You're very handsome yourself tonight." She instantly wanted to take those words back the moment after she spoke them. She didn't want him to think she was interested in him outside of the friendship they had so quickly formed. The last thing she needed right now was a man pining after her as she tried to save the world.

"Are you ready to go?" Slade offered her his arm with a smile.

"Yes." She did feel very beautiful tonight even if it was far from her normal, country girl comfort zone. The reflection in the patio doors caught her attention as they walked past. She stood with her hand in the crook of Slade's arm and the couple that reflected back was the most glamorous she had ever seen. *Wow, my life has taken another strange turn*, she thought as they walked out into the night.

Chapter 4

Nicole looked around as they entered the room further, taking in all the people that were seated around large tables covered in crisp white linens as well as the guests standing in groups talking in low mumbles. Everyone was dressed so perfectly and in the highest fashion money could buy. The glitter of diamonds around fingers and hanging from ears added to the ambiance of the room as the women moved gracefully about in their cocktail party attire. Nicole smiled lightly when she didn't see a woman wearing a dress she loved more than the one she wore.

A waiter approached them quickly carrying a tray of champagne filled glasses. Slade handed one to Nicole before taking one for himself. Nicole watched curiously as he downed one glass then quickly grabbed another before the waiter walked away. She shifted uncomfortably when she realized everyone had turned their attention on them. She flashed a small smile at the watching eyes then took a small sip of her drink.

Slade grinned a smug, half smile at her, "You ready to meet a bit of Ireland's high society assholes?"

Nicole let her eyes drop down to his half empty glass then back up to his eyes, "Are you?"

"Just a small word of advice," he leaned over and whispered in her ear. "Keep an open mind because I'm sure tonight is going to be interesting." Slade straightened back up and clinked his glass off of hers before taking another long drink.

Nicole's brows knitted together in confusion over his words, "What do you mean?" She asked, but only received a sly wink in response from Slade.

He smiled large enough to show the dimples in both of his freshly shaved cheeks then placed his hand on the small of her back as he guided her further into the room. Nicole felt a small shiver that raised goose bumps on her arms as they moved forward. It seemed like her body was trying to warn her but it was so weak she didn't know were the unease was coming from. *Now's not the time to get jumpy Nicole. Get it together,* she told herself as they approached a group of smiling people.

"Ah, Slade, so nice of you to join us," said a tall, slightly graying man. "And with such beautiful company too," he gave Nicole a tight smile as he reached to shake her hand.

Nicole shook his hand lightly then moved back to Slade's side. The shiver began to dance a bit stronger across her skin. She rubbed her arms, trying to subdue the tingling as she looked around the room.

"Nicole, this is Mr. Casey and his beautiful wife Calumina."

"Please call me Cal," said Mr. Casey's wife as she smiled broadly. "So Slade, have you given Nicole the grand tour of your hotel yet?"

Slade finished off his second glass of champagne before answering the question. "No, unfortunately I've been a bit tied up with business but she did get to see most of the spa today."

"Oh, the spa here is to die for. The masseuse has the hands of an angel. But you must make Slade walk you around the gardens. They are beautiful," she smiled as she patted Nicole on the arm then stepped back to her husband's side.

"Thank you, I would love to see them," smiled Nicole. It was nice to find a friendly person in a room of strangers. She could feel the eyes of others on her, watching her like she was an intruder in their world. But wasn't she really just that? Pretending to belong just so she could find her path. Hoping that some useful information would make it to her ears as she tried to act normal among Irish high class.

Nicole heard someone call out Slade's name from somewhere in the crowd. He rolled his eyes as he snatched a glass of red wine from a passing waiter, "If you'll excuse me for just a moment Nicole, seems I am needed for business again." He pulled her hand to his lips, pressing a tender kiss into her fingers, "I won't be long, I promise."

Nicole watched as Slade made his way across the room, stopping every now and again to say hello to overly pushy men and women, practically begging for his attention. She noticed a tall brunette step in his path who traced each inch of his body with her eyes like she was mentally undressing him. She leaned up to whisper in his ear, placing one black lace covered hand on his cheek as she spoke. After a few seconds the woman's piercing, green eyes locked onto Nicole's over his shoulder. The edge of her red lips turned up as she placed a kiss on his cheek and stepped around him, walking in Nicole's direction.

Slade turned to meet Nicole's eyes with his steely gaze. His jaw clinched as he lifted the glass to his lips and finished off his wine.

Nicole was sure she saw a flash of regret in Slade's eyes before the woman cut off her view of him. She let her eyes meet the woman's cat like orbs as she approached. The tingle she felt when trouble was near was growing in her body with each step of the woman as she drew closer. It felt like the fight or flight instinct that most people have built in was telling her this was a bad situation, and she need to get the hell out of there. But she fought it, forcing her feet to hold their place and her chin to raise high. She held the woman's gaze, refusing to be bullied by her soul-deep stare. Nicole pasted a smile on as the woman came to a stop in front of her.

"Hello, dear," she extended her glove clad hand, grabbing just the tips of Nicole's fingers in a light shake. "I'm Morena. I'm a *close* friend of Slade's," she purred putting extra emphasis on the word "close" like Nicole was too dumb to catch the underlying meaning.

Nicole took a sip of her now warm champagne, "Nice to meet you Morena, I'm Nicole." She stared into Morena's eyes unblinking. Her face was powder white with high, sharp cheek bones; a stark contrast to her bright red, full lips and her almost glowing eyes. She wore a short, black dress that hugged each curve of her body. The deeply cut neckline gave the room a good look at her ample cleavage. Her long hair draped around her shoulders with the top pulled back into an elaborate braid. The silence began to stretch between them but Nicole didn't offer to pick up the conversation. She hoped the brunette diva would get the hint and move her ghostly ass on to the next target.

"Are you enjoying Ireland, dear?" Morena asked with what sounded like genuine curiosity in her voice.

Nicole nodded, "Yes. I've only been here one day but so far everything I've seen has been beautiful."

"Yes, I imagine it's much different from your small home town in the States," she chuckled as she raked her eyes across Nicole. There was a taunting undertone as if Morena was pointing out how far from home she truly was.

"Oh, is it that obvious that I'm American?" Nicole smiled then took another sip of her drink as she slowly counted to ten in her head. She could tell this woman had it in for her and there was no way to getting around it.

"No, I only know because Slade told me this afternoon over drinks. He mentioned you had just flown in from the U.S. and that you were kind of," she paused tapped her chin like she was searching for words that were foreign to her, "Oh yes, he said you were backpacking around Ireland."

Nicole was enjoying Morena's soothing voice and company about as much as she enjoyed the sound of fingernails raking across a chalkboard. She understood that Morena was marking her territory over Slade and she wasn't about to fight her over it. He was a wonderful man who had been very kind to her but that was the extent of things. Realizing the silliness of the situation, she now had her gut's fill of the Snow White Diva for tonight. "Listen Morena," Nicole stepped up to whisper in her ear, "I know what you're trying to get at so you can lay off the snide, low class jokes. I'm not after Slade nor do I plan on sticking around here for long. So get your snooty, plastic nose out of my business before you get on my bad side." Nicole leaned back, taking in Morena's wide eyes and tight lined lips then continued, "It was so nice to meet you, *dear*. Do take care." Nicole made a subtle flicking motion with her hand as if she was swatting away a fly then watched as Morena turned on her heels and walked away.

Nicole shook her head as she wondered how she managed to get herself into such odd situations. After a few moments of glancing around the room to see if anyone else had noticed the unpleasant encounter, she decided it was time for action. Powers or no powers, she had to figure out if anyone knew Loch. After all that was why she was here and she wasn't going to let anything, not even a jealous woman, stop her from reaching her goal tonight.

She spotted Slade in a group of chatting men. He was downing another glass of wine as if it was water to a man who had walked out of the desert. "Why in the world is he drinking so heavy?" she asked herself as she made her way around the large room. She had only walked a few feet when she started to catch random words in her head. She stopped where she was, afraid that if she moved she would lose the flicker that was trickling in, and listened. *Some nerve he has, flaunting her like a trophy,* an unfamiliar gruff, male voice spit. *That bitch better be glad I can't lay a finger on her right now.* A mischievous grin turned up the edge of Nicole's lips as she listened to the female ranting. She had a good idea whose thoughts those were without digging too deep.

Nicole made her way to a chair in a shadow darkened corner and took a seat, afraid that if she didn't get out of sight someone would notice her distracted stare. She could feel her power starting to flow more freely with each passing second. Her whole body began to tingle as the energy crept through every vein. It felt as though a giant bolder had been blown to pieces, releasing the caged tiger that lay waiting inside her. The voices became crystal clear, like everyone was talking directly to her, but uncaring about what they were telling her. *Our time is finally here.* Nicole could feel eyes on her as she sat wrapped up tight in her mind. She forced her staring eyes to scan the room, searching for voices that matched the ones in her head. *This will earn him a seat at Loch's right hand. That should be my place,* came another voice, thickly laced with venom.

Nicole's heart beat quickened and a knot formed in her stomach. The mention of Loch's name was the first clue she had gotten that she was on the right track since she arrived in Ireland. Her eyes darted from face to face, meeting many eyes that quickly looked away. *Him?* She wondered, *Are they thinking about Slade?* Her mind was racing with questions but was detoured as another of her keen senses kicked in—the ability to feel the location of other warriors. Her mind was instantly in a tug of war as it split off into many different directions all at the same time. It was an ability that all warriors possessed, allowing them to coordinate attacks in battles. This room had at least ten warriors in it, half near all the exits and the rest mixed in among the party goers. The stone faced men and women made her realize at that moment, she was in enemy territory. There were people in this very room who were on Loch's side and that meant she was in trouble.

She took a deep breath, trying to calm her nerves and decide what she to do. *I've got the upper hand here. It seems they don't know about my powers so I should be able to walk out of here. Yes, I'll tell Slade that I'm not feeling well and that I'm going back to the room...*she told herself as she forced her legs to move from the shock frozen state. She started cutting a trail across the packed floor, doing her best to be polite as she made her way through the crowd. When Nicole spotted Slade her mind began to spin an idea. She reached her powers out to try to hear Slade's mind. That would be the best way to get her answers so she would truly know if he was on her side or not. For all she knew she could be walking into a trap.

Nicole slowed her pace and wrapped her power around Slade, only wanting to hear what he was thinking, not the rest of the room for the moment. She froze in her tracks as her energy hit an invisible wall—a wall that wouldn't allow her inside his mind. *He has something to hide,* her mind screamed as the wheels in her head began to process everything. *Slade seems to be keeping her well under control. Loch said she was powerful.* Nicole looked up meeting Mr. Casey's stare as she processed his mind's words. "Slade has been blocking my powers," she mumbled to herself as she backed away from the group.

Chapter 5

Nicole frantically searched the room for an exit fighting to keep her body from shaking and her feet from running. She needed to get out of this room and she needed to go now, before anyone realized that Slade didn't have her powers locked away any more. She spotted two large doors opening to the outside pool area with many people coming and going. That was her way out. She started moving forward, mindful to keep each step slow and steady as she came close enough to feel the breeze dancing in from the night air. "Nicole, wait," came a voice from behind her but she kept moving, pretending to not hear her name being called above the voices of the large crowd.

She scanned the area as she stepped outside, quickly noticing a softly lit, cobblestone path leading into a garden. She pressed forward, moving a bit quicker than she intended because of her warrior speed flooding back into her body.

She moved forward in the shadows of the tall trees using her speed and the stealth of night to stay hidden.

Soon she found herself lost in a maze of green hedges and beautiful, fragrant rose bushes. The crescent shaped moon provided her only light as she slowed to a normal pace but her mind continued to race miles ahead. *Slade betrayed me. I thought I could trust him but he was working for Loch all along. He's the enemy.* Her mind stated facts as she struggled to find a way out of the maze. She could feel the pain of betrayal cutting her heart deep. She trusted Slade and had been sure he was a friend and the way he looked at her made it seem that he wanted more than friendship so how could he treat her like this?

"Nicole, please! Just stop and hear me out," Slade's voice rang out from somewhere behind her. She pressed forward again, working her way around the edge of the hedges, making turn after turn trying to put some distance between her and the man she no longer knew. The man who just hours ago she believed to be her only friend in this foreign land.

She made her way to the end of the path and took a left only to run into a dead end. "Damn it," she cursed, staring up at the top of the hedges. After a few seconds she shook her head at her lack of thinking, "You dummy, you can burn a hole through the bushes," she told herself as she called her power to her hands and watched as her palms glowed bright red. Just as she reached forward to touch the bush a hand grabbed her shoulder and spun her around. Nicole was face to face with Slade and froze in place for what felt like an eternity, staring into his eyes.

As she took in his pain lined face she forced her hands to move up between their bodies and created a wall of wind that shoved him backwards. She couldn't bring herself to hurt him even if he did betray her. Some feeling deep inside of her was stopping her from setting him on fire so she could escape. When she was sure the wind was going to hold him she started inching her way around him.

"I wanted you to hear everything, Nicole. Don't you understand? I'm on your side," Slade pleaded. "I had to be drunk for my power to weaken enough for you to use your abilities. That's the only way to turn off what I have," he struggled to turn his head toward her, fighting against the winds that were holding him in place.

"You expect me to believe that. After all I've heard tonight, the only thing I know about you is that you're Loch's prized pupil," Nicole sneered through her gritted teeth. "You've been using your powers to make me weak so I would stay by your side until you could take me to Loch."

"It's not like that," Slade yelled. "Give me a chance to explain, you stubborn woman. Don't you think I would have already turned you over to him if that was my plan? I would have driven you straight to him from the airport."

Nicole stood for a moment in silence, processing Slade's words. Maybe that was true, he did have the perfect opportunity then, especially since she didn't know anything about Ireland. She wouldn't have known until she was standing in front of Loch that Slade was the enemy. So why wait? Why flaunt her in front of people who were loyal to Loch? She sighed with frustration when she realized nothing was adding up. "Why? Why are you showing me off to his people then?"

"Because I need them to believe that I am one of them. They need to think that I am loyal to Loch so I can get close to him. The closest I've ever been is via phone call; the first call was when he sent me to retrieve you from America and the other today when he called to tell me we will be meeting in a few days. I need to get close enough to kill him. Don't you see, we want the same thing," he pleaded with his eyes as he searched Nicole's face for any sign of understanding.

Nicole's brows crumpled together as she paced in front of Slade. "How do I know you're not telling me a lie? You keep me blocked from inside of your head so you must be hiding more from me?"

"Didn't you hear me? My power is always on, like a constant protective force-field that I can't turn off. The only way you were able to hear what you needed to tonight is because I drank so much alcohol. It dulls my powers, but it takes a lot for it to allow someone inside of my head." He sighed as he tried to shift his body into a more comfortable position. "You can think of me as a peace keeper. I'm useful in heated negotiations where people of both fae and warrior origins would be tempted to kill each other. I neutralize everyone's powers so hopefully a peaceful solution can be found.

"That still doesn't prove I can trust you, Slade. It just proves that you can make me a weak lap dog if I stay around you. I can't be weak, I can't afford to be weak. There isn't time."

"So you're going to do this alone? Just go out there and try to find Loch by yourself?" Slade chuckled. "Sage told me you were hard headed."

Nicole's eyes widened at the sound of a familiar name, "Sage told you about me?"

"Yes, my sister told me a lot about you and how powerful you are. And if you would let me go I will prove it to you."

With a sigh Nicole sent the wall of wind up into the star filled night sky. She watched as Slade smoothed out his tux then faced her again. She tensed as he slowly moved his hand. He push back the curtain of silky blond hair that covered his ear revealing a pointed tip—the pointed ear that is found on all fairy kind.

"I guess that's why I couldn't do it?" said Nicole softly.

"Do what?

"Hurt you. I couldn't figure out why I hesitated but now I know it's because you remind me of Sage." Nicole smiled softly as she realized she missed that crazy gothic fairy almost as much as she missed her dad and her best friend, Kat.

Slade beamed a bright smile at Nicole as he reached forward picking a small twig from her hair then let the back of his fingers gently slide down her cheek, "Remind me to thank my dear sister later." He winked at her and gently said, "Come on, we better get back to the party before we're missed."

"Go back? You must be kidding? How do you expect me to go back in there when I know everyone is my enemy?"

"You're safe, Nicole. You are my guest and no one would dare cross me. They all know that I am expected to bring you to Loch."

"That doesn't mean everyone in that party likes it," snorted Nicole as she started to pace the small trail. "There are people in that room who think you are crossing a line by having me here."

Slade's face turned hard as his jaw muscles flexed with tension. He was quiet for a few moments, lost in his thoughts. "I can't imagine what you must have heard tonight already but I'm afraid it may be a good idea for you to go back in there and continue to listen." After a few moments Slade's face returned to its normal, confident state. "Just listen for anything out of the ordinary. You know, things that will help us see if we have any allies who are looking for a way to stop Loch too."

"And what will you be doing while I'm snooping?" Nicole asked reluctantly, giving in to the fact that she had to return to the hostile party full of hate-laced glares.

The corners of Slade's lips turned up into a sly grin and a mischievous twinkle lit up his pale blue eyes, "I'm going to enjoy a few more drinks as I mingle with my comrades." He flashed a quick wink, "All in the name of helping you use your powers. The foggier my head is, the clearer yours will be."

Nicole rolled her eyes at the obvious joy Slade was getting out of being able to turn loose and drink all he wanted. "Men," she groaned letting him take her hand and lead her back through the maze of tall shrubs. When they stepped back onto the cobblestone path Slade stopped and turned to Nicole. He pulled her hand to his lips, kissing it gently, "If the pressure gets to be too much in there, signal me and we will leave."

Nicole took her hand back slowly, not sure how to take his protective attitude and tenderness now that she knew they were on the same team. She thought for a moment that all the alcohol he had downed was bringing a new side of him out. But as she studied his face she realized she had seen that longing look in his eyes before. She smiled nervously, "I will." She took a deep breath then started forward, "Let's do this."

~*~**

As soon as they entered the room, Nicole's mind was swarmed with questions and racy allegations. Similar to how it would feel if a hundred red wasps were buzzing around her, looking for a vulnerable place to attack. All she had to do was show one small sign of weakness and everything would fall apart.

He'll lose interest in her fast. She's too easy, Morena's venom filled voiced cackled in her mind. Nicole mischievous side began to creep to the surface as she listened to everyone speculating the reasons she and Slade had left the party. She stretched up to whisper in Slade's ear, "You'll never guess what everyone thinks we've been up to." She giggled.

Slade flashed the sexiest smile she had ever seen then pulled her gently against his chest as he moved closer to whisper back in her ear, "Well, you must forgive me if I don't rush to put an end to that rumor," he pressed a kiss to her cheek before turning his attention back to the party. "I think I'll find another drink, my love."

Nicole stared after him as he strode into the crowd. She absentmindedly touched the warm spot on her cheek where Slade's soft lips had been seconds ago. Her stomach knotted tight as she tried to reason out what just happened. *I sure as hell hope he was playing along for the crowd because I can't deal with this right now.* Her mind raced as she fought to put on a confident face for the room. But in the end wasn't it better to let everyone think that she and Slade had escaped to be intimate? At least that way no one would suspect she was any wiser about Slade's involvement with Loch than she had been before their escape into the garden.

I will kill him, echoed through her head, sending a heart stopping shiver down her spine. The familiar voice, a voice she had been longing to hear, caused a large lump to form in her throat. She spun around in the direction of the soul deep pull as a warm woodsy scent danced around her on the breeze from the open doors. "Luke," she whispered staring past the glowing pool into the dark shadows of the garden.

The tall, broad warrior who was standing guard beside the door turned to stare out the same direction as she was. Nicole knew the built in GPS that comes standard to every warrior had given Luke away. She started towards the door as the hard looking warrior moved outside but was grabbed by the elbow. "Let go," she hissed, jerking her arm away before she realized it was Slade.

"You can't go to him. He can't be part of your life anymore," he whispered to her, careful to keep his voice from being heard by the other party goers.

"I think I can choose who is in my life, Slade," she said, fighting to keep her voice low as anger and panic began to fill her. "I can't just stand here and do nothing while those goons capture him." She started to move forward again but Slade grabbed her by the hand.

"We both know they won't catch him. Nicole, please, you don't want him to get hurt so you have to let him go," Slade looked at her with compassion and pleaded with his eyes. "What do you think Loch will do if he finds out Luke is here?"

Nicole thought about his words as her eyes searched the dark night. She could feel Luke moving away from the hotel, leaving the goon that was pursuing him far behind. Hadn't that been the reason she walked away? Protecting Luke from the dangers of her life was why she came to Ireland alone. Tears began to swim in her eyes as she realized Slade was right. She couldn't run into Luke's arms, no matter how bad her heart longed for him to hold her. The danger was too real. She had to keep things together for everyone even if it meant sacrificing her wants; her wants that included having Luke.

Slade turned her to face him then lifted her chin so he could look her in the eyes, "You're doing the right thing." Seeing her misty eyes, he pulled her into a hallway that provided a small amount of privacy.

Nicole nodded as a single tear escaped making a wet trail down her cheek. Slade pulled her into his arms and she didn't resist. She needed someone to understand her pain and Slade was that person. He was her only ally in a new world that she could barely fathom and at times feared. "Thank you for helping me," she whispered into his chest.

"I know this is hard on you." He slid the back of his fingers across her cheek, drying away the tears. "I'll do whatever it takes to help you but Luke can't be involved. Luke will only make things tougher for you," he pulled back from her so he could see into her eyes as he spoke. "There's always the chance he will turn on you for his father."

Nicole's eye's widened at his words. "He wouldn't turn on me," she shook her head as she took a step back from Slade. "I know Luke is loyal to me," her muscles began to tense as her anger bubbled to the surface.

Slade reached forward tucking a stray strand of hair behind her ear then he cupped her face in his hands. Forcing her to look into his pale, pity filled eyes while he spoke, "If he hadn't let Loch out of prison we wouldn't be standing here, on the edge of this battle. Nicole, you are too kind for your own good. You're a cop for god's sake. You have to use what you know and not let your emotions force you into bias decisions."

Nicole pulled her face out of his hands and backed away again. She glared at him, biting her bottom lip as she carefully thought through her words before speaking. "You don't know a damn thing about him or me." She walked back out into the crowd, now thinking it was much better to face their glaring eyes than Slade.

~***~**

Nicole spent the next hour mingling among her enemies, sampling their minds and making mental notes on who she needed to watch out for, but not coming out with any new information that she thought was useful. After a bit she settled into a chair next to Cal, Mr. Casey's chatty wife. She seemed to be one of the few people here who was genuinely kind and had no dark, hidden motives lurking in her thoughts.

"Are you enjoying the party dear?"

"I guess so. I've met so many people but I'm sure I will never remember half of their names," Nicole replied.

Cal chuckled softly, "Don't worry, most of those snoots aren't worth remembering."

Nicole smiled back at the gray haired woman who's eyes sparkled with a fiery, youthful glow. "I take you're having as much fun as I am tonight?"

"I hate these cocktail parties. They are always full of power hungry leeches," Cal leaned in close to Nicole, lowering her voice into a whisper. "I'm sure that's what's driving Slade to drink so much. If I had to put up with those people clinging onto my every breath I would be downing ever drop of alcohol I could find too."

Nicole leaned back in her chair as she looked across the room to where Slade was standing. Morena had her arm laced around his as he finished off another glass of wine. He glanced in Nicole's direction, a pained look met her behind his glassy eyes but his attention was quickly brought back to the group as Morena giggled loudly and placed a hand on his chest. Nicole sighed as she thought about how she had left things with Slade earlier. He really did want to help her put an end to Loch and here she was being a royal bitch to him.

"I wouldn't let that tramp worry me too much. She's been trying for the longest to latch onto Slade but I think he sees past the pretty face and fake boobs."

Nicole could feel her cheeks heat as she realized Cal thought she was jealous of Morena, "Oh, no...It's not like that between Slade and me. We're just friends."

Cal studied Nicole's face for a moment then patted her on the arm and nodded, "Yes, well, I don't guess an old woman like me should be meddling in things like that anyway. I was just thinking out loud. It's a bad habit of mine—a sign of getting old, dear," she chuckled.

"I know you're not meddling," Nicole smiled. "It's nice to find someone who is looking out for me in a room full of strangers. Talking to you kind of makes me home sick. My dad was always the one who would give me advice about everything, men included." Nicole swallowed hard trying to keep her voice from giving away how much she truly missed her old life. She always had her dad to lean on when times got rough and she didn't realize how much she had been taking him for granted all these years.

"Well I'm sure if your dad was here he would be telling you the same thing. That girl is trouble and I see the way Slade looks at you. Hell, he doesn't go a few minutes without looking at you." Cal looked back in the direction of Slade then continued, "But if you just want to be friends, I think now is the time to prove how good of a friend you can be."

Nicole followed the woman's gaze out into the party and was shocked as her eyes fell on Slade. He was making his way over to them in a zig-zag pattern and this wasn't some covert, warrior inspired move. This was

Slade when he had finally met his limit of drinks. She hurried over to him and slid her arm around his waist to offer some support.

Slade pulled back from her to attempt to glare at her with his unsteady vision, "You and I need to talk," he slurred.

"Sure thing, but I think we should talk tomorrow when you're sober."

"No we....are going to...talk now," he said as he weaved on his feet, fighting hard not to fall on his face.

Nicole put her arm back around him as she took a deep breath to steady her nerves for the fight that was about to happen, "Let me get you back to your room and then we will talk."

Slade stared at her for a few seconds, mulling over her suggestion, then nodded in agreement. "Fine," he snipped.

His brows were pinched together and his lips were drawn in a hard line but his coordination reminded Nicole of a toddler. She bit her lip to hold in the giggle that was fighting to escape as they started moving forward.

"Where the hell do you think you're taking him?"

A hand wrapped around Nicole's shoulder from behind, jerking her to a stop thus causing her grip on Slade to loosen. He began to stumble forward and she hurried to steady him before he fell and then turned to face Morena. "I'd suggest you keep that hand off me if you want to keep it," Nicole whispered trying not to draw any more eyes on her than Slade already had with his drunken display.

"I know what you're trying to do and I'm not going to stand by and let you get your country bumpkin claws into him," Morena took a defiant step towards Nicole with her chin raised high.

"Morena, I've already had this conversation with you once and I'm not going to repeat myself so take your jealous ass somewhere else. I'm just taking him back to his room so he can sleep this off." Nicole readjusted herself under Slade's shoulder and started moving towards the door again.

They only made it a few feet when Nicole was jerked to a stop and spun around, causing Slade to go crashing into a table and then roll to the floor. Morena stood nose to nose with her, a one sided smirk pasted on her face, "You are not leaving with him," she hissed as she swung her hand, slapping Nicole across the cheek.

Nicole's body began to shake as she touched the throbbing spot on her face, "You can't say I didn't warn you." Nicole sent one, well aimed punch to the center of the powder white face of Morena, taking joy in the cracking sound that accompanied the blow. Morena crumpled to the floor screaming as she cupped her bleeding nose.

All eyes turned on Nicole causing the pride of knocking Morena off her pedestal to deflate. She stood frozen in place, debating on what she could do to smooth things over when she heard chuckling coming from beside her. Cal walked up with a wide grin on her face as she looked down at Morena sniveling on the floor, "I knew it would happen and it's about time," she laughed. "Come on honey, I'll help you get Slade off the floor."

They moved over to where Slade was sitting with a smug look on his face as he had watched the scene play out. They pulled him up and Cal helped Nicole get under his arm again, "Now, I don't think you'll have any more trouble getting him out of here.

"Thank you Cal," Nicole said over her shoulder as they moved toward the door.

"No, thank you dear. This has been the best party I've been too in a long time," she winked then looked back to where two men were helping Morena up from the floor and chuckled again.

~**~**

Nicole sighed with relief when she finally released Slade onto his bed. She helped him take off his jacket and shoes then went to work turning down his bed covers. "We still need to talk," slurred Slade as he fumbled with the button on his dress shirt.

Nicole couldn't stop herself from blushing when she realized she was watching with deep amazement as each button popped open, revealing his marble hard chest a little at a time. She gave herself a good mental slap and turned her attention out to the terrace. She pretended to be interested in the view of the night sky outside the large glass doors. "I think that we should leave that conversation for another time Slade. You need to sleep."

Without any warning Slade was standing behind her, his breath warm on her neck as he placed his hand on her shoulder. "It's because of him isn't it? Luke is why you won't give me a fair chance." He leaned in close to whisper in her ear, "I think you're using him as an excuse to push me away. Secretly, you want me as much as I want you."

"Truthfully, you're are drunk off of your ass and don't know what you're talking about," shot back an irritated Nicole as she tried to step back from him to only find herself pressed against the glass doors.

A seductive smile curved Slade's lips as he placed his hands on the glass doors, one on each side of Nicole. "I can give you a world you never dreamed of Nicole. Money is no object. Anything you could ever want would be laid at your feet like the queen you are." He inched forward until his lips were just centimeters away from Nicole's, "I am the only one who can give you the one thing you have wanted since your powers started to emerge."

Nicole swallowed hard as she fought the feelings his sultry look was stirring inside of her. She knew he was being this forward because of the alcohol—alcohol that he had consumed to help her, but still she was mesmerized by his words. Unable to look away or move she whispered, "And what would that be?"

He slid one finger along her cheek and down her neck, slowly tracing the outline of her bare collarbone before he spoke, "A normal life. No more blocking out the voices or struggling with the power inside of you. You wouldn't have to pretend anymore. I can keep all of that locked away forever and you can live a carefree life for the rest of eternity."

"Eternity?" Nicole's brows knotted together as she absorbed his words, "You're saying I'm immortal?"

An amused glint filled his eyes as he bit the edge of his bottom lip, "That warrior isn't good for you Nicole and that proves it. He didn't think you needed to know you are an immortal?" Slade laughed. "He wanted you to feel like you needed his protection. He wanted you to feel like you needed him in your life forever."

Slade lifted her chin up with one finger as he closed the space between their bodies, pinning Nicole up against the cold, glass doors and causing her to gasp in surprise, "I think you should be able to choose who you spend forever with without blinders. That's the kind of man I am Nicole," he whispered.

Nicole held her breath as she digested Slade's words. *Would Luke really betray me like that*? she wondered and then asked herself, *Why would he keep the fact that I'm immortal hidden from me?*

"That doesn't add up," she said weakly as Slade brushed his lips across her cheek, then moved smoothly towards her lips. Her self-control was now gone and all she could think of was the heat of his body pressed against her own. The smell of his skin drew her in even though her mind was struggling to break free of his....spell.

Snap out of it you idiot! Sage's voice shouted inside of Nicole's head. Nicole's eyes cleared as if a vail had been lifted. Sage's energy was clear to Nicole and she had missed the strength of it almost as much as she missed her friend and trainer.

She pressed hard against Slade's chest, shoving him back from her just as his lips grazed hers. A bright red glow lit the space between them as power seeped into her palms, waiting on her command with the loyalty of a pit bull. "I'm going to chalk your babbling up to you being a drunken asshole but let this be your warning," Nicole took one defiant step towards him, looked firmly into his wide eyes. "You will not lay another hand on me. I am grateful for your help but I will not be bullied into anything...not by you or by Loch." Nicole let the power recede back inside of her then strode over to the open doors of the room. She grabbed onto the door frame focusing on controlling her temper that was threatening to explode before turning to face Slade's hardened face, "You know... you shouldn't be so hard on Luke. He's a better man than you give him credit for," she sighed deeply then left the room, leaving him alone to recover from the alcohol and hopefully, rethink his view.

Chapter 6

Nicole lay awake in her bed staring at the ceiling as her mind raced. She had tried desperately to reach out to Sage over and over again but kept coming up empty. She knew she hadn't imagined Sage's voice in her head. There was no doubting the distinctive, snippy tone of the sharp-edged, Gothic fae that had truly set all of her powers free. Sure, she had almost killed Nicole in the process but in the end, it was worth the risk. Nicole remembered how different things were the second she woke after Sage sent her to death's door. She wasn't limited to hearing just the evil thought of others any longer. Now she could hear everything along with commanding the power of wind, fire and water with remarkable ease. If it wasn't for that hard-nosed fae, she was sure her best friend, Kat, would have died that horrible night at the airfield. There was no way she would have been able to call upon the rare, white healing fire that only one other fae in history had controlled: her grandmother, Queen Titania.

She let out a long frustrated breath as she flipped

over to her side and hugged her pillow tight against her body. There hadn't been a sound from Slade's room since she left him alone. She hoped that he had passed out but thought it was more likely he was brewing over the rejection. Slade didn't strike her as a man who heard the word "no" often....actually from the way Morena was clinging to him she figured he had *never* heard the word.

"Oh God! Did I really punch her in the face?" Nicole groaned as she rolled over onto her back again, covering her face with her pillow. "I don't need more enemies in this place. I've already got enough haters lining up."

"Do you always talk to yourself?"

Nicole flung the pillow from her face and leaped from the bed. Her hands were glowing with a faint light as she searched the room for the intruder.

"Wait, wait," The bedroom light came on revealing Slade's broad frame filling the doorway with his hands stretched wide to show he wasn't armed.

Nicole let the near absent power recede back into her body as she took in Slade's placid demeanor. "I see you're about sober. That would explain why my power is weakening," she sighed.

"Yes, I'm feeling a lot better," he leaned up against the door frame crossing his arms over his bare chest. "I....well," he stumbled over his words as a small grin lit up his eyes.

Nicole looked down at herself and quickly realized what was causing his reaction. She was standing in the open, wearing a black lace camisole and panties. She gasped pulling the sheet from the bed and wrapping it around her. Her face felt like it was on fire as her cheeks heated. "You know, most normal people knock before coming into someone's room," she grumbled trying to cover her embarrassment with sarcasm.

"I didn't think you would hear me as loud as you were talking to yourself," he chuckled then bit his lip as he tried to slate his face. "Please don't be mad at me. See that's why I came in here," he said quickly.

Nicole stared at him with a crinkled nose, "Was that some form of an apology?"

Slade shifted his weight from foot to foot with his eyes on the floor then he settled his body back against the door frame, returning his attention to her face. "Yes...do you accept?"

"That was the worst damn apology I've ever heard." She poked fun at him, fighting hard not to let the giggle escape, but honestly she was glad to see he wasn't mad at her. She didn't want to lose their friendship to some drunken mistake.

"I'll make it up to you, I promise," Slade said.

He had the biggest puppy dog eyes she had ever seen. She smiled at him realizing he wasn't catching on to her playful mood. "I'm not going to act like tonight didn't happen but I'm not mad at you anymore. You did a hard thing for me tonight and I'm sure you will have one hell of a hangover in the morning to show for it," she winced as she thought of her last hangover. "So let's just call it even, okay?"

He nodded, smiling as if a huge weight had been lifted from him, "That's not really fair. I can get drunk off of wine but I won't have to deal with a hangover," he shrugged his shoulders. "Just one of the many perks of being a fairy," he winked. "So the way I see it, I still owe you. If you'll let me, I'd like to show you a few places tomorrow. I'll give you the grand tour around some of my favorite sites of Ireland."

"Slade, that is nice of you but I think we are losing focus on why I'm here. I need to get to Loch and soon. God only knows what he's planning while I sit here, in the lap of luxury, with you," Nicole sat down on the edge of her bed being careful to keep the sheet pulled tight around her.

"Nicole, we can't do anything until he calls me again and trust me, he will. You are the one thing he wants more than anything so he won't keep you waiting long," he sighed as he raked his hand across his face in frustration. "I can't let you sit here and just wait for, well....who knows what kind of situation."

"He didn't tell you what he was planning?" Nicole asked with curiosity written all over her face. These were the questions that she was dying to know the answers to but so far, no one had been able to tell her what she needed to hear. The only thing she knew was she was unique, being as she was the only warrior/fairy mix. A trait passed to her when her grandmother, Queen Titania fell in love with her warrior, Alaois, and conceived a child of mixed bloodlines. Unknowingly, they created a powerful being that had the best of both fae and warrior powers. The queen was forced to hide the child away in the human world and to cast a spell that locked the power away so the child wouldn't be found by the warriors who loathed the product of the union. The power would only be awakened when it was needed to protect the bloodline and that was how it was found in Nicole. First it was subtle, simply hearing thoughts laced with malice and evil but the closer the warriors came to capturing her, the more her power evolved to give her the tools she needed to protect herself. But none of what she knew told her why Loch wanted her alive.

He had his chance to kill her years ago, doing away with the tainted blood line once and for all but he didn't.

Instead, that night on a Florida beach, he set everything into motion. He wanted the power to surface in Nicole, he wanted her to discover what and who she was but why?

Slade studied her face before answering, which had given her the time to get lost in her thoughts. She realized that he was pondering his answer before speaking, “He has never told me but I would say it’s to control your power. I mean, you are the rightful heir to the throne that was left empty when Queen Titania died. If he had you under his thumb then he would control the kingdom,” he shrugged his shoulders.

She thought back to the sad story Sage had told her of how Queen Titania had allowed herself to age, giving up her immortality because she could not live her life without her love and their child. But even Sage didn’t say much when Nicole asked what it meant for her. “Does he really think I plan on ruling a kingdom? I’m no queen. I can barely rule my own life,” she chuckled trying to lighten the mood but was only met by Slade’s annoyed glare.

“It is your place to rule,” he said firmly.

Nicole was startled to see the anger that was radiating from Slade. He had always seemed very well put together but something in her words was touching a nerve with him and she didn’t want to push the issue so she only nodded.

Slade took a deep breath then exhaled slowly, “Nicole, there is so much you still don’t know about yourself and your place in this world. I would love to be the person to guide you and help you learn everything but,” he rubbed his eyes then placed a finger over his temple, “I don’t think I’m running on all cylinders yet.” Slade smiled softly at her then walked over to stand beside where she sat on the bed, “I couldn’t let myself rest knowing that you were upset with me. I'm so ashamed with how I acted earlier," he slid his hand down her bare arm before taking a step back. "I'm not going to deny that I'm jealous of the feelings you have for that warrior," he held up his hand stopping the protest he could see building in Nicole. He looked down at the floor before meeting her eyes again, "Just, please, give me a chance to prove that I'm not the jerk I acted like tonight. I want to show you a bit of my world and I promise I will have my phone on me so if Loch calls we will know."

Nicole stared at her lap as she tried to process the jumbled thoughts that were tumbling around in her head. There was no way that she was even considering the relationship Slade was pushing for. She knew her heart belonged to Luke even if she had never spoke the words. She missed him every second they were apart. There was a deep void in her heart that could only be filled by Luke. "Slade," she let her eyes meet his, "I'm very grateful for everything you've done for me but I won't pretend to be interested in you just so you'll keep helping me," she watched as Slade's eyes took on a hard look. Her heart jumped up in her throat causing her to swallow hard, "I'd like to be able to call you my friend, Slade, but if that isn't good enough for you….I'll leave."

The creases around his eyes softened as he studied her face, "No," he shook his head slowly, flashing a small smile in an attempt to hide some of his disappointment, "I don't want you to leave." He walked back to the door and stood staring out into the darkness, lost in his thoughts, before he turned to face Nicole again. "It's killing me to think you're mad at me Nicole, so if friendship is all you will allow me to have….I will take it," he smiled softly at her. "Good night, my love," he winked as he flicked the light-switch off then walked out of her room leaving her alone in the dark.

Nicole flopped back onto her bed and covered her

face with a pillow, letting out a muffled, frustrated groan before tossing the feather filled silencer roughly to the floor. The sound of Slade's laughter drifted to her before he closed the doors to his room. "Men," she sighed, settling under her covers and praying for sleep to take her. This had been the busiest day of her life and it was just her first day in Ireland. She was afraid to imagine what day two in this foreign land would hold for her.

~**~**

The darkness of peaceful sleep drifted away from her as a familiar and ancient graveyard began to take shape out of the haze. This place had become Nicole's sanctuary where she could find guidance and wisdom from a surprising source. Queen Titania sat underneath the sweeping limbs of a giant weeping willow that took precedence in the center of the long forgotten resting place of the dead. Her long white hair cascaded around her lean, strong shoulders as her kind, pale blue eyes looked expectantly at her granddaughter. "Come my dear, sit with me and talk," she motioned for Nicole to sit beside her on the bed of green moss that covered the ground around the base of the tree.

Nicole smiled softly at the beautiful woman as she moved underneath the gently swaying limbs. "I've missed you, Grandmother."

"And I have you too. I feared the worse when I no longer felt your power reaching out to me. Where are you now my child?" Queen Titania placed her hand over Nicole's when she settled down into a spot next to her. Concern was written on the woman's face as she waited for Nicole to answer.

"I'm in Ireland. You were right. The only way for me to save those I love is to fight so I've come to find

Loch."

"Yes, sadly this was the only right choice and I'm proud of you for moving forward. I was afraid," her voice trailed off as she studied Nicole closely. "You are weak Nicole. Even now I can feel your spirit pulling away from me. Where are your warriors?"

Nicole bit her lip nervously as she thought about how to explain. It would seem the spirit of her wise grandmother had been shut out the past few days thanks to Slade's power. He must be able to keep other peoples power from touching her as well as keeping her from using her own gifts. His powers acted as some sort of shield or a dome that was covering her. "I have no warriors," she whispered. "I released Luke of his oath then trapped him, Rhys and Sage in a prison of wind so I could leave the United States without them." Nicole could see the anger building behind the pale blue eyes of Queen Titania so she pressed on, "This is my battle and I will not risk losing anyone I love."

Softness replaced the hard lines creasing the Queen's forehead as she raised a hand to touch Nicole's cheek, "I know what it is like to lose someone you love, my dear. I also know what it is like to see the man you love risk his life for you," she sighed as she brushed the hair from Nicole's face. "Luke will not fail you. Even after you sent him away he still follows you, I can feel his presence very close to us. He does not do this because of an oath to me; he does this because he loves you."

"You can't know that for sure," Nicole rushed to say as her heart jumped in her chest. The idea that Luke may actually love her had her both happy and scared at the same time. She knew that she loved him, even if she had been too stubborn to admit it to him but she had never dreamed that he would return her feelings. After all, he was an immortal warrior who had lived for hundreds of years, what could he really see in her?

A small smile turned up the edge of her grandmother's lips as she studied Nicole's eyes, "You are sitting on the edge of a great war, one that has been building for generations, and your only fear is love," she chuckled creating a sound as magical as wind chimes singing in a summer breeze.

"I guess you're right," sighed Nicole, "It is a bit teen drama for..." Her words were cut short as a gut wrenching pain shot through her body. The world around her began to spin as pain contorted her face.

Queen Titania fought to steady Nicole by the shoulders, "You're being forced away from me. Who are you with?"

"He can't help...this," stammered Nicole as she tried to think past the darkness that was closing in on her.

"Who, Nicole? You must tell me who is doing this to you," the woman forced Nicole's rolling eyes on her face, searching desperately for the answer that was quickly slipping from her grasp.

Nicole began to fade from the magical realm though she fought with all she had to not sink into the darkness that was pulling her under like quicksand. "A fae...named...Slade," she watched the Queen's face twist into a shocked, wide eyed stare. She could see the old woman's lips working frantically to form words that never sounded in her ears. She awoke with a gasp, struggling to fill her tight lungs with air as she sprung upright in her bed. The beads of sweat on her forehead caused goose bumps to rise on her skin. The cool night air danced in the room around her, sending a few loose papers floating gracefully down to the floor. The last of her power, power that had summoned the protective wind to her, drifted away. She leaned back into her pillow as her heart beat slowed back into its normal, steady rhythm, "Slade must be completely sober now," she sighed.

~**~**

Nicole sat on the patio outside of her room with a large, black fleece throw wrapped around her. The morning sun was warm on her cheeks and the birds were singing in the trees of the beautiful garden around her. The flowers that surrounded her were truly something she would have imagined seeing in the Garden of Eden. All the blooms were picture perfect with their vibrant red, pinks and violets, each giving off a unique scent that mixed together to form a heavenly perfume. "Slade does have a beautiful place here," Nicole admitted to herself aloud as she took in a deep breath of the morning air. She was trying hard to shake the visit from her grandmother in her dreams. Everything seemed to be fine until the end when she was being forced out by Slade's returning powers. The queen's face was seared into her memory. *Why did she get so upset at the mention of Slade's name? Maybe she didn't hear what I was saying, after all, I was being ripped back into my world*, Nicole wondered to herself as she picked at the edge of the blanket.

A soft knock sounded on the closed patio door behind her. She turned to see Slade standing on the other side of the glass. He opened the door slightly and stuck his head outside, "Do you mind if I join you?" His face twisted comically, as if he was waiting on Nicole to throw something at him.

Nicole bit her lip trying to keep from laughing at his pitiful display and motioned for him to join her. She watched a relieved smile stretch across his face as he moved towards the table where she sat. When he reached her side he knelt down beside her gently kissing her cheek then placed a single white rose on the table in front of her, “I know I’ve already apologized but it didn’t feel proper without a flower.”

Nicole tried to ignore that he had managed to sneak another kiss as she looked down at the beautiful rose in full bloom, “White? Like your raising a truce flag,” she chuckled.

“Exactly. Time for us to start over, a new beginning where you don’t think I’m a jack ass.” Slade sat in the chair next to her with excitement radiating off him like a five year old on his birthday. “I’ve got a wonderful day planned for us. First breakfast then I’ll give you a tour of the gardens, followed by sightseeing around some of my favorite spots in Dublin.”

Nicole felt her stomach start to churn as she stared into Slade’s expecting face. There was an unease tugging at her mind but she wasn’t sure if it was real concern or her worry over what happened with Queen Titania last night. She knew that he was trying to make up for yesterday but what was his reason for wanting to keep her so close to him? Was he really trying to be her friend and protect her until Loch shows his face? She sat up straight in her seat pulling the blanket tighter around her shoulders, “Slade, I think my time should be spent working on a plan. I’ve got to figure out how to fight Loch.

“Nicole, we’ve already talked about...”

“No, you told me what you wanted me to do but it’s not what I *need* to do. I have a purpose in being here and many people’s lives depend on me doing it,” she pleaded with her eyes for him to understand.

“You don’t know what you’re walking into!” Slade face twisted with anger as he stood up, towering over her. "Loch is powerful and he will get what he wants."

"What are you trying to say, Slade? That I should sit here and do nothing at all?" Anger was filling her voice as she watched Slade move into a defiance stance.

"I'm saying you should stay with me. You take your rightful place as ruler of the fae kingdom with me by your side as king. Together no one will be able to touch us, not even Loch. I can show you a world you never dreamed of and with my powers you will get to live a normal life for all of eternity. I know that's all you really want Nicole, to be as normal as an immortal can pretend to be and I will let you have that."

Nicole's heart sunk at his words. This was his plan all along, to win her love so he could rule the fae kingdom. He never cared about helping her figure out how to stop Loch. There was no concern for the war that was building and the threat that was on her friends and family's head. He wanted the one thing his bags of money and good looks couldn't give him—the fae kingdom.

Nicole stood and stepped forward until she was staring up into Slade's ice cold eyes, "I will not be used." She pushed past him and walked back into her room. She began to pull her clothes out of the bureau and the closet, tossing everything onto the bed. She dug around under the bed, grabbing her backpack from where she had hid it. When she stood up Slade was standing behind her. He spun her around by the shoulder and shoved her roughly onto the bed.

"I don't think you understand what's happened. You have two choices here," he leaned down pointing a finger in her face as he spoke, "You go be Loch's lap dog, help him destroy all fae then when he is done, he will destroy you. Or you join me," he grabbed her face between his hands, as an evil, power hungry look filled his eyes and his lips curved into a smile. "We will rule together, side by side. We will rid the world of those low life warriors and the fae kingdom will be strong once again."

Nicole jerked her head away from his hands then quickly backed off the bed so there was some distance between them again, "That's your big plan? You're no better than Loch," she hissed taking a step backwards, getting closer to the open patio doors. "I will not be killing anyone but Loch…and if you get in my way…I will kill you too."

She turned to run out of the room but Slade was already standing in front of her. She gasped as he grabbed her by the arms and pulled her hard against his chest. She could feel the heat of his breath blanketing her neck as she tried to break free from him.

"You know, that's what really attracts me to you Nicole—your spirit. You're beauty is beyond any I've ever seen and you know what you want, just like I know what I want but your spirit is unlike any I've encountered," he let his lips brush across her earlobe as he pulled her struggling body tighter against him. "Am I really that hard to love?"

"Love," she hissed with wide eyes, "Do you really think you can force me to love you?" she laughed as she leaned her head back, putting some space between her face and his. She was trying to come up with a plan to get away from him but her anger was building inside of her with each breath, making it hard to think past the moment. "I will never love a man like you," she spit in Slade's face.

Slade closed his eyes and took a deep breath, slowly releasing his hold on Nicole. He wiped the moisture from his face with the back of his hand before letting his anger darkened eyes meet hers again. "You can love that traitor warrior but not me?" He stood staring at her then he let his eyes drift over her shoulder. After a few moments he shook his head defiantly, "You need time to think my offer over. After all, you are a smart woman who doesn't make rash decisions and I can respect that," he walked around her to the French doors that lead back into the living area of the hotel room before he stopped, speaking over his shoulder, "I'll leave you to your thoughts but be forewarned, if you haven't made your decision by the time Loch calls," he paused looking back at Nicole with a mixture of hurt and anger written on his face. "I will take you to him and your fate will be sealed. He will use you and you will have no choice but to obey him."

Nicole watched as he walked out of the room, shutting the doors behind him. *Is this really what has become of my life?* She thought, turning to look back outside as she fought to form an escape route in her head. But as she stared movement among the green caught her attention. A large form materialized out of nowhere, its towering presence was familiar and unsettling to Nicole. The warrior that had left the party in pursuit of Luke last night stood at the edge of the garden, hands locked in front of him and feet shoulder-width apart. He raised his chin so he was looking down at Nicole. When their eyes locked he shook his head slowly from side to side, sending her a warning without saying a word.

"Damn it," she cursed under her breath as she slammed the patio door closed and locked it, blocking the chilling glare of the warrior. She leaned against the door and slid down to the floor with her elbows on her knees and her hands gripping the sides of her head. "Nice job Nicole, you can't even keep yourself out of trouble for two days, how in the world are you going to save a kingdom? And to top it all off, I chose the only person in the world that could make my powers completely useless as my friend.” She sighed deeply as she realized what kind of trouble she was in. She had cut ties with the only people who could truly help her: Luke, Sage, and Rhys. She thought it would keep them safe but she was more than wrong. She could see that now that she was a prisoner and forced to see the truth. They were sent to help her put an end to Loch, not only by training her but also by fighting at her side.

Nicole rocked her head from side to side in her hands, frustrated by her own stubbornness. She didn’t know how to even begin to fix this mess. Luke and Sage were somewhere in Ireland but they couldn’t get close enough to help her; not with all of these warriors who were on Loch's side. Plus now there was Slade to deal with. How could anyone fight someone who could make everyone’s powers completely useless?

Leaning her head against the cold glass of the door, she could feel tears make warm trails down her cheeks as she closed her eyes tight and prayed.

Wenona Hulsey

Chapter 7

The next two days were a blur of nothingness and self-pity for Nicole. She believed herself to be a weak, powerless woman who could do nothing to change becoming Slade's prisoner. She spent most of her time locked in her room, lying on her bed and staring at the ceiling lost in thought. There were times when she was forced from her bed to accompany Slade into town when he had business. Whenever they were out she looked for any opportunity to escape but the warriors that went with them made it impossible for her to try anything.

Several times each day a warrior would enter her room carrying a tray of food. The warrior, a new one each time, would stand against the wall while she ate then after she was done, would gather everything up and leave but not before asking if she had an answer for Slade.

Today she had enough of the questions. "I have a question for you," she retorted, "Why do you serve a traitor to his own people? Slade isn't a warrior, he's a fae, and if you truly want a war then why do you obey him?" Nicole crossed her feet underneath her as she leaned back against the headboard of her bed.

The warrior in her room studied her face for a moment before moving towards the door. "Do you have an answer for Slade," he asked again with no show of emotion.

"You're being controlled by the fae you hate and it doesn't bother you," she chuckled hoping to get a reaction out of the stone faced man. She could see the tension flexing in his jaws and the tightness in his muscles as he stood with a hand on the door. "He keeps you weak just like he's doing me. I mean really, how much good would you be if a fight broke out while Slade was around to suck up all of your power," she clicked her tongue against her teeth, tsking him slyly. "That makes you no more than, I don't know....Tinkerbell's puppy, all bark and no bite."

A change in the wind around her was all Nicole registered before the warrior was next to her, towering above the bed with a dark look filling his eyes and anger shaking his body with each panted breath he took. His hands were held out to his sides, both glowing with red flames, and his lips curled into a smirk as he realized he had startled her with his display. "But I thought you couldn't use your power if Slade was around," she stammered as she tried to hold her ground under his glare.

"Well, I guess you shouldn't trust everything that your told, now should you princess," his smile became wide as he realized that he had the upper hand in this conversation. "Now, do you have an answer," he asked as he let the glow of his hands die out.

Nicole bit the inside of her cheek to keep the arrogant warrior from seeing how much he had gotten to her. She shook her head from side to side and bit out her words slowly, "It's the same answer he's been told for two days so stop asking and get the hell out of here," she pointed towards the door and was relieved when the broad, muscle bound man nodded and walked out, carrying her half eaten breakfast with him.

Her fingernails dug into her palms drawing blood as everything started to become clear to her. Slade had planned this entire charade out so well. Even the fact that they were seated together on the plane had been planned so perfectly by him. *He wanted me to feel abandoned and weak so I would lean on him. He made me think Luke had turned his back on me at the airport and lead me to believe that he had no control over his powers so he could keep me tamed. I'm such a fool. How could I let him manipulate me like that*, she groaned banging her palm into her forehead. "Big, bad, city boy—one, sheltered, trusting Alabama girl—zero," she muttered to herself as she leaned back across the bed.

The day turned into evening as the light in her room began to dim with the setting sun. Nicole was vaguely aware of the change as she lay unmoving on the bed. She had settled into an unnerving pattern of waiting. Waiting for time to pass, waiting for an unknown hero or waiting for the call that would send her into the hands of her enemy. An enemy, that at one time she was foolish enough to think that she could take on alone. Instead, she chose to ignore her years of police training that told her how to research her target well: study his every move and desire before taking him down. Then there wouldn't have been any surprises like this. She would have known what she was up against and avoided turning into a prisoner.

The sound of heavy footsteps approaching her door drew her attention from her thoughts. It was too early yet for her meal to be brought to her so her body tensed for the unknown as the door swung open. "Shower and dress for dinner. I will be back in an hour to escort you down," the same stone faced warrior from earlier informed her. She noticed his eyes were still tight and cold like they were earlier when she challenged him. He laid a long garment bag across the foot of the bed then sat a shoe box beside it before turning on his heels and exiting without another word.

Nicole found a bit of joy in the fact that she had gotten under his skin so easily. "Nice talking to you again, Rover," she chuckled as the door slammed behind the gorilla-like warrior. She slid to the end of the bed and opened the bag to see what she would be wearing. She pulled out a blood red dress that bordered on hooker attire. The front draped around her neck with a sharp v-cut that barely covered her breasts with silk strips of material. The dress didn't join together again until below her belly button, leaving a lot of cleavage and most of her stomach exposed. The bottom half of the dress was much more modest in a length that reached to her ankles but the long split that stretched to the top her thigh put an end to any comfort she had put into keeping some of her dignity intact.

"You have got to be kidding me!" her jaws clinched as she opened the shoe box. She pulled out matching red shoes with six inch heels that strapped around the ankle. "Well if he wants to kill me this is sure one way to do it. I will break my neck in these trashy things." She went to toss the death traps back into the box but an envelope caught her eye.

My love,

I hope this letter finds you on much happier terms than I left you. I am sure you are shocked by the attire for tonight but I must insist you wear it. You see, this is not what I would choose for such a beautiful woman, but it is what Loch would choose. He has requested you be brought to him tonight so our time together is running out.

I will see you at dinner and I hope, with all that I am, that you will have reconsidered my offer otherwise you must get accustomed to looking as you do tonight because you will forever be Loch's whore.

Slade

Nicole let the paper fall from her hands and land silently on the carpet near her feet. Her heart was beating so loud that it drowned out the chaos in her mind. The breath in her lungs came in with ragged pants as she let herself sink to the floor. This was it, the fight she had been training for was finally here but she no longer had a weapon to battle with. All that training and preparations was useless without her power. "How in the hell am I going to win this now?"

~***~**

Nicole entered the eloquent dining area of the hotel on the bulbous arm of the warrior that hated her deeply. She had been given strict instruction not to try anything or she would regret it. Holding her head up high, even though she looked like she had just walked off a street corner, she strode with confidence past the staring eyes of the other diners. There was no way she was going to let Slade have the satisfaction of seeing how humiliated she was so she smiled confidently as they approached his dimly lit booth.

Slade stood as they neared the table, "Thank you for joining me, Nicole."

"Like I had a choice," she retorted taking her seat across from him.

Slade smiled slyly at her as he sat back down in his seat, "Well, I'm beginning to see that you don't make very good choices if given options." A waiter approached with a bottle of red wine and two glasses, filling them promptly then walking away just as fast as he appeared.

Nicole watched the nervous demeanor of the waiter with interest. It seemed that everyone took their job seriously when Slade was around. She found herself wondering if the reaction of the man was because his boss was in the room or if it was fear because people knew what type of deceitful and power hungry man Slade really was. Finally, she let her eyes turn back to Slade who was staring back at her with an unreadable look, "When it's a choice between the lesser of two evils, there's never a good choice."

Slade nodded then took a slow drink of his wine, savoring the taste. "You look," he paused, searching for the right words, "ravishing tonight. Red is a good color for you. It matches the fire I see in your eyes."

"You want to see fire, then stop holding my powers away from me," she winked with a one dark smile curving her lips.

"Now, now, my love. You know I've not had enough of these tonight for you touch that caged beast."

"Do I? Well, you will have to excuse my doubt in you now that I know what you really are," she bit back the urge to call him a bold faced liar, thinking maybe she should keep that information under her sleeve for now.

Slade leaned forward placing his glass down on the table then steepled his fingers in front of him, "You know that I want what is best for our people, Nicole. We were once a very powerful and respected Kingdom that held the warriors in their proper place for centuries. But foolish people let foolish ideas of a perfect union between the two races, making them equal, get in the way and caused the fall of our people." He sighed, folding his hands in front of him on the table, "We can do that once again, don't you see? The fae people shouldn't live in fear of the warriors that once served as our slaves."

Nicole could feel the anger building inside of her. Didn't he realize that she was the result of that union of races? Was he completely unaware that she was so powerful because her blood was a mixture of both fae and warrior, created not to be used as a weapon of war but out of love? She looked down at the bright white cloth that covered the table as she gathered her thoughts, "Do you think Loch will just walk away if I don't show up tonight? He's been waiting for this day for a very long time so I'm sure he will come for me if you hold me here."

"But my love, you will go to him tonight," he smirked with self-confidence gleaming in his eyes. "You will be accepted into the warrior's domain with open arms along with me as your humble escort. He will make you an offer and you will accept, then when the time is right, we will destroy Loch's kingdom from the inside out. He won't know what has hit him until it's too late," he slammed his fist into his palm as he smiled, showing the dimples she once admired.

"We," Nicole laughed. "And what exactly will you be doing to help out, Slade? I mean, isn't your greatest power being a leech," she smiled as she leaned forward, lowering her voice to a whisper, "Of course, I say that in the most flattering way possible."

Slade glared at her smirking face, not finding any humor in her words, "I can make those warrior's powers useless then you can destroy them all."

"But you see, this is where you and I don't see eye to eye, my friend. I have no desire to kill anyone but Loch. I take him out then this whole war is over."

"That's not good enough!" Slade slammed his fist down on the table causing his wine glass to fall over and shatter. A trail of red seeped across the table then began to pool on the floor. "There will be another warrior waiting to take his place so this war will continue until one race is gone. I will not sit by and let it be the Fae."

Nicole's muscles tensed in response to Slade's display. She could feel all the eyes in the room turn on them as she fought to keep seated. Crossing her arms over her chest, she leaned back into the plush cushions of the booth seat. *What's the point in fighting this, he isn't going to budge so now is the time to play it smart. He's willing to help me get to Loch and that's my goal. Why not use that to my advantage?* Her mind spun around the idea with surprising ease. She wasn't raised to use people and knew if her dad was here she would get a serious lecture but Slade could be a useful tool to end this war and she would be stupid not to take advantage of it.

Nicole stood up and was quickly followed by Slade jumping to his feet, "Where do you think you're going?"

A smile played across her lips as she watched the goon she had affectionately nicknamed Rover push off the wall he was leaning against. He watched her every move as if she was about to attack. She gave him a quick wink then turned her attention back to Slade, "If I'm going to war, I'm sure as hell not going looking like this."

Slade studied her face, his brows pinched together in thought, until whatever he was looking for was satisfied. He nodded to the warrior, "Escort Ms. Keenan back to her room so she can change. I will meet you at the car."

Nicole spun on her heels and started making her way out of the room but was stopped by the arm, "Don't try to screw me Nicole, you will regret it," Slade whispered in her ear.

"Now Slade, I thought you wanted me to give you a good screwing. You're such a confusing man," she purred with a sarcastic undertone she was sure would leave Slade wondering. She left him standing there to watch her walk away on the arm of a warrior.

Chapter 8

Nicole hurried into her room with the warrior following close behind, "Sit boy," she pointed to the couch in the living area of the suite. "I've got to change and I won't need your supervision."

The man studied her for a moment then slowly nodded his head, "You've got five minutes then I'm coming in after you." He leaned against the wall crossing his arms over his broad chest.

"You're such a sweetheart," Nicole rolled her eyes at the warrior then quickly went into her room, shutting the door behind her. Her mind was running in a hundred different directions all at the same time. "One step at a time girl," she spoke to herself as she started to slide out of the atrocious dress. "First I figure out how to take out Loch, then I move onto getting rid of Slade all while not getting myself killed. Simple," she said sarcastically.

Her chest began tightening with every breath and her throat was shutting off as her nerves went into over drive. She tried to swallow down the building emotions and just concentrate on changing into some comfortable clothes. She managed to slide an Alabama football T-shirt over her head, but the world around her began to spin as she fought for control. Her knees wobbled slightly so she quickly dropped to the floor, taking deep breaths to fight off the blackness overtaking her vision. This wasn't her nerves. No she could tell this was an outside force trying to press its way into her head. But it wasn't strong enough to drill past Slade's shield.

The door to her room crashed open and Claude and Slade came pouring in with the guard taking position in the doorway. Slade glanced down to where Nicole sat in the floor then turned his attention out her patio door, "Send the others to capture them then you come back here with us."

Claude nodded then he and the guard were gone from the room in a blink of an eye. Slade walked over to Nicole, "Get dressed. We need to go now," he snipped reaching down and pulling her to her feet by one arm.

Nicole's vision was still blurred but she managed to remain on her feet. The weakness seemed to be dissipating rapidly with each passing second, "What's going on?"

"Seems my dear sister and that warrior of yours are trying to get to you. I almost forgot how strong Sage's powers were too." He shook his head as he let his eyes drift back out the door and across the darkening garden. "No matter now. All she managed to do was give you a headache and alert the warriors to her location. I'll have them soon enough."

"Leave them alone, Slade! I swear if you hurt them I will make you regret ever hearing my name," Nicole hissed.

Slade grabbed her jeans from across the bed and

shoved them in her hands, "Put them on or walk to the car in only your shirt and panties, decide now." He turned his attention back to the door, her threat having no effect on his demeanor. He glared out into the darkness following an unseen chase as he shifted uneasily.

Nicole put on her jeans but before she could get her shoes tied Claude appeared at the end of her bed with a wisp of wind following behind him, "The rest of the guards are trailing them," he reported.

"Let's go then," Slade pulled Nicole off the bed by her arm as she struggled to not trip over her untied laces.

"Just us? Wouldn't it be wise to bring more guards, sir?"

"There's no time. It's best to move while they are running for their lives."

Claude nodded in agreement and followed Slade and Nicole out of the room. They started down the hallway of the hotel. Slade and Claude were on constant alert, swiveling their heads from side to side and cautiously approaching every corner before moving forward again.

Nicole cleared her throat and tried hard not to let the irritation of being pulled along like a small child show in her voice, "You know, if you'd let me use my powers we could all be in the car in the next few seconds instead of you all having to go at human speed with me." Nicole hoped her voice of reason would overpower Slade's suspicion but the look on his face told her she was getting nowhere with him.

"Nice try, love," Slade pulled her forward toward a side exit of the hotel that opened to a private parking area. The black limo sat waiting in the center of the lot.

Claude rushed forward in a blur of speed towards the car. He started the limo and was waiting with the door held open before they closed half of the distance.

"Don't you understand that I miss my powers? It's really not fair of you to continue to hold them from me especially since you expect us to work together in defeating Loch," she climbed into the car and sat drumming her fingers on the armrest as she waited for Slade to join her. She knew she was running out of time to help Luke and Sage. The only way she stood a chance of helping was to attempt convincing Slade into giving her power back. "The way I see it, you owe me for lying all of this time."

Slade stood gripping the top of the open door for a moment then bent so he could see Nicole inside the car, "I'm keeping the power at bay to protect you."

"Protect me? How is keeping me from being able to defend myself protection?"

Slade snorted with an arrogant grin as cold as his hardened eyes, "I'm protecting you from the stupid decision you would make to save your friends. Even now, you're trying to figure out a way to help them. You would sacrifice accomplishing your goal to make sure they are safe," he shook his head with a look of disdain on his face. "I won't let you do something that you will regret." Slade climbed into the car, his stature filling the space and giving Nichole a sense of claustrophobia.

"How can you say that? Sage is your sister. Aren't you the slightest bit worried about her?" Panic filled Nicole's voice as the car started to move away from the hotel. Her window of opportunity was shrinking by the second. "You're not that cold, are you?" Nicole's voice quavered with her last words. She could see the look of complete detachment in his eyes at the mention of his sister's name.

"Blood is the only thing Sage and I share." He waved his hand dismissively then leaned forward until his face was inches from Nicole's. "You just worry about being a good girl when we meet Loch. He must believe that you are willing to join him. Don't mess this up Nicole or *you* will be the one regretting the day you heard *my* name," he reached up in the blink of an eye, grabbing Nicole by the back of her head. He pulled her head back roughly by a fist full of her hair causing her to gasp. "Do you understand me, my love?"

Tears glazed over Nicole's vision as she tried not to scream in pain. She could feel hairs, one by one, turning loose from her scalp as Slade tightened his grip, pulling her head farther back. "I understand," she spat.

Staring down into her eyes he smiled softly, liking what he saw, and then let loose of his hold on her head. "Good," he sat down next to her instead of taking his seat across from her in the limo.

Rubbing at the tingling area on the back of her head Nicole shifted in her seat, trying to put some space between herself and Slade. She could feel the pressure of him invading her personal space as he sat next to her, letting his leg brush against hers like they were longtime friends. She had to bite back the urge to go for the door as the limo crawled slowly down the winding drive that led away from the hotel. She knew she wouldn't get far but a few moments out of Slade's reach seemed worth the risk.

"You know you're forcing me to be this kind of person, Nicole," Slade reached over and took her hand away from the spot on her head and kissed it gently.

Nicole jerked her hand back as if the touch of his lips against her skin had been the deepest pain she had ever felt, "Don't touch me again."

"It doesn't have to be like this. I can make you happy and give you a wonderful life. We could be so much more than," he paused searching for the right word then smiled. "Business partners I guess would be the best label for us. We are both working together to reach a single goal for individual gain, but we could have so much more together."

Nicole's eyes were wide and her mouth agape as she tried to fathom the words that had just oozed from Slade's mouth. She took in his serious and expecting eyes as he waited for her to respond and realized that he was delusional enough to believe that after all that had happened in the past few days, she would consider having a real relationship with him. "You have got to be kidding me. You are a power-hungry, deceitful psycho that has no trouble kidnapping and roughing up a woman. Where I come from, the only thing you would get out of this relationship is the business end of a shotgun."

Slade's face turned hard for a moment. He leaned back into the smooth leather seat staring forward in silence until a smirk softened his glare, "Well, you still have time to come around to the idea and..." He let his eyes meet hers as his smirk turned into a full grin, "In the mean time we will have to keep the shotguns put away."

~***~**

As the limo came to a stop in front of the large estate where Loch would be, Nicole's stomach balled into a tight knot. The building was constructed of beautiful white stones and stood three stories high with enormous white columns marking the entryway. Gleaming windows adorned the face of the luxury home and a large balcony sat high above. The lawn was groomed with vibrantly colored flowers and green bushes all placed precisely, creating a picture perfect view to the casual eye. It was all beautiful, but Nicole saw so much more. One look around and she noticed armed men tucked away just out of sight from the untrained eye. Two men were on the roof, one on the balcony and she had spotted four more guards along the edge of the yard who were blurring their way to the limo. "Warriors with semi-automatic weapons. Wonderful," muttered Nicole as the men surrounded the car.

"Just keep your mouth closed," Slade shot back at her as Claude opened the door. Slade stepped out with the confidence of a man who owned the world, "I believe your master is expecting us." He held out his hand and waited for Nicole to take it as she emerged from the car.

Nicole begrudgingly took his hand and let him let him help her from the car but before she could get her bearings she was shoved against the door by a warrior dressed in black. He held her tight against the car as another warrior moved to restrain Slade with surprising ease. "Slade my sweet, it doesn't seem we were expected guests after all."

"We've been expecting you," said the guard with a shove to the back of Slade's head.

Slade jerked his body in an attempt to break the warrior's hold on him but with little effect, "Then you should know that this is unnecessary of you." He jerked his arms again but was pressed harder against the car by the guard.

"I'd say it's quite necessary." A shrill and familiar voice caused goose bumps to dance across Nicole's skin.

"Morena, so nice to see you again," Nicole purred. She couldn't help the smile spreading across her face like honey when she noticed the dark bruises on each side of Morena's nose. The woman had made a valiant attempt to conceal the black and purple marks but had failed horribly. Nicole had wondered if Morena had any powers, other than being a super bitch, but judging by the slow rate she was healing it was clear to her that Morena was a simple human.

Morena gave Nicole a dismissive glance as if she didn't exist and then turned her cold glare onto Slade.

"Slade..." she clicked her tongue against her teeth as she stopped a few feet in front of the limo. "What a peculiar situation you've allowed yourself in. I had such high hopes for you...for us, but now," she shook her head as she turned around and began to make her way back up the path that lead to the door of the elaborate estate. "Lock them up," She ordered over her shoulder to the guards holding them at the limo.

"You can't do this. You can't let your jealous ways come between what we are trying to accomplish," Slade shouted.

Morena stopped where she stood but did not turn around. She seemed lost in thought then with a shake of her head she started forward again, "You have made your choice and I've made mine."

Chapter 9

The sound of the tumblers clicking into place and the key sliding out of the lock was like a death sentence to Nicole. "This isn't working out at all," she mumbled cradling her head in both hands. Her steps echoed on the cold concrete floor as she paced the small room. The smell of mildew in the stale air coated her throat and left a thick film in her lungs. She walked back up to the steel door and banged her fist against the metal, "I came to you so you shouldn't be locking me up. This is crazy!" She listened intently for any response but silence filled the space around her. She was completely alone.

A single guard had taken Slade up to a higher level while two guards escorted Nicole to the basement level; they refused to speak to her or answer any of her demands to see Loch. Both guards kept their handguns aimed on her until they shoved her inside the dark room and closed the door quickly behind them. She guessed they must have heard about her powers and were scared she might turn on them. Nicole's mind began to spin around the idea that there had to be a limit to

Slade's power. She wondered just how far away he could be and still keep her powers from her.

She placed her hand out in front of her and tried to call the powers from their hiding place deep within her. She closed her eyes digging deep to where the power usually lay inside her while it waited for her call. She cracked her eyes open just a slit to look into her open palm. No glow of power met her gaze but she wasn't deterred. She closed her eyes again and widened her stance bringing her left hand out in front of her and pointing both palms towards the cold, steal barrier holding her in this room. Taking a deep breath she opened her mind to let any waiting power pool to the surface but just as she began to push she heard the click of heals on the concrete floors outside of her prison.

The echo of steps ended on the other side of her door so Nicole dropped her hands and took a step back toward the far wall as the door swung open. Morena stood in the doorway with her hands on each hip. Her red fingernails, a perfect match to the crimson sheath dress that hugged each curve of her body, were tapping a smug rhythm as she glared at Nicole. "Oh my dear friend, what an awful situation you find yourself in. But it's your lucky day because I'm willing to forgive our difference over a silly man and help you find your way out of this place."

Nicole crossed her arms over her chest, "That's so very kind of you but I have a feeling that you're not doing this from the kindness of your little, black heart, Morena. What's the catch?"

Morena took a step closer to Nicole with a grin on her red lips, "Nicole, honey, you've got me figured all wrong. I just want to help you make it back home to your 'normal little country girl life' that you had before all of this," she waived her hand around the small brick room with a look of disgust on her face. "I'm sure deep down that's all you want too...a chance to go back to your dad, your friends and your normal routine in your safe life. That's what I'm offering you, all you have to do is say yes and I'll have you on a plane within the hour."

That was the closest to the truth Nicole had heard anyone speak since she arrived in Ireland. The chance to turn her back on all of these troubles and go back to the normal life she once had was like holding the winning ticket in the lottery between her fingers. All she needed to do was cash in and walk away into the sunset. "What happens if I walk away right now and never look back? Where does that leave my people if I take the coward's way out?" Nicole watched the smug smile fall from Morena's face and her glare turn ice cold.

"What do you care? You can't really claim to be loyal to either warrior or fae so why make yourself choose. Just take what I'm offering, you stupid girl and walk away. This is your chance to go back to what you had before all of this war pressed its way into your life." She stepped forward again so her face was only inches from Nicole's, "Don't be a fool."

Nicole raised her chin and met Morena's hate-filled gaze, "I'm not a coward like you, hiding behind whichever man I can get my claws into just to use his power. I will fight."

The anger radiating from Morena was almost tangible in the air around her as she took a step back. "Have it your way, you stubborn bitch," the angry woman spouted before turning away from Nicole. She walked back through the prison door stopping just outside, "I had a feeling you wouldn't see things clearly so I've brought you a gift to keep you company while I give you a little more time to think my offer over."

Nicole watched Morena nod down the hall to

someone out of her line of sight then step clear of the doorway. A warrior dressed in black army fatigues came through the opening with a body slung over his shoulder. He dropped the lifeless form onto the floor at her feet causing Nicole to gasp when she got a look at the person crumpled on the floor, "Sage."

Nicole dropped to her knees on the floor beside her friend unsure of what needed to be done. She slid the ebony hair away from Sage's face and tucked it behind her pointed ear, "What the hell did you do to her?" The question rang out loud and fierce as Nicole turned her hardened eyes towards the closing door. She caught sight of Morena watching the scene with great pleasure, "She's not dead but if you don't make the right decision, for both of your sakes, she may not be so lucky next time."

The door closed just as Nicole was ready to lunge after the smug lady in red so she turned her attention instead to her friend. "Sage, come on honey, wake up," she shook her shoulder then patted her cheek gently but didn't get a response. Nicole leaned in close to Sage's face to listen for air leaving her nose because she couldn't see any movement resembling breathing coming from her chest.

"Umm, you smell nice," was whispered in Nicole's ear causing her to gasp. Sage gave a weak smile as she rolled herself out flat on the floor. She reached a hand up and rubbed a spot on her head tenderly before letting her hand rest on the cold concrete below her.

Nicole shook her head trying to clear away some of the fog from being startled, "Are you okay? What happened to you?"

"Well, I had to get to you somehow so I let that dumb brute warrior catch me. He got a bit rougher than I expected," she groaned as she pushed herself up on her elbows. The black leather pants, matching black corset adorned with small silver spikes and knee length leather boots Sage was wearing should have sent a clear signal to anyone that this fairy shouldn't be taken lightly but Nicole didn't think it was the right time to point that little fact out.

"You let him catch you?" Nicole asked as she helped Sage up into a sitting position on the floor, "Why would you do that? Have you lost your mind?"

Sage rolled her eyes as she tried to stretch some of the soreness out of her petite body, "Okay, I love you girl but I've not gone crazy. Now Luke...he may be a different story." She snorted sarcastically before letting her eyes meet Nicole's again. "We've been trying like hell to get to you for days but your boyfriend's hotel is too heavily guarded and..." she sighed, "Slade's power is a real fucking downer so this was the next best thing we could come up with."

Nicole stood up and started to pace beside Sage, "Okay first of all, your brother is not my boyfriend. He managed to trick me into thinking he was just a nice guy who wanted to show me around Ireland and I needed time to figure out where Loch was so I didn't—"

"Wooaa girl, hold up and take a breath. I'm not pointing fingers. I know how twisted Slade can be when there's something he wants. After all, he is my loving brother," she laughed dryly. "It just looked to us like you were enjoying his attention. And the night that I managed to get into your head for just a few moments, well, let's just say your body was running pretty damn hot."

Nicole leaned against the wall and slid to the floor. She cradled her head in her hands, "I don't know what happened to me. I was like some hormone enraged teenager when his eyes locked on mine. Everything else didn't matter and all I could think about was him." She raised her head from her palms and studied Sage's questioning face. "What? You don't believe me? I wouldn't lie to you, Sage."

"No, I know that. It would seem my *brother* has learned a few new forbidden tricks since the last time we were together," the venom when she said “brother” was thick in her mouth. Sage pushed herself up off the floor and walked to stand beside Nicole offering her a hand up.

"What do you mean?" she asked as she took her hand and let Sage help her up. Standing beside her friend again gave her a small amount of confidence back. Up until that moment it felt like it had been years since she was near someone she cared about. Just a few days secluded from everyone had been weighing on her more than she had realized and, though the situation wasn't a good one, she was grateful to have Sage with her.

“Centuries ago there were some dishonorable fae abusing certain powers. These fae were eventually punished and said powers became illegal for any other fae to use. The dishonorable ones were some barbaric fae who would use persuasion to gain power and, at their darkest and most destructive moments, to take the bodies of unwilling partners."

Nicole's eyes widened as Sage's words started to make sense, "They would use their powers to rape women," she gasped. "Do you...I mean...you're not saying that Slade."

"You would remember if he did. Your mind is half warrior and so far you have gotten every good power of both warrior and fae. Meaning that if this theory holds true to this as well, you may not have been strong enough to not be affected by his power but you were strong enough to break the spell," she reached out and pulled Nicole into a hug. "I'm sure that he would want you to come to him willingly."

Nicole nodded into Sage's shoulder as she processed the night that he had drank so much and tried to kiss her. It was like reliving a shameful moment that burned deep in her heart but she was sure that Sage was right.

"I remember everything from that night and he definitely wants me to come willingly. He thinks that he and I will destroy the warriors then reign as king and queen of the Fae Kingdom."

Sage hugged Nicole tight then stepped back to look her in the face, "That's my brother through and through. Always was stubborn about getting things he wants but he's crossed the line...again." She walked to the far wall and stared out the small barred window as silence filled the room.

"Does his power affect you like it does me?" Nicole asked softly. She wasn't sure if that was an appropriate question to ask in the magical world. She didn't want to make Sage mad at her but she needed answers. The princess fae/warrior had learned the hard way that she had no real clue what she would be facing now that she was under Loch's roof. Not being rude was shoved aside as she was hard pressed to learn as much as she could in the little time she had left to prepare.

Sage didn't face Nicole, but instead kept her gaze on the small ribbon of moon light filtering through the dirty glass and bars, "You know, when you're a kid, even in the fairy world, everything is happy and the whole world is yours for the taking. You have dreams, you have friends and good times, but that's all you worry about. Slade and I were the same growing up. I loved and looked up to my big brother, he was my best friend." She turned toward Nicole slowly, wrapping her arms around herself then leaning against the wall. The beam of light reflected off the strands of silky black hair hiding Sage's face as she gathered her thoughts.

"But once we became teens our power, like all fae, started to really develop and it began to drive a wedge between us. We both have the speed and strength that matched our parents but my telepathy was at a level unheard of in our family history. Not only could I hear thoughts but I could control others through their minds. Be it as simple as compelling someone into changing their views on a subject by tampering with their memories or as extreme as taking complete control of a person's body and have them walk up to their best friend and slit his throat."

Nicole reached up and covered her neck with her hands as Sage's words took hold of her mind. She knew that her Gothic fairy friend looked dark and dangerous but she had thought it was all a play for attention, like a teenager with green spiked hair. Now she was looking at Sage in a whole different light.

"Don't worry, I'm not going to hurt you Nicole," she said with a slight smirk. "It would seem a power of this kind found the right fae to live in because those few who have come close to touching this amount of energy used it for vain and selfish reasons. Ruining lives and destroying all that was good around them," she sighed deeply then brushed her hair away from her cheek with a black fingernail. "Slade, on the other hand, was gifted with the power to level the playing field. He can neutralize anyone's powers so no one can use them. I thought it was a wonderful gift but he despised it. He said the Gods were laughing at him and had spit in his face by give his power to a mere girl." The pain was easy to hear in Sage's voice though she was trying hard to seem unaffected by the memories.

Nicole's own heart ached for her friend's hardship and ruined relationship with her brother. She had never known what it was like to have a sibling but she knew it hurt like hell to have Kat mad at her so she could imagine it was much worse with your own flesh and blood. "Is that when you stopped talking to Slade?"

Sage nodded, "Pretty close. After a little while I thought things were getting better between us. He started coming around again and spending time talking to me but before long all talk turned towards my powers. Seems he thought he could learn how to create the power in himself if he could understand how it worked. He started dealing with shady people in the magical world, people you don't ever want to meet, let alone end up owing anything too. He tried to pry information from me but once I knew what he was up to I walked away from him." She gave Nicole a weak smile, "We haven't spoken in half a century."

"I'm sorry Sage."

"Don't be," she shrugged then reached into her back pocket and pulled out a tube of lipstick, "He chose his life and I've chose mine." Sage opened the gold cylinder and started smoothing the crimson color over her plump lips. Nicole had long ago come to think of that red as Sage's trademark color. The way it glowed against her pale white skin reminded her of a portrait by a skilled artist who only accented one piece of the puzzle and left the rest in black and white for the observer to interpret.

"Well, I hope you have more than lipstick hidden on you if we are planning on breaking out of here."

Sage capped her crimson lip paint then shrugged her shoulders, "Sorry, this is all I've got. You want some," she winked and blew a kiss in Nicole's direction.

"No thank you," Nicole rolled her eyes as the playful Sage that she remembered started to surface. "Now what do we do? Please tell me you had a plan when you let that guard capture you," begged Nicole. She leaned against the wall and picked at the edge of her warn white t-shirt. The feeling of being confined was starting to close in on her with each second that ticked away while she was in the tiny room that served as her prison.

Sage bit the edge of her lip and squinted her nose up slightly, "Well, it was kind of a split second decision on my part. I just knew I needed to be inside here with you but...no, I didn't really think much past getting here." She put her arm around Nicole giving her a hug. "But at least you're not by yourself anymore."

Nicole giggled, "You and your bright sides." A moment of silence settled over the room as Nicole thought. "Is Luke alone?"

"Yes. He and I have been trying to get to you—"

The sound of approaching footsteps had both the women focusing on the door. Nicole could feel her body's reflexive reaction gravitate to the spot in her chest where her powers once lived but unfortunately came away without the slightest tingle of energy.

The door slung open quickly and three muscle bound guards, dressed in all black military fatigues, came barreling inside. One took hold of Sage's arm and the other two guards each took one of Nicole's arms. Neither woman struggled; although Nicole was sure she heard Sage mumbling profanities under her breath as the goth fairy turned her attention on the hall outside of the doorway.

"My dearest sister, how nice to see you again after all these years," Slade stood in the hall with his hands casually tucked in his pockets and a slight grin on his face.

Sage tried to take a step forward but the guard pulled her to a stop, "If you weren't blocking my powers right now I'd have these gorillas rip you to shreds but we all know that my big brother doesn't fight fair."

Slade let out a deep, rumbling laugh, throwing his head back and revealing his perfectly white teeth, "Now that's the Sage I remember." He turned his attention to Nicole, "Love, we have an audience with Loch. I've gotten all the confusion straightened out for you so there's nothing to fear." He reached his hand out toward her, "You're not going to cause any trouble right?"

Nicole studied his eyes for a moment. She starred into the depths of his ice blue orbs searching for hope that he was still on the side of the fairies and hadn't really joined up with Loch. With a heavy heart and a large lump in her throat she reached for Slade's hand. The guards released their hold but still kept a cautious eye on her every movement as they started down the hall. Nicole glanced behind to make sure that Sage was coming too and was met by the anger filled gaze of her friend. There hadn't been time to explain so Sage would just have to trust her.

The pressure was eating away at Nicole as she walked fingers laced with a man whom she knew had his own motives for helping her. She just couldn't be sure if he was on her side at all anymore. The warmth of his body heat next to her own was a torment, knowing that she couldn't ask questions even with them being this close to each other.

Seeming to sense Nicole's turmoil Slade gave her hand a slight squeeze then began to trace small circles on her hand with his thumb. The sensation caused Nicole's stomach to knot even tighter as a confusing sense of longing started to tug at her heart.

The group came to the top of the stairs that brought them out of the dark basement area and into the brightly lit and posh interior of the estate. Nicole was in awe of the exquisite oil paintings lining the eggshell colored walls. One in particular caused her to drag her feet as they passed so she could study it. It was of a beautiful woman with long flowing, brunette hair standing on a balcony that overlooked the sea. A white stone castle was perched on the edge of a high cliff but the beauty in the strokes of the masterful painter wasn't what held Nicole's attention: it was the look of deep sadness on the woman's face— a face that Nicole had seen in her dreams.

"Nicole," Slade gave a gentle tug on her hand trying to encourage her to keep moving, "come on. We are expected and it would be very rude of us to be late." His voice was soft but firm.

"Who is that woman?" Nicole asked, gesturing toward the painting with a nod.

Sage spoke up, "Oh does she look familiar to you? She should and I pray to the Gods that you are half the woman she was," hissed Sage. "Queen Titania gave up everything to save the Fae Kingdom and I hope your grandmother didn't do it in vein."

Sage's words shot threw Nicole's heart like ice cold daggers but before she could respond Slade turned to her, "That's enough out of you, sister. If you can't be quiet I'll send you back to the cell I just saved you from." He stood nose to nose with her in a battle of unspoken words until Sage took a step back but she did not try to mask the hate radiating from her. Slade nodded then started down the hall again, taking Nicole's hand in his just as they reached two large oak doors with guards standing at attention on each side.

Just as the guards moved to open the doors a loud

commotion sounded back down the hallway in the direction they had just came from. Nicole turned in time to see a guard being slammed violently into the wall, sending sprays of sheet rock crumbling to the floor. Her breath caught in her throat when the man stepped away from the crumpled body lying on the floor. "Luke," she gasped and started forward.

"Stop her," the voice of Morena boomed out from the now open doors behind them.

Before Nicole could take two steps a large arm wrapped around her neck pulling her hard backwards. She struggled to slip from the man's grip as more guards began to swarm the hallway from behind Morena.

Luke tackled the guard running toward him and in one fluid motion of brute strength snapped the man's neck, letting him fall heavily to the floor before moving onto the next. There was no show of fire or super strength in this battle. All men here were fighting on fair ground because of Slade's unwavering and unbiased powers blanketing everyone as thoroughly as the air they all breathed.

Nicole could see the sweat starting to bead on Luke's forehead as he moved from man to man, cutting a path toward her with each swing of his fist, letting nothing stand in his way. Her eyes darted to her side where Sage was struggling to free herself from her captor as well. The slight woman expertly centered the guard's stomach with a blade-like elbow then copied the motion to his face when he bowed over in pain. Just as she Nicole began to slip from the hold of her own captor the feel of cold metal on her temple followed by the clicking of a hammer froze her in place.

"Enough," yelled Morena as she pressed the barrel of her gun to Nicole's face, "I've tolerated all I will of this game." She turned her hard glare onto Sage and Luke,

"Now, if you two don't want your pretty little friend's brains on the floor in the next five seconds I'd suggest you stop."

Sage and Luke froze where they stood. Luke let the guard he choked close to unconsciousness fall at his feet gasping for breath. For the first time Nicole was able to meet his hardened gaze as he panted for breath. There was no tenderness in his eyes as he stared at Nicole. There was only anger, hurt and determination. He looked away from her to Slade then back to Morena as his body trembled and muscles flexed with anticipation, "Just give her to me and there won't be any need for more bloodshed."

"You're in no position to be making demands warrior," retorted Morena. "Slade, take Nicole inside," she motioned toward the open oak doors. "Guard, take those two down to the cells until I can ask Loch what he wants done."

Slade stepped up behind Nicole taking her by the arms as the guard stepped aside. Nicole's vision blurred and the room around her was warping into odd shapes from the lack of oxygen up until the second that the guard released his hold on her neck. Her legs went weak just as Slade took hold and she found herself falling but before her knees hit the floor Slade slid his arms around her waist pulling her back to her feet, "Hold on love," he whispered pulling her close to his body. "Don't pass out when I'm about to do something extremely stupid."

Slade turned Nicole with lightning speed, spinning her out of the line of Morena's gun then let loose his hold on Nicole. He spun sending Morena's gun sailing across the floor. Almost in the same fluid motion he swept his leg out and sent the guard holding Sage to the ground. Sage quickly seized Morena in her stunned state and downed her with a sharp blow to the back of her head, sending her into an unconscious pile on the floor. Seeing his cue Luke ripped his arms from the grasp of the guards that fought to hold him.

Nicole watched the two men fighting side by side to dispose of the final guards. She had let herself forget that Slade still possessed his supernatural speed while everyone else was basically human. He moved with the magical speed and inhuman grace Nicole had seen Sage display but he killed with the brute force and the cold, hardened look of a warrior. Never hesitating as he twisted the neck of his target then stood looking down at his dead enemy with complete confidence. But what was even more unbelievable to her was that Luke was completely powerless but yet he made quick work of the guard that sought to subdue him as well. It was like watching a master fighter moving about without a thought, always knowing what his next move will be then swooping in for the kill without the slightest sign of doubt. If it wasn’t for the rapid rise and fall of his chest when he finished Nicole would have never known his powers were held out of his reach just as hers were.

Nicole found herself mesmerized and staring unabashedly at Luke. His dirt stained gray shirt clung to his muscles as the sweat made the material darker in spots on his chest and down his lean stomach. Even the littlest details like the small tears in his shirt exposing his golden, tanned skin drew her attention. She had honestly believed she would never see this man again. Her heart stopped as the world paused its forward motion in the moment their eyes locked. A deep longing to run into his arms and have him hold her tight pulled at her as she searched his eyes hoping to see the same, but coldness was all she found in his deep, pristine, hazel pools staring back at her.

"Let's go," shouted Sage as she turned to run back down the hall.

Before Nicole could move from her trance Slade was standing in front of her, blocking her view of Luke. She blinked her eyes trying to pull herself back into the moment as Slade took her hand, "Come love, this is no time for daydreams."

"Get your dirty hands off of her," Luke shouted as he charged Slade. With a thunderous boom they crashed into the wall. Luke landed on top of Slade and drew his fist back, "You are not going with us traitor."

With one shove of his hands Slade sent Luke sliding down the hallway on his back, "Seems you forget that I still have my powers, warrior." Slade stood up knocking the dust off his black sport coat with an unamused air then turned his cold gaze on Luke who was pulling himself from the floor, "You will not decide where I go."

"Will you two stop it," shouted Nicole. "We don't have time for this. We've got to get out of here." She turned to Luke, "We need his help otherwise we will be facing warriors with full powers without him."

Luke stood with his jaw muscles flexing and his brows knitted together, "Fine, bring the traitor. I'll deal with him when we're out of here." He stepped up to Nicole looking down into her face, "Unless you're attached to him and would like to stop me princess?"

Luke's heated breath brushed across Nicole's cheek as she tried not to back away from his hardened stare. A million things rushed to the tip of her tongue but before she could say a word Luke turned away from her and started down the hall in the direction Sage had gone.

Nicole stared after him both hurt and confused as Slade slid an arm around her shoulders and nudged her forward, "Nice boyfriend you have there, love," he chuckled.

"Hey wait," Nicole shouted, ignoring Slade's snide

remark. "We can't leave Morena to go tell Loch, can we? I mean," she stammered trying to say what she was thinking gently, "You killed the guards so shouldn't you also...dispose of her?" She was amazed at her own coldness as she watched Slade, Sage and Luke exchange glances.

"She's right. Morena is a loose end but we could use her to our advantage," spoke-up Luke.

"How so?" Sage asked as she ran back to the group.

"You wipe her mind then I'll implant a new memory," Luke spoke to Sage, "A memory that would clear the traitor of any wrong-doing in Loch's eyes."

Slade snorted, "And why do you care about clearing my name?"

"I don't," he stared Slade down with malice in his glare. "But you could prove to be useful if we need someone back on the inside again before this is over."

Nicole knew Luke was right. The only person remaining alive that witnessed Slade's betrayal to Loch was Morena. They could use her mind to allow Slade access back into Loch's good graces, if they thought he was kidnapped by Luke. "There are two problems with this plan," sighed Nicole. "Slade can't just walk out of here looking like he went willingly and he won't let us use our powers."

Sage and Luke exchanged a look then Nicole watched as a smirk turned up the edge of Luke's lips, "That can be fixed." Without a warning he swung his arm catching Slade on the chin. An echo of knuckles clashing against Slade's jaw bone bounced off the walls of the hall just before he collapsed to the floor. Instantly power rushed through every vein and out every pore of Nicole's body. She felt light and free, like a hundred pound chain had been lifted from around her neck as her hands began to glow.

Luke watched her with a glimmer in his eyes, enjoying the happiness radiating from Nicole, "Better, princess?"

"Yes," she smiled then looked down at the limp man in the floor. She thought of reminding Luke that they could have given Slade a chance to pull his shield away which would have allowed them to use their power but decided to bring up another point instead, "You know you're going to have to carry him out of here right?"

He groaned throwing up his hand, "Couldn't you let me enjoy punching him for just a few more minutes before you tossed that bit of information at me?" He shook his head then turned to Sage, "Time to work your magic."

Chapter 10

Once away from the estate Luke lead the group deep into the woods away from the roads and any sign of civilized world that could be seen or heard. The sun was rising, causing the early morning dew to glimmer on the leaves of the green underbrush of the forest. Nicole's eyes traveled across the landscape half on guard and half admiring the untouched beauty of the world around them.

No one in the group had spoken a word after they escaped Loch's estate. When they were far enough away Luke had tossed Slade to the ground and Nicole tried to gently coach him awake. Before he could fully focus Sage kicked him in the leg "Stop whining and get your ass up."

For what felt like hours, because they had no concept of time, they moved forward along a hidden trail without uttering a word to each other. The tension was thick and almost unbearable to her. Luke and Sage walked slightly ahead of Nicole, never looking back while

Slade insisted on walking at her side like a silent shadow.

When Nicole finally had her fill of the silence she stopped and spoke with the stubborn jut of her chin, "Where are we going?" She placed her hands on her hips.

"We are taking you somewhere safe," Sage replied with a sharp tone.

Nicole rolled her eyes at the evasive answer, "And where would that be?"

"Does it really matter?"

"Yes it matters, Sage. I want to know," snipped Nicole. She knew she was being hard to deal with but the silence was killing her. If she had to pick a fight to get the real issues to the surface she was ready.

"Do you want to know or are you worried for your boyfriend," spat Luke as he turned to face her.

Nicole took in a sharp breath at his words and prepared to set the record straight right then and there but Slade spoke up, "Oh, is the poor warrior worried that the princess may choose her fae side over her warrior side?" Slade took a step towards Luke with a cocky grin, "Is that what's got a bug up your ass, Luke? Well, I'm not going to act like that's not what I want but so far Nicole has been an elusive creature."

Luke looked past Slade to where Nicole stood, "I want to hear it from you Nicole. Are you taking a side in this war?"

Nicole was hurt and taken aback by his question, "I'm still standing where I was when I left you behind in Alabama. I came here to put an end to Loch and that's still what I want. I want to stop this war from happening."

"But then what," demanded Luke. "When you finish Loch where will your loyalty lay? Will you go with him?" He threw a daggered look in Slade's direction as he spoke.

"Is this really what you want to know Luke," Nicole pushed her way past Slade and stepped up to Luke. Her body was beginning to shake and her words were rushing past her lips before she thought, "Are you asking me which side I'll choose in this war or are you asking me—" She reached forward and shoved with all she had on Luke's chest, causing him to take a step back with wide eyes. "Or are you asking me if I'm choosing you or Slade," her voice echoed through the forest. She stepped back, taking a deep, unsteady breath as she ran her shaking hand through her hair.

Sage came forward and took Nicole by the hand, pulling her back in the direction the group had been walking leaving the two men standing alone. "Nicole, there will be time for this when we get you safe. We are taking you to one of the few remaining gateways to the Fae world. It's hidden away deep in the forest and has been forgotten by most."

Nicole shook her head trying to clear her anger clouded mind and focus on what Sage was telling her, "What do you mean 'gateway'? Are you talking like...to another world?"

Sage snorted, "Yes." She shrugged her shoulders like Nicole was asking the dumbest questions she had ever heard. Sage's powder white skin was glowing in the morning light. Rays of sunshine that found their way past the dense canopy of leaves and were dancing off her black hair making it glitter like something out of a fairytale.

Nicole watched her friend like she was seeing her for the first time. The dark Gothic fae, whom always dressed in black clothes and adorned spiked dog collars as if it were the height of fashion, had a magic radiating from her in a way Nicole had never seen before.

Sage glanced over at the staring Nicole and crinkled her nose, "What? Do I have dirt on my face?"

"Ummm, I promise I'm not coming onto you but your skin is beautiful," Nicole stopped walking and pulled Sages arm up to her face like she was a scientist inspecting a great find. "You're freaking glowing like a lighting bug," she gasped with a large, teasing grin on her face.

Sage pulled her arm back, "I'm not a freak, Nicole. You're the only mutant here," she snorted with grin. She took Nicole's hand and lifted it up in front of her friend's face, "You're doing it too so don't get all jealous of my fairy sexiness," she winked.

Nicole gasped as she stared at the light radiating from her hand. She turned her hand from side to side then lifted her other hand up to see the same glow on her hand and up her arms until the point where her sleeve hid her skin away, "I've never done this before," she whispered.

"That's because you've never been near a Fae gateway before. Our magic is the strongest in our own realm. You will love your kingdom, Nicole," Slade spoke from behind her in a proud tone.

Nicole turned to see that Slade also had the glow that she and Sage were emitting. It was as if she was seeing his spirit on the surface of his skin in all its captivating beauty. There was so much she was still learning about the world and it made her wonder how she could possibly save a world from war when the basic workings of the very people she was trying to help were so foreign to her. She looked from Slade to Sage then finally let her eyes rest on Luke who had taken his place up in the back of the group. He stood with his arms crossed over his chest as he took in the spectacle playing out in front of him.

"It's time we get moving again. She's not safe here," Luke demanded looking straight at Nicole but speaking around her.

"Damn Luke, you don't have to be so snippy. We don't have far to go," Sage retorted with a roll of her eyes as she tugged Nicole's arm to follow her.

"I guess the chap is just feeling a bit left out right now. I don't blame him...all warriors should envy the fae powers," Slade winked at Nicole then fell into step behind her.

Luke snorted laughter, "If I wanted to be a sparkling fairy tale creature I'd find a vampire to bite my arse."

A chuckle escaped Nicole's lips before she could hide it away. Sage gave Nicole a cross but playful look causing Nicole to giggle harder.

"You've got to admit that was a good one, Sage. And Slade does keep that look of constant pain and despair on his face like those twinkling vamps from the movies." The more she talked, the more she laughed and with one glance back at Slade, Sage nodded and joined in with her bell-like laughter.

Slade gave a groan from where he stood shaking his head. Nicole chanced a glance back at Luke and caught a fleeting glimpse of a smile as he stared at the ground around his feet. When he looked up his eyes locked with Nicole's for a brief second then any hint of his happiness in the moment was gone. Hurt and anger lined his face again, "Let's move."

~*~**

Another ten minutes the group traveled in silence. Nicole shadowed Sage as she followed a trail that could only be felt by a pull deep inside the soul of a fae. She knew they must be nearing the end of the journey because the trees were unusually vibrant green and there was an abundance of animals: from large, beautiful deer to small, bright green humming birds darting about. There was also a vibration of energy in the air and at times she could see small electric orbs appear only to disappear again like tiny, blue fireflies dancing under the shade of the trees that sheltered them from the midday sun.

The thick forest gave way to a large clearing blanketed in small yellow flowers and in the center of the opening stood a huge Weeping Willow with its long, dangling limbs creating an umbrella that covered the entire center of the opening. Nicole stood in awe of the magic she could feel dancing in the air around her but at the same time a strange sense of familiarity swept over her. "I've been here before," she whispered.

Sage shook her head, "That's impossible."

Nicole took a few steps into the clearing then turned taking in all that was to be seen, "It's the same but different," she shook her head her brows pinched together in thought. "I have these dreams...no, more like visions because they are so real and I've seen this tree," she pointed to the willow just as a breeze caressed its green limbs causing them to sway like the full skirt of a pirouetting ballerina.

"Are you sure it's this exact place or is it just the tree that's familiar to you," Slade asked as he came to stand at Nicole's side. He had long ago dropped his sports coat and was wearing the top three buttons of his white dress shirt undone. His long blond hair was hanging in a disheveled frame around his sweat beaded face.

"The place is different but the tree is the exact one. I would know it anywhere."

Slade and Sage looked to each other before Sage spoke, "This is the spirit tree. It," she pointed to the willow with a smile, "is at every fae gateway."

"It," repeated Nicole with a shake of her head. "The same tree is moved from placed to place?"

"Not exactly and yet, yes." Slade took Nicole's hand and lead her to the tree with a proud smile. "This tree is the embodiment of the fae spirit and magic. It is the only way that one can travel in or out of the realm. This exact tree is located in two places in your world and two places in mine at this moment because it is made of spirit. Spirit can divide, protect and grow."

"It's easier to think of the tree like the feeling of being in love," spoke up Luke from behind Nicole.

Nicole's heart sped up as he barely spoke above a whisper. She didn't dare turn to face him for fear of meeting his cold eyes again so she laced her hands in front of her and looked down at her feet that sat on a pillow of bright yellow flowers and green moss.

"You can be in one place but your heart is always with the one you love. A part of you is with her always and you can feel her worlds away, sending you strength and filling your soul with happiness," He stepped up to Nicole's side but never looked at her.

Nicole stared up at the eloquent limbs of the beautiful willow. She fought to whisper past the lump of emotion in the back of her throat, "I know what you mean." Taking a deep breath she tried to clear her head of Luke's words. "Where are all the gateways at? I mean, couldn't just anyone run up on this place?"

Sage smiled a knowing smirk at Nicole, obviously enjoying the building tension radiating from Luke. "Well, the placements of the gateways were based on prophecies made centuries ago and it would seem the old bat was right. One gate is," she did a perfect curtsy that almost looked lady-like if it wasn't for her tight, black leather pants, "conveniently located just miles from where we needed to escape from today. Another is in the forest that connects to your father's land back in Alabama."

Nicole's eye's got wide, "I wondered how you and Rhys seemed to just appear at my house out of nowhere." In the same second another question ran to the front of Nicole's lips, "Where is Rhys? He's not here too is he?" The thought of the crude but incredibly sexy warrior brought bittersweet feelings rushing to Nicole. He had fought by her side and helped her save her best friend but his pushy advances had caused her to say some harsh things to him and she never got a chance to apologize.

"He's with your father and Kat. He and Kat wanted to come with us but Luke sent them back to be with your dad," Sage said as she placed an impatient hand on her hip. She didn't like to be interrupted and she wasn't afraid to let it be known. "Now, if you would like to let me finish or do you already know this story?" She raised her eyebrows waiting for Nicole's response. Nicole tossed her hands up in front of her as an apology for her rudeness and waited for Sage to continue. "There was a forth gateway but....it was lost."

"How do you lose a gateway?"

"Not really sure but it would seem that it was sealed away from us. The fae and warriors have searched for years for the gate but it was never found."

"Why would someone want to hide it," asked Nicole.

Slade, who had grown silent after Luke had joined the group, spoke up, "The gateway led to the fae burial grounds. It's how those fae who chose to give up immortality can pass on their powers to the next generation. The spirit tree recycles the power into the fae children, which are very rare now. No child can be conceived in the fae world unless there is power waiting to be granted to the baby. The tree is near empty so the fae race is weakening with each fairy who chooses to pass on without being allowed to give back the power." Slade shook his head as if shaking off the depressing topic, "Right now it's important for us to make sure you're safe inside the fae realm then we will figure out how to defend our kingdom from the war that is sure to come." He leaned forward so he could see Luke, "I'm sure we can at least agree on that one thing."

Luke nodded then moved the low hanging branches so Sage and Nicole could step under the canopy. "Just one question," he turned back letting the branches block Slade from following, "Do you think your people are going to welcome you with open arms? Surly they know what kind of traitor you have been to the kingdom." Luke crossed his hands over his chest, "You're not going to cause Nicole any more trouble. I know what you are."

Slade went toe to toe with Luke, not backing down from his challenge. "Where do you think I got my orders from? I'm overdue to report in anyway so this little trip is perfect timing. Though the welcoming may not be warm for you when I tell that you personally fucked up a plan that has been years in the making with your little show of heroics." Slade moved in to whisper in Luke's ear, "You're not going to win this fight...or the girl." He pushed past, bumping Luke's shoulder roughly with his own. After a moment of muttered profanities Luke ducked through the green curtain to follow the group.

"It's pretty simple really, you place your hands on the tree and the portal opens," explained Sage to Nicole as she placed her hands on the thick, rough bark around the large base of the willow.

Nicole stared with wide eyes not wanting to miss the second the magic started to happen but as time ticked away she realized that Sage had forgotten one key thing, "How can you open a magic portal without your magic?"

Sage placed her hands a little closer together then closed her eyes tight with a frustrated snort, "I was hoping that I could at least make this work." She sat still and focused for another moment then groaned, "Damn it Slade. Where's your off switch? Pull your power back so we can open the doorway."

"We could just get rid of him," Luke turned toward Slade, "he's only going to turn on us again anyway. Let's save ourselves some suffering now and end this."

The edge of Slade's lips turned up into a taunting grin, showing the glimmer of his perfectly white teeth, "You could try." He motioned for Luke to try him with a flick of his finger in a “bring it” motion.

Luke didn't hesitate, moving forward with a guttural roar, but a squeal from Nicole stopped him in his tracks. He spun on his toes and lunged forward, ready to attack the unknown enemy without a second thought but the sight he beheld stopped him cold.

"I did it," gasped Nicole as she beamed. The center of the tree had liquefied into a swirling pool of blue and white that pulsed with a heartbeat of its own. "It's so beautiful," she whispered as she pulled her hands away from the tree.

Sage put her arm around Nicole's shoulder and kissed her on the cheek. Turning her eyes on Slade she said, "Well, it would seem you aren't as strong as you thought, dear brother. Looks like Nicole is becoming resistant to your overpowering charm."

Slade stared into the vortex with tension showing with each flex of his jaw, "She's unlike any I've ever known." He tried to conceal his unhappiness but Nicole noticed the flash of anger in his eyes before he pasted on a smile, "Shall we move then?"

Chapter 11

The world around Nicole became surreal as she stepped out from the gateway. The view was no longer that of the green willow branches but a deep crimson that blanketed the world around her. She reached her hand out and touched the leaves of the willow, "It's beautiful," she breathed. She had never seen a tree such as this. The leaves were smooth like velvet between her fingers. A blue magical glow twirled along the veins of each red leaf and twisted around the surface of the bark.

Sage took Nicole by the hand a pulled her from under the limbs, "Just wait until you see the rest of your world," she smiled.

Nicole let Sage guide her out from under the canopy of leaves to where she stood on vibrant green grass. The smell of salt water danced on the breeze and the warmth of the morning sun kissed her cheeks. The willow was on a cliff high above the sea water below. Stepping to the edge Nicole took in the view of the perfectly white sands of the beach below then let her eyes drift along the area around her.

"Look," Sage pointed, "There is your kingdom," she beamed. A massive white stone castle clung to the edge of the cliff with stained glass windows near the top of each tower glimmering in the sun like diamonds. A town lay at the castle's feet and even from where Nicole stood she could see it was full of people coming and going.

Nicole shook her head as emotions clamped down on her chest like a vise. She fought back the tears that were filling her eyes, "It's so beautiful but...this isn't my kingdom or my people," she whispered as thoughts of her dad and Kat started to consume her. She missed them so much and hated that the only way to protect the both of them was to leave them behind. Her powers had already caused them so much pain. She had to finish this war so they wouldn't need to worry and she had to see it through to the end. That would be the only way she could keep everyone safe—her dad, her best friend and two races of people that were all depending on her.

"It's your kingdom when you're ready," Slade put a hand on her shoulder but she kept staring blankly toward the sprawling green land and grand castle that kissed the white beaches of the sea. "You must take your place, Nicole. You can't fight destiny, love."

"She doesn't have to do a damn thing Slade so back off," snarled Luke as he yanked Slade's hand from Nicole's shoulder.

"Gentlemen," a strong but feminine voice sounded from behind them. Nicole turned to see a group of warriors flanking a small fae woman with snow white hair reaching past her waist. Her skin was equally as white and smooth as her hair was and set off by deep, dark brown eyes. Slade, Sage, and Luke all bowed low at the sight of the woman leaving Nicole standing in confusion. "Slade, it would seem you have forgotten your medallion," she looked down into his face as he stared up at her.

"Yes, I'm sorry my Queen. There was no time for me to collect my things before we changed realms," he apologized with what Nicole thought was genuine fear in his voice. The queen motioned to the guard nearest her and he pulled a silver chain from his pocket and threw it at Slade's feet.

Slade begrudgingly retrieved the necklace from the ground. Nicole only caught a fleeting glance of the silver dollar sized medallion before he placed it around his neck and tucked it inside the sweat stained white shirt but within seconds she knew its purpose. The air around her crackled with power and warmth took over her whole body. The familiar ball of fire sprung to her palms without a command being thought and a rush of words flooded her mind. The walls that had been blocking her powers fell away. She leaned her head back and sighed with relief then she turned her eyes on Slade, "You've had a way to turn this off all along and you never did?"

Slade looked at her and started to speak but, after a look of defeat, he drew his lips into a tight line, "I'll explain everything, just not right now, love."

"Yes you will," she bit off her words, "and stop calling me love."

Nicole turned her attention back to the group but not before hearing a small grunt of laughter from Luke as he stepped up to her side.

The woman moved closer to the group with a tender smile on her thin, pink lips, "Nicole, we have been waiting for you my dear." She touched Nicole's face like a mother would her child, there was so much tenderness in her eyes as she pulled her into a warm embrace.

Nicole smiled back after the woman released her, "And who are you," she asked.

"Oh, yes, how forgetful of me. I am Teya. I have been acting Queen since the passing of my sister Titania many years ago," she sighed. "You look so much like her." Teya got lost in her own thoughts for a moment and the smile fell from her face but she soon recovered and reached for Nicole's hand. "Come dear, you must be dreadfully tired. Let's get you a hot bath and a warm meal."

Nicole fell into step with Teya. She noticed that even though the Queen was a small woman she carried herself so strong. The large warriors that were escorting her didn't seem as intimidating as the petite fae in the beautiful white dress. Even Nicole felt herself wanting to cringe back from her and walk a step behind but she held her ground, "But how did you know we would be here?"

"I see everything that goes and comes through the gateway. I can feel the change in the air when the portal is opened. It's a gift that only the King and Queen of the Fae possess. It helps us keep the kingdom safe," she smiled warmly as they continued down the path that was bringing them closer to the gates of the town.

Nicole's gaze drifted ahead to the people who were scrambling about to reach the side of the path, "What are they doing," she whispered.

"They all want to see you. This kingdom has been lost without a true Queen sitting on the thrown or so that is what I'm told," Teya laughed a beautiful, bell like sound as she patted Nicole's hand.

Nicole weighted Teya's words for a moment and was about to ask why the people felt that way but Teya spoke instead, "You have really got to remember to put the guard up in your mind dear. I can hear your questions spinning at an alarming rate," she turned her eyes on Nicole and though she was wearing a smile on her thin lips her eyes reflected a bit of smugness.

"Oh, so sorry. I've been without the use of my powers for so long I guess I'd forgotten to block everyone out of my mind." Nicole was feeling a bit overwhelmed as the power rushed back to her on top of taking in all of the new world that she had just stepped into.

"Well, it's best to fix that now because most of the fae in this kingdom can hear your thoughts and some of those you need to keep to yourself, dear."

Nicole wondered if she was imagining a hint of a darker warning in the Queen's words. She decided it was best to not speak and focus on the world around her. The closer they got to the gates the more the sides of the cobble stone streets filled with smiling and curious faces. Nicole was amazed at the warm energy and excited thoughts she was sampling from the crowd.

"Princess," squealed a soft voice from the growing sea of faces. A small, pointed ear girl came into view and just as her mother was reaching to stop her she darted forward at a speed that was just slightly faster than that of a normal human child.

Nicole looked down just in time to see a blur of white lace and golden ringlets wrap tiny arms around her leg. She smiled down into the young fairy's big green eyes with a laugh and spoke, "Well, hello there."

The little girl squealed with delight and hugged Nicole's leg tighter. Her mother reached for the little living doll, "Zeva, let go please." She smiled up at Nicole as she pealed Zeva's small arms off, "I'm so sorry,

Princess, she is a very free spirit," she gave a nervous laugh.

"She's very beautiful," called out Nicole as the young woman led the tiny fairy away. Nicole glanced around and didn't notice any other children. Then she remembered Slade saying that children were rare because of the lost gateway. It was lonely at times for Nicole to be an only child in her house so she could imagine it was a hundred times harder for little Zeva who looked to be the only child in this town.

Zeva followed her mother with her bottom lip quivering and un-shed tears shining in her big eyes. When her mother reached the edge of the road she stopped suddenly and pulled her hand away, "Wait," she whispered in an urgent tone. Her white and yellow dress billowed out around her as she crouched down. She looked up at her mother eagerly and after a moment's hesitation her mother nodded with a smile.

Zeva clapped her hands together like a child receiving a new toy then lowered her hands toward the ground.

Nicole stepped closer to the golden haired child to get a better view of what had caught her eye. She couldn't imagine what kind of shining trinket or crawling bug hid in the crevice could cause such enthusiasm.

Zeva smiled over at Nicole then turned back to the small spot of dirt between two glistening cobblestones. She lightly touched the rich soil with her tiny fingertip then pulled her hand back as if encouraging something to come out of hiding.

Within seconds a small sprout sprung from the ground causing Nicole to gasp. The seedling weaved and danced. It stretched higher and higher, forming bright green leaves on a long, thick stem. Then, with one last flick of Zeva's finger, the large bud on top opened up into a beautiful, royal blue tulip. Nicole stared in amazement at the once empty spot among the stones that was now glowing with color. "It's beautiful, Zeva. I'm absolutely sure that is the most enchanting flower I've ever seen in my life," she breathed.

The rosy cheeked fairy took in Nicole's impressed stare then let out a beautiful giggle as she plucked the flower from the dirt. She placed the tulip in Nicole's hand then took a step back to curtsy like a perfectly trained lady.

Nicole kissed Zeva's round cheek, "Thank you, it's almost as pretty as you." The little girl beamed a proud smile as she stepped back to her mother's waiting arms. Nicole admired the flower then turned back to join the group. She thought she caught a hint of a smile on Luke's face but she dropped her eyes to the path ahead of her. She refused to focus on the pain his tender side brought to the surface of her heart. Not having him by her side hurt like hell but people change—grow apart—and now wasn't the time for her to dwell on her own loss. She had a whole kingdom of people to think about.

Chapter 12

Luke followed the group into the castle. He stood in the grand vestibule taking in the still somewhat familiar surroundings of the place he used to call home many centuries ago. The ornate statues of kings and queens of the past lined the stone walls but a new one was sitting in the center of the floor—the acting Queen Teya. The figure was imposing and heavily ornate compared to the modest likeness of the other tributes. The realistic replica sat atop a pedestal in the center of a flowing fountain. Luke walked up to the fountain's edge and admired the array of colored exotic fish that swam about in the frozen queen's shadow. They darted away from him creating glimmering rainbows in the dark waters.

He glanced up seeing the group was being lead to rooms but he didn't need to follow to know where Nicole would be. With his renewed powers he could once again feel her every move as her warrior blood called to him. He wondered if she could still feel him or if she even cared to notice any longer. The lure of the fairy life is one that anyone could easily fall into but would she forget that she was also like him?

He rubbed his hand across the back of his neck as he thought. The stress was getting to him and not about the mounting war—he was trained for wars but not for dealing with women. Knowing that he needed to talk to her he bounded up the right side of the staircase in the direction that he could sense her. *It is time to stop being a jealous ass and tell her the truth*, he thought to himself as he rounded the corner and walked down the hall. The castle wasn't stuck in the old ways like most would have thought. Hardwood floors lined the hallways and a deep burgundy was painted on the walls with wide, white crown molding covering the once cold stone block walls. The fixtures were also modern insets that dotted the ceiling, dropping down just enough light to cast a warm glow to the walkway. "More of Teya's touches," he grumbled as he reached the end of the hall and turned to the right again.

Luke could feel Nicole moving about but it was in small bursts so he figured she was getting settled into her room. He was hoping to catch her before she had too much time to dote over the grandeur of the place and, more importantly, before she had more time to think about what a childish pain he had been. He turned right again at the end of the hall and noticed the pull was leading him up into the tower room at the top of the stairs. He took the first two steps in one lunge making quick time up the spiraling incline but stopped short of the last three steps. At the top of the stars he could see Slade standing in the doorway of Nicole's room. He was talking softly to her as she studied him. "Please, I just need a moment to talk to you," he took her hand and kissed it lightly but she pulled her hand back from him.

Luke could see the doubt and unease in her eyes as she listened to Slade. "Slade, there's nothing we need to talk about. I know what your motives were back at

Loch's and I'm sure they haven't changed. You are in this for your own gains and I will not help you."

"Please, you've got me all wrong. If all I cared about was myself, I wouldn't have helped you and everyone else get out of there," he said tenderly. "Just let me come in and explain. There's so much you still don't know, love," he whispered.

Luke watched with his heart beating in his throat. He wanted her to tell him to leave, to shut the door in his face, any sign that there wasn't a chance she was going to listen to his lies but instead she let her shoulders sag in defeat and stepped back to let Slade in.

When Slade was inside Luke stepped out into sight hoping to get Nicole to change her mind. Just as she was closing the door she noticed Luke. She froze staring into his soul with her deep blue eyes. He could see the confusion and hurt just as clear as he could see her standing in front of him. He tried to think of something to say, anything at all, but the whole world seemed to stand still in the moment. Then she dropped her eyes to the floor and closed the door.

He ran his hands roughly into his hair. "Fuck!" he groaned pacing the floor. "I'm such an idiot. She wants to be with him." He punched the wall with a guttural roar. Sheet rock crumbled around his fist along with some brick of the block wall hidden behind. He shook with anger as he turned back down the stairway, "If that's what she wants then I'll let her have it but he's not going to keep me from doing my job."

~*~**

"He follows you around like some lost puppy." Slade opened the French doors that led out to the balcony of Nicole's room.

Nicole crossed her arms over her chest, "You knew he was out there?"

"Of course, love. I wouldn't be the man I am today if I wasn't always aware of what's going on around me. There's always someone looking to take what I want," he faced her with a smile.

"Oh, you mean you're always having to watch your back so someone wont steal what your trying to take," she could feel her temper starting to rise the more she looked into his smug face. "Slade, I don't have time for your bull. Thank you for helping us get away from Loch but I'm not giving you what you want. I do not want to rule this kingdom; I only want to put an end to the war, so you will not gain power by using me."

Slade dropped his eyes, a genuine look of hurt replaced his calm and distinguished demeanor, "Nicole, I'm not the cold blooded man you think I am. I care about these people," he took her hand and led her out onto the balcony.

Nicole could see the whole town stretching out below her. She pointed to the cobblestone road that ended at the castle gates, "What is that?"

"That is for you. A parade in your honor, love." He pointed to the line of people all making their way down the street to place flowers, food, and ornate gifts at the foot of the gate."

"But why? I don't understand why all the fuss."

"These people believe in you, Nicole. They know that you will be the one to bring happiness and peace back to our world. They want to pay tribute to the new queen."

Nicole clutched her hand to her chest, "New queen! But I don't want to be the queen." She shook her head and backed into the cover of her room, "That's not what I came here to do."

"But it's your place," Slade said firmly with his brows pressed together in frustration.

Nicole threw her hands up in the air, "No it's not Slade." She stomped over to the door and opened it, "It's time you left."

Slade studied her face with a cold look in his eyes, "Fine, but this conversation isn't over." He walked past her but stopped before he was completely through the doorway, "It's your decision what you do with the throne but I have a say in how you feel about me." He slid the back of his finger down her cheek, "I care about you love, and I'm not giving up that easily."

Nicole stepped back from his reach and closed the door. She leaned against the wall and listened to the echo of his boots as he turned and walked away. "Damn it, I don't need this. Not any of this," she cursed. She sat down on the edge of the huge four post bed and stared out the open doors of the balcony into the bright, midday sky. She didn't want to rule a kingdom, she didn't want to fight a war, hell, she didn't want to be anywhere right now other than in her own bed back in her own, little, Alabama home town safe under the covers.

She dropped her head down into her hands. "What happened to magical worlds staying in story books?"

"Well like it or not the fairy tale is as real as this fairy standing in front of you," snapped Sage.

Nicole jumped, "Where did you come from?"

Sage pointed a finger to the open bedroom door as she stood with one hand on her hip, "It wasn't locked so I walked in."

"Well most normal people knock, Sage."

Sage laughed, "Well good thing I'm not normal. I brought you something to wear tonight," she pointed to a garment bag draped over a high back chair in the corner of the room. "You're welcome," she smirked.

"Oh, umm...sorry. Thank you," Nicole rubbed her temples.

Sage jumped onto the high bed and leaned up against the pillows, "Your bed is bigger than mine," she stated as she fluffed the pillow behind her head. She patted the spot next to her and Nicole leaned back and stared up at the white canopy above her. "Well, you've gotten too damn good with guarding your thoughts so you're going to have to spill it."

Nicole kept staring up into the space above her, "I wouldn't know where to begin."

Sage slid down so she was lying flat on her back just like Nicole and stared up into the void too.

"Well, let's not deal with the heavy right now. How about we talk about the two boys fighting over you? It will be just like a slumber party." She pressed up onto her elbows so she could look down into Nicole's face, "I'll even braid your hair."

Nicole turned her eyes on Sage raising one eyebrow in disbelief, "Who are you and what have you done with the irritable, cold-hearted Sage I love?"

A genuine grin spread across Sage's red lips, "Stop flattering me or I'll go back to flirting with you just like my brother and Luke. I am one step ahead of them already," she winked.

"One step ahead of them...what do you mean?"

"I've got you in bed." Sage gave a comical wiggle of

her eyebrows causing Nicole to giggle.

"You are so full of yourself, Sage," Nicole laughed as she let her eyes drift back to the space above her. Sage settled in beside her again still laughing.

"Well at least you're smiling. You shouldn't let those guys get you down. Right now you should worry about taking a long bath, drinking a glass of wine and then getting ready for the ball tonight."

"Ball?" groaned Nicole. "Can't I just hang out in my room for a few days and pretend to be sick?" She hated the idea of facing the world right now. All she wanted to do is hide away and pretend like life was normal again. No powers, no kingdoms in jeopardy and defiantly no men fighting for her hand. She longed for the smell of pine, the taste of sweet tea and the company of her dad and Kat.

"Really, Nicole. You can't hide away from this. You need to talk to Luke. As much as I detest warriors...I feel bad for him. He's going off the deep end."

"I should talk to him? Sage, I don't think you see what I see. When he looks at me he's always so cold. He's not the man I knew before I left him behind."

Sage rolled to her side and thumped Nicole on the arm, "Don't you see? That's what made him like this. You refuse to let him be by your side in any form because you're too stubborn. If nothing else you have to understand his job is to protect you." She sat up crossing her legs under her, "You may not love him Nicole but I can tell he loves you so the least you could do is let him be your warrior again."

Nicole stared at Sage like she was seeing the dark haired, pointed ear, snow white fairy for the very first time, "Listen to you. Since when do you believe in love and letting a man protect you?"

Sage dropped her eyes and a serious look turned down her lips, "I've had a lot of time with Luke since you left and well...we both can agree that we care about keeping you safe. All romantic feelings aside, he truly is miserable without you."

Picking at the pillow behind her head Nicole let her mind drift back to the Luke she left in Alabama. Life had been so crazy that she never really allowed him to get too close to her. Before she knew that he was a warrior it was the fear of him finding out that she had hidden powers that kept her distant from him. But even after they knew the whole story about each other she had still pushed him away to protect him. She didn't want anyone to suffer for her, especially those she cared about so pushing him away was the best thing to do then...but what about now?

Sage darted off the bed in a blur that made Nicole motion sick for a moment, "When you see this dress you are going to change your mind about going to the ball." Sage said, pulling Nicole from her thoughts. She unzipped the garment bag and revealed a long dress in a stunning deep green. Beautiful black swirls delicately danced across the velvet bodice with precisely placed pearls in the center of each turn. It was sleeveless with the top made to define a small waist and then turned into a long and flowing silk skirt.

Nicole rose from the bed. She felt the crush of the velvet beneath her fingers as she traced the intricate design of the dress, "And what fairy tale princess did you steal this from?"

Sage snarled her nose, "Those primpy little things don't have shit on this dress. This one was made for a true leader, one with a mind of steel and blood of fire." She placed the dress in Nicole's hands with a wink. "Now hang this up and go enjoy a good soak. I'll stand guard out here and keep the men away."

Nicole gave a sarcastic laugh, "I don't think you will be too busy. I've managed to make them both mad at me within minutes of each other."

Sage walked to what Nicole thought were two doors leading to a closet and slid them open. Hidden in the wall was a huge, flat screen television and shelves lined with movies and books. The fairy thumbed through the movie titles as Nicole gawked, "What? Did you think just because we live in a castle in a different dimension we would all be using torches and chamber pots."

"I wasn't expecting...."she pointed to the home theater set up then shook her head, "Just forget it," she laughed. "I'm guessing I'm not going to be taking a bath in fire heated water either am I?"

"Not unless you count the gas hot water heater as a fire. But if you like, you can go take a bath in the river and I'll enjoy your Jacuzzi tub—just so you feel like you're getting the 'true story book experience'." Sage flopped down on the bed with a remote in her hand and a sly grin on her crimson lips.

Nicole smiled at the prospect of a nice hot bath with powerful jets soothing away the soreness in her muscles, "I'll pass. Enjoy your movie, Sage."

"Yell if you need company," shouted Sage as Nicole shut the bathroom door.

"I'll pass," Nicole repeated with a laugh.

Chapter 13

Sage sat in front of her vanity mirror finishing the final touches on her dark lined eyes. The jet black pencil was almost a nub but she expertly glided it around her oval shaped eyes then dropped it down on the glass tray littered with eye shadows and lipsticks. She leaned back in her chair and took in her reflection, "You are one hot fairy." She kissed at the image staring back at her then began packing up her curling iron, hairspray, and every hair clip she could find into a small travel bag.

After she had the bag ready she slipped a button up shirt over her black strapless bra then walked across the room to grab the pair of gray yoga pants. Just as she slipped them on over her slender hips a knock sounded on her bedroom door, "Come in," she yelled not looking up as the door swung open.

"What do you want, Destiny?" asked Sage with a bored tone. The young fairy stood in the doorway watching Sage dart about her room gathering items and stuffing them in a bag.

"Where are you going dressed like that?" Destiny asked but with a snarl of disgust twisting her pale face in a comical way.

Sage stopped in front of the teen girl, "If you must know, I'm going to help the princess get ready for tonight," she waved her hands across her body, "I didn't want to get anything on my dress so I'm going like this." She rolled her eyes as the girl just stared at her with a dimwitted look on her face, "Was there a reason you came here?"

"Oh...yes," stammered the girl as her cheeks tinted red. "You've been summoned to Queen Teya's chambers."

"Now," huffed Sage. "I'm a bit busy."

Destiny's almond shaped blue eyes gleamed with joy at the chance to be mischievous, "Do you want me to tell the Queen that? You know I will."

Sage laughed a dark giggle, "That would be a sight. No, I'm coming."

Within minutes Sage was waiting outside the Queen's room as Destiny announced her arrival. After a few moments Destiny opened the door and waved Sage inside as she stepped out, closing the door behind her.

The room was dimly lit with the thick red drapes pulled closed so no sun could seep inside. The drapes matched the coverings on the grand canopy bed that was perfectly dressed; not a pillow out of place or a wrinkle in sight. Sage stepped deeper into the room finding the small framed queen sitting quietly in a chair with an open book in her lap, "Come," Teya waved her hand at Sage motioning for her to take the Victorian high back chair across from her.

"Sage, I've brought you here to speak of something

very important that mustn't leave this room. I'm about to ask you to do something that may seem...a little out of the ordinary but I'm sure that you want to do what is best for this kingdom as much as I do," she smiled but the emotion didn't touch her eyes.

"Of course what you tell me will remain between us," agreed Sage. Though her voice was confident unease was creeping under her skin as she stared into the queen's eyes.

Teya placed the book onto the table beside her then folded her hands in her lap, "I need you to wipe Nicole's mind of us. You need to take her back to a point where she can return to her happy life in her little town without the burdens of our world."

Sage wrinkled her nose as words bubbled in her chest, "Have you gone insane? I will do no such thing. This kingdom needs her like she—"

Teya held up a hand, "I know you care deeply about the princess, Sage but this is for her own good. I'm sure if the princess thought it through this would be what she would want. She's not cut out for war."

Sage shook her head as she tried to wrap her mind around what she was being asked to do, "You want me to wipe her memories clean of us? And what do you plan to do about her powers? You can't just wipe those away."

"No but you can convince her to wear this," she held out her hand and dangled a tear-shaped emerald that was wrapped in silver Celtic knots. The intricate knots wove into the chain that held the shimmering jewel creating a complete link. "Tell her that it was her mother's and that she never takes it off."

"Made to contain her power just like the one Slade wears," Sage stood up and stared down into the unreadable face of the Queen. "Is it for Nicole's own good or is this because you're jealous of the princess?"

"How dare you talk to me that way. Have you forgotten who I am?" She raised her chin high as her eyes lit with fire. The beautiful young woman instantly looked hard and dangerous as the power whipped her long, white hair wildly around her face. Sage covered her eyes and took a step back just as the table between them flipped up and slung across the floor, splintering when it slammed against the wall.

Anger ripped through Sage. She would not be bullied by anyone. What the Queen was asking her to do was wrong and she wouldn't dare do anything to hurt Nicole. She took a defiant step forward into the energy that was threatening to drop her to her knees, "How dare you speak of doing such things to your future queen," Sage screamed over the roar of the power around her.

"She will never be queen. She does not know what these people need or how to be a leader," she smiled indifferently then leaned back in her chair as casually as if they were talking about the weather. "If you care about your friend, Sage, I would suggest you do as I say."

Sage laughed coldly, "Or what, you're going to kill me?"

"No, I know your loyalty to that half bread runs too deep for that threat to work on you my dear," she cocked her head sideways as she studied Sage, almost as if she was looking into her soul. "But if I kill the princess you would lose this fight. It would be easy to take her life away."

Sage fought to keep her voice strong and her eyes focused even as her heart tried to beat out of her chest, "You would be caught. No one can murder inside this realm and get away with it. There are many fae that are truth seers living within the very walls of this palace."

Teya smiled a toothy grin, "Very well. I'll prove to you how easy it is." She turned her eyes toward the door leading back out into the hall where Sage had entered, "Destiny, come." The door opened only seconds later and the witty teen fae with shimmering, shoulder length blond hair came through the door using as much enthusiasm as a young girl being grounded for skipping school would have.

"Destiny dear, seems we had a slight accident," Teya waved a hand at the shattered tabled on the far side of the room. "Mend it for me."

After giving Sage a curious glance Destiny stood in front of the shards of wood and shattered glass waving her hands through the air. Like her fingers controlled the strings of a marionette, the rubble moved and swayed. Each piece edged its way into the proper spot guided by the flick of Destiny's fingers.

Sage watched the simple but fine-tuned power of the young fairy with awe until movement to her side drew her attention away, "Sage, you wanted proof," said the Queen in a volume that could be heard by everyone in the room and hinted of darkness. Teya closed her eyes as her power returned to the room. It whipped and danced through the air like wind from a hurricane racing across the space to where Destiny stood with her back to it unaware of what was looming over her as she worked her magic on the wounded table.

Sage stepped in between Teya and the unsuspecting girl, "No, you can't do that." She pleaded holding her hands up in a sign of resignation, "I'll do it. Just don't hurt her."

The queen stopped her forward motion and opened

her eyes. She glared at Sage, "You will watch and you will see first-hand what I will do to Nicole should you fail." Her voice was hard and intimidating as she stared unblinking at Sage. With a nod of her chin the pulsing gray fog split into two streams. The first cloud wrapped around Sage from her ankles all the way up to cover her mouth as she fought to scream. The second rushed toward Destiny as she spun around to see Sage dangling inches above the floor.

Destiny stared wide eyed but before the gray viper of power could reach her she whipped her hand around her head like she was winding a lasso. The table she had just mended slung through the air toward the queen at lightning speed. The flying furniture hit its mark leaving Teya temporally dazed and confused.

The power holding Sage weakened slightly allowing her to free her face. She looked over to the confused girl, "Run!"

Destiny shook her head, "I can't leave you," she yelled moving closer to Sage.

"Don't be a hero Destiny, run you damn stupid—"

The rope holding Sage tightened until she couldn't breathe, cutting off her plea. Teya's dark, taunting laughter echoed around the room like a ghost, "Destiny dear, you just made killing you all the sweeter. You're too much like Sage and one of her in this kingdom is already one too many."

Destiny shook her head as she backed away but it was too late. The gray power struck out, cocooning the beautiful young fairy. All Sage could see were Destiny's big, blue eyes as they filled with glimmering tears. The girl struggled to break the power's hold on her but within moments she collapsed to her knees.

"Stop it," Sage wheezed with what little air was

being allowed to fill her own desperate lungs. Panic raced through her veins as helplessness consumed her heart. Her own vision started to blur and warp in odd shapes but it didn't keep her from seeing the life slipping away from Destiny with each ticking second. The girl's features slacked as tears streamed down her snow white skin and disappeared into the gray mass that greedily took every last emotion from the girl. Sage closed her eyes, she didn't want to see Destiny take her last breath but she couldn't help but hear her lifeless body hit the floor with a sickening thud.

Moments later Sage was dropped to the floor and left gasping for air. The power was slithering its way back to Teya like a trained serpent to its master. "How could you," Sage screamed as her lungs burned and her chest heaved trying to recover.

Teya looked down at Destiny's lifeless body, "Such a powerful feeling." She whispered admiring a job well done. "To be a God—decide who should live and who should die," she sat down in her chair then turned to Sage. "I make good decisions in the interest of my kingdom. I will never hesitate to kill for us and you needed to see that for yourself, Sage. Do not doubt my conviction."

"I don't doubt that you're fucking crazy," Sage hissed as she pulled herself to her feet.

"Call it what you will but I believe we understand one another now, don't we?"

Sage stared into the Queen's face and for the first time, could truly see the darkness lurking under that pure skin and innocent eyes. She wasn't sure if the queen truly believed that she was doing the best thing for the fae people but she was sure that there was no way around doing this.

~**~**

Sage walked back up to her room in a trance. Her mind kept screaming out how wrong all of this was even though she didn't have a choice. *It would be better for her to forget all of this. She doesn't want this for her life,* she thought to herself as she opened the door to her own room. She sunk down in front of her bed and stared out the open window across the room. *She would rather live out a normal life, even if it is a lie, than to be dead.*

She watched the clouds rolling by outside as she tried to clear her mind then gave up and dropped her head down into her hands letting the tears fall that she had been holding back. Images of Destiny's lifeless body falling to the floor played out when she closed her eyes, reminding her that this wasn't a bluff. She had cost the young girl her life, a life that she had just began to live, by butting heads with the Queen. She wouldn't risk Nicole's life.

Drying the tears away roughly with her fingers she took a deep breath, solidifying her resolve to do what was best for her friend even if Nicole wouldn't understand. "It doesn't matter anyway. When I'm done she won't remember me so she can't be mad," Sage sighed then grabbed the bag of beauty supplies from her bed and hurried out the door.

All too fast Sage stood staring at the large oak door that served as the last barrier between her and carrying out the plans that would change Nicole's life forever. Her heart beat in her chest as if it was trying to escape the pain that was waiting on the other side of wall. She pulled the enchanted necklace from her waist band and stared into the emerald stone as it dangled from her hand, "I can't do this." She hid the jewel back in her pants then backed away from the door knowing this would be her own death sentence.

Have you forgotten so quickly, Sage? Teya's voice rang out in her head stopping her where she stood. The tone of the queen's voice was sickly sweet making Sage's stomach tighten into a knot.

"No," Sage whispered. Defeat was suffocating her with each passing second. She swallowed hard to push back the bile rising in her throat.

Fail me and you will suffer a fate much worse than death, my dear.

The words were so clear that Sage looked around the small space expecting to see the queen standing behind her but only found an empty stairwell. She took a deep breath as she tried to think of a way out of this spiraling disaster but before she could release the air from her lungs a searing pain rippled through her body from head to toe, dropping her to the floor. She wanted to scream out but her mouth was clamped tight by the electricity streaming into her muscles. The energy twisted and contorted Sage's body causing her back to arch painfully and her legs to draw up to her chest.

Sage began to pray for death, begging for the end of her own life, the suffering was too much. Then, just as quick as the pain had arrived, it left; giving her control again over her limbs. She rolled to her back letting her body lay flat on the floor. The torment was over but the reminder was still sitting in her strained and hot limbs. Tears dropped silently from her eyes as she once again pleaded for death to take her.

Chapter 14

Nicole lay across her bed wrapped in a white robe. The long bath helped to relax some of the tension from her muscles but couldn't erase the thoughts of everything that was pressing on her mind. A looming war, the feeling of not fitting in on either side, and then the struggle in her mind between Luke and Slade was eating away at her sanity. She let out a slightly hysterical giggle at the irony of the situation. She didn't really fit on either side of the war but belonged a little with both and, like some sick twist of fate, she didn't truly fit with Luke or with Slade but felt drawn to both.

Her mind drifted back to just a few months ago when she was a semi-normal police woman in her small town. *I didn't know how good I had it,* she thought to herself. *Police work was easy, I got to talk to my dad every day and I had Kat there with me to cheer me up when things got crazy. And Luke,* she sighed remembering how kind and chivalrous he was even then, before she knew that he was a warrior. A small smile lit her face as she rolled onto her stomach and hugged a throw pillow. *I guess he's always been able to melt me even if I never told him.*

The door to her room swung open causing her to jump. She swept her wet curls from her face so she could see Sage, "You scared me to death!"

Sage tossed her bag into the chair without saying a word. She sat down then eyed Nicole, "Were you sleeping?"

Nicole studied Sage curiously, "No, just resting." She pushed herself up against the headboard leaning against the pillows, "Where did you go?"

Sage rolled her eyes, "I decided to get a shower too then I had a few things to take care of."

Nicole could feel the tension radiating off of Sage but was afraid to ask so she attempted to change the subject. "Oh...well, what's in the bag?"

Sage looked over at the bag lost in thought for a moment before she spoke, "I wanted to help you get dressed for the night. I'm actually really good at hair and makeup." She attempted a smile as she motioned for Nicole to go sit at the dark oak vanity.

Nicole sat down and stared at Sage as she worked the brush through the tangles in Nicole's long curls. Something was weighing heavy on her friend's shoulders and judging by the smudges of Sage's normally perfect makeup she could tell she had been crying, "Sage, what's wrong?"

"Your hair is ridiculously long," quipped Sage as she brushed Nicole's hair, working her way from the tangles at the bottom to run the brush down the length of Nicole's brown locks in one smooth motion.

"Sage, stop dodging me. I can tell you're upset about something...so spill," she glared at Sage who was still refusing to make eye contact with her.

Sage continued to work with Nicole's hair for a moment then dropped the brush down on the vanity top. She rummaged through the bag pulling out hair pins and a can of hairspray, "I'm just worried about you. You have a lot ahead of you and I know it's hard."

"I'll make it," Nicole gave her a small smile but still had a feeling she hadn't heard the entire story. "Is that what made you cry?"

Sage froze staring down at her hand still inside the bag, "Nicole...Do you ever wish this wasn't your life? If you were given a 'do over' by the 'do over Gods' would you take it and not enter into this world?

Nicole laughed, "You have 'Do over Gods' here too? This place is freaking amazing."

Sage placed her hand on her hip and waited for Nicole to answer her. The scowl on her face made it clear that she wasn't playing around.

Nicole could see the worry in Sage's eyes and it made her heart break. She stood up and wrapped her arms around her friend's neck hugging her tight, "Sage, I'm fine, I promise. I'm not going to lie, there were moments in the beginning that I wanted nothing to do with this life. I wanted to hide away from it all but then I realized that I couldn't."

"But what if you never knew about this life at all? Don't you think you would be happier?"

Nicole pulled away to look into Sage's eyes, "What? And miss the chance to have you as one of my best friends? No," she shook her head. "I wouldn't change anything now. I know we can't predict what's going to happen but I'm where I should be right now."

Sage took a in a shaky breath as she hugged Nicole back again, "Okay, enough of all this sappy shit. We've got to get you ready."

Nicole sat back down and let Sage go to work on her hair. She watched in silence as each pin was carefully inserted. Every spiraling curl had a place that only Sage could fully understand but as the moments ticked by Nicole looked more and more like royalty instead of the rough around the edges country girl she was. The finished look was eloquent with all her hair twisted up on her head except for a few well-placed curls that hung loose.

Without a word Sage went to artfully applying Nicole's makeup with light touches. The tension between her and Nicole had died down in the silence but the darkness of Sage's task still weighed heavy on her heart. Sage took a deep breath then asked, "Do you not miss your family back home?"

"Of course I do. I miss them something awful," Nicole tilted her head back so she could see her friend's eyes. "Why the random question?"

Shrugging her shoulders she pulled a round makeup brush from the bag and dabbed it into face powder, "I just figured that if you had the chance to go back to your family without all of this you would take it."

Nicole was fed up with the odd way Sage was acting so she pushed her hand away, "Tell me what's going on Sage. There's something happening and you're not being honest with me. Are you trying to tell me to go back home?"

"No, that's not what I'm saying."

"Then what?" Nicole's voice was a bit louder than she intended.

"Nothing, Nicole! I'm just....worried."

"So that means, to make you feel better, I should go

back home and pretend like none of this is going on? You want me to let this war play out and people die while I stick my head in the sand?"

Sage spun away from Nicole and in a flash she threw the small brush across the room where it slammed against the wall, "Would that be so fucking bad Nicole? You would be safe. Let Teya and Loch fight this out and you go on living your life like you used to."

"That's not possible and you know It Sage. For one, Loch wouldn't let me live; he's already made that pretty damn clear," Nicole stood up and stomped over in front of where Sage stood glaring at her. "And I can't just forget my powers or my destiny, Sage."

The mention of the word "destiny" had Sage's heart in her throat. A flash of the young fairy dead on the floor consumed her thoughts for a moment. She watched as the memory warped into a vision of the future and Nicole lay on the floor with her lifeless eyes staring at the ceiling above. She cringed but the image drove home the fact that she had to talk Nicole into this so Teya couldn't do the same to her best friend. It was the only way to save her from a fate she knew her friend wasn't strong enough to keep from happening, "I can help you forget it all, even your powers." She pulled the emerald necklace from her waistband but kept it hidden in her palm.

As the meaning of Sage's words hit Nicole her eyes widened and she struggled to form words, "You know I don't want that."

"But it would be safe. I would watch over you and so would Luke. You would never know we were there and you wouldn't have to deal with the weight of this war on your shoulders." Sage pleaded for her to understand.

Nicole could see genuine worry lining Sage's snow white skin around her eyes and mouth. She placed her hands on the small fairy's face, "Thank you so much for caring enough about me to want to protect me but this is my war to fight. Loch must be stopped—by me. I can't do that without knowing who I am and," she hugged Sage tight then went to sit in the chair again, "I can't do this without you on my side. I need you to support me, Sage."

Running her hand across her face Sage nodded her head. There was no way to convince Nicole to do this so she would just have to do it without her consent. She sighed deeply then walked over picking up the discarded makeup brush from the floor, "I knew you were too damn stubborn to talk any sense into," she gave a dry laugh, "so let's finish getting ready for tonight."

She stepped up beside Nicole and picked up the loose face powder and dabbed the full brush into it before swirling in small circles around Nicole's face. Once she was done she picked up a dark brown eyeliner, "Close your eyes and lean your head back for me."

Nicole followed her instructions then said, "Don't be upset with me please. I know you want to protect me but I'm doing what needs to be done."

"And so am I," whispered Sage as she placed her fingertips on each of Nicole's temples. She sent energy jolting into Nicole's head causing her to jerk for a split second then she stared up into Sage's face with dazed, doll like eyes. "Nicole, listen carefully to me," Sage's lip began to quiver as she tried to form the words she needed. "You must..." her voice trailed off as she stared down at the necklace twined in her own fingers. She let it drop loose so she could see the green jewel shinning in the light of the room. Her mind began to spin with a million scenarios at once. What to plant in Nicole's head so her life would be happy? What should she do when she's done? How to deal with Teya once the deal is finished?

She placed her hands back on Nicole's temples, "This is the right thing for you, Nicole. You're my best friend and I love you." Tears flowed down Sage's cheeks as she looked down into Nicole's blank gaze and then froze. How could she let herself be forced to betray her friend? Nicole had been through so much already and now she was about to wipe away all her self-sacrifice as if it meant nothing; giving her a few blank pages filled with lies in place of all the memories of her struggles. "Screw this," She stepped back, "Teya can't kill me without people noticing me missing and I'm sure as hell not going down without a fight. I'm not her little bitch and I'm done acting like one."

"Hey," she snapped her fingers in front of Nicole's face causing her to blink. "Stop day dreaming on me, we've got to finish getting you ready."

Chapter 15

The sun dipped deeply in the sky all too fast for Nicole's liking. She would be happy to spend the rest of her day chatting with Sage as she came and went or sitting on the balcony alone like she was now. She stared out past the town below and into the pink and orange sunset that decorated the horizon. Her fingers absentmindedly stroked the velvet of her dress as her mind drifted to Luke. She hadn't heard from him since she shut the door in his face this morning. There was no doubt that he was off somewhere fuming over her letting Slade into her room but strangely she couldn't feel him anywhere around through their warrior link. Letting out a deep sigh she decided that tonight she was going to find him and talk this out. She couldn't say the words that he wanted to hear but she could tell him that she wanted him to be her warrior. "Time to toughen up girl," she mumbled to herself. "If you can't handle men then you sure as hell can't handle this war."

A knock came at her bedroom door and she knew it

couldn't be Sage because she would have shown herself in. Sage had left over an hour ago to finish dressing for the night, she said would meet her at the ball later.

Nicole opened the door to see a tense Slade dressed in a classy, black tuxedo, "I was hoping you'd let me escort you to dinner." The meekness in his words took Nicole aback. He wasn't being the cocky and self-assured man she had gotten to know. He rubbed the back of his neck and avoided her eyes, "Listen I really want to apologize for how I've been acting, Nicole. I...didn't mean to be such a—"

"Jerk? Egotistical male? Power hungry maniac...you choose but I'm sure they all fit the bill pretty well," Nicole interrupted as she crossed her arms over her chest.

Slade gave her a small smile and lifted his eyes to her face for the first time since she opened the door, "I deserve each label and I promise if you'll give me a chance I'll prove that wasn't the real me. I've been working this undercover job in Loch's world for so long that it's hard to turn off the man I had to be and be the man I am but, Nicole," he reached out and pulled her hands away from her chest holding on to just her fingertips, "I just need a chance to show you."

"Slade–" she started but he jumped back in.

"You look beautiful tonight," he laced his fingers with hers and tugged her out the door. "You will outshine everyone there just as you always have."

~**~**

Nicole pulled her hand away from Slade's just as he opened the door to the ball room. He looked at her confused for a moment then nodded as they stepped into the eyesight of the other party goers, "We are seated next to the queen for dinner." He said placing his hand on the small of Nicole's back as they walked into the chamber.

The room was set up with white linen covered tables, each with settings of gold embossed plates and gold flatware on one side of the room. Then on the other half, under the largest crystal chandelier Nicole had ever seen, was a marble dance floor. But what drew her attention the most were the stairs leading up to two large thrones, one of which was occupied by Queen Teya.

Slade lead Nicole to the foot of the stairs and he bowed to the Queen while Nicole stood there staring up into the beautiful woman's face. She thought about how innocent and young Teya appeared before the queen's voice pulled her back into the moment, "How beautiful you look tonight my dear. Though," she paused to rise from her seat and descend the stairs to stand in front of Nicole, "you do not look like you have gotten any rest. Are your chambers not to your liking?"

"Oh, no, the room is wonderful. Thank you," Nicole smiled softly.

"Wonderful." The Queen turned her eyes on Slade, "I'm glad you are keeping an eye on our princess Slade but let me suggest that you teach her proper etiquette for when she walks into the room where the Queen sits." She turned on her heals, "Oh, and Nicole dear, Sage had some unexpected business to attend to so she won't be joining us tonight." She tossed the words casually over her shoulder then climbed back up to her throne above the crowd.

Nicole's mouth struggled to form words for a moment as she stared after Teya then when the words did come she had to bite her tongue to keep them contained. Slade took her hand and placed it at the crook of his arm, "Come, let's take our seat love." He didn't seem fazed by the Queens rudeness as he led her to their table.

Once seated Nicole nodded and smiled politely at the other people sitting around them then leaned in to whisper to Slade, "What the hell was that about?"

Slade smiled as if she had said something funny then leaned back to her, "Not now, love. After dinner we will take a walk."

"Well, what about Sage?" Unease crept under Nicole's skin. She knew that Sage had planned on coming to the ball when they last spoke a few hours ago. What could be so urgent that it would pull her away?

"I'm not sure but it's not unusual for assignments to come up suddenly. It's all part of being one of the Queen's elite. Don't worry, I'm sure she will be back soon."

Nodding in agreement Nicole turned her attention back to the room. She searched the chatting crowds for familiar faces...well one in particular but he was nowhere to be seen either. The people were still filing in two by two, all men stopping to bow and women doing polite curtsies in front of the queen before making their way to the tables. She hoped to see him enter the door as she watched.

"He left."

Nicole turned back to Slade and was shocked at how close his face was to hers. She could feel the warmth of his breath caressing her cheek, "What are you talking about?"

"Luke left. He asked the Queen's permission to use the gateway shortly after we arrived at the palace and then he left," he studied her reaction as he took a sip of his champagne.

Nicole's heart sank though she fought to hide her disappointment. She knew that she hadn't been able to feel Luke's presence for a while but deep down she had hoped that it was just that she was getting good at blocking out that awareness. How could he just walk away from her? Then the reality of what he did hit her. He left her behind just like she had him.

Feeling Slade's eyes still studying her as he waited for her to speak she reached for her own flute of golden courage and took a deep drink.

"I'm sure he has a good reason. He doesn't have to check in with me when he makes a move," she stared ahead for fear that Slade would see through her tough front. Her mind was spinning between fear and hurt as she tried to reason away his sudden disappearance.

Slade grabbed the bottle of champagne and refilled Nicole's empty glass then his own, "I'm sure he does."

~**~**

The meal went forward without Nicole stepping on any more royal toes. She played things safe by nodding politely as the Queen spoke and smiling to the various people who introduced themselves as the night progressed. Everyone at her table played a role in running the Fae kingdom but she was most intrigued by General Moyer. He was a hard-nosed warrior with dark, deep eyes. His body was broad and thick with muscle but, unlike most gym rats Nicole knew back home, his demeanor was wise and intelligent. When he spoke he commanded the whole room's attention with the gentle roll of his voice. People were eager to cling onto his every word no matter if the subject was the decadent chocolate desert he was eating or the rotation of the warriors around the kingdom.

"Tell me, princess," the general turned his dark, lined eyes on Nicole, "how has your training been with the warriors that were sent to you?"

The mention of her warriors brought the question of Luke back to the surface again, cutting deep and threatening to pull her mind into spiraling, worried thoughts.

"They have been very helpful for what time we've had to train." She tried to clear her mind of the past and thrust herself into the moment as she focused on the general.

He studied her face then nodded, "Yes, I have heard that things turned ugly very fast. I only wish that we'd been allowed to retrieve you sooner."

Nicole's brows furrowed together, "Sooner? What do you mean? Luke has been there since the day my real powers surfaced."

"Ah yes, but you did have some powers before the day you were shot. I was denied the request to bring you here and start your training after the incident in Florida. Seems some were still doubtful if your power would ever fully surface," he glanced sideways to the Queen as he casually ran his finger along the condensation on the crystal flute in front of him.

The reality of his words hit her like a knife to the chest, "How long did you know? How long did you leave me fumbling my way around in the dark before you decided to send help?" Nicole fought to keep her anger under control as hushed whispers echoed around her. She felt Slade's hand give a gentle squeeze on her knee as she locked eyes with Teya.

"My dear," chimed in Queen Teya, "You have always had someone checking in on your family from time to time for generations long forgotten. The power had never fully surfaced in any of your ancestors so there was no reason to think you would be any different." The queen patted Nicole's hand, her voice was haughty and patronizing but at the same time sweet.

"But I am different and I have been for years. Loch knew it so that tells me you did too," she pulled her hand from the queen's embrace and passed a hard glance between both Teya and the general waiting for answers.

Slade cleared his throat, "Love, I think I've had a little much to drink. Do you mind walking with me into the garden for some fresh air?" He stood and pulled out Nicole's chair not giving her a chance to respond.

Nicole let Slade guide her past the filling dance floor and out the doors that lead into a softly glowing garden. Though the anger was still swelling inside of Nicole's chest she couldn't help but to be taken aback by the beauty of the star filled night sky and the enchanted garden surrounding them as they walked down the stone path. Every plant, large and small, glowed with a mesmerizing light. The deep crimson roses gave off a slight echo of red light and the violet iris left blue trails like a small comet as they swayed in the soft, summer breeze. Nicole let her eyes take in everything from the smallest blade of grass to the tallest apple trees as Slade lead her farther away from the swarms of people.

Nicole let out a deep sigh when she could no longer hear the sound of the music playing or the chatter of uppity royalty. She looked down at Slade's fingers intertwined with her own as they walked and felt a ping of guilt. She pulled her hand from his, "Thank you for getting me out of there."

Slade smiled as he put his hands into his pants pockets, "You're welcome, love. I could feel the heat radiating from your temper," he chuckled. "It's a wonder you didn't catch your chair on fire. You've really got to work on controlling your powers before it gets you into trouble."

Nicole gave a small laugh, "Yeah, I've been told that before." Her mind drifted back to the afternoon she almost caught her dad's couch on fire because Luke had made her mad. He was trying to talk some sense into her about her destiny in life not being a burden but a blessing...but she didn't want to hear it. She had wanted to be left alone to live her mediocre existence as a cop in her sleepy country town, not be forced to master the powers she didn't want or to defend a world she didn't care about.

She shook her head when reality hit her. Selfish and living in denial didn't even begin to scratch the surface when analyzing who she was back then. Adding obstinate and a pain in the ass into her title would get you moving more in the right direction but things were different now. She understood that if she didn't put an end to the war there would never be peace for anyone around her. It was time to put her self-serving wants and needs away so she could be the person that those she loved needed her to be. No more crying or bitching; it was time to dig in with both feet and do what was needed to be done.

"Hey," Slade touched Nicole's shoulder, "What are you thinking so hard about?"

Nicole looked up to see they had emerged from the garden into a large opening that looked out across the sea. The smell of salt water was refreshing; filling Nicole with a sense of freedom from the weight of the world.

The moonlight glistened off the crest of each wave as it danced up towards the beach below. "I was just wondering..." Nicole struggled to regain her focus on the night's excitement and not reveal that her mind was on Luke, "Why do I get the feeling Teya doesn't care for me?"

Slade pointed to a bench placed at the cliff's edge, "Sit with me and I'll give you my thoughts on her." He led her over and removed his jacket, placing it on the dew covered seat. "Here, so you won't get your dress damp. Did I tell you how beautiful you look tonight?"

Nicole couldn't help but admire the tenderness Slade was showing. He was so different from the man she had met back in Ireland, surrounded by all the best money could buy and all the power hungry people. She wondered which persona was the true side of Slade: the playboy who was out for power or the gentle, caring man she had seen since he helped everyone escape Loch's grasp.

"Yes, you have and thank you," she said as she sat down and looked out across the water.

"The truth is I'm really not sure where the Queen's loyalty lies. She has taken running the kingdom very seriously after the passing of your grandmother; always looking out for the best interest of the fae but..." he paused sliding a hand through his light blond hair as he let out a sigh. "I'm beginning to think she is jealous of you."

Nicole turned her eyes on Slade, "Jealous of me? But why?"

Slade shrugged his shoulders, "I'm sure it's because by all rights the throne is yours, not hers. This whole kingdom," he glanced around at all the beauty that surrounded them, "It belongs to you and you're the only person who holds the power to rule it; a power much greater than any King or Queen before you. I'm sure that scares the hell out of Teya." He chuckled as he took in Nicole's bewildered expression. "Don't you see? That's why your Grandmother's love for her warrior caused such an outpouring of hate from a few. They all feared the power that the child created with both fae and warrior blood would hold."

"I'm not sure that matters now. What's done is done and I'm here now. I don't want the throne. I just want to stop this war and leave my people to live in peace," Nicole crossed her arms across her chest as a slight chill raised goose bumps on her bare arms.

Slade reached out and rubbed his hands across her arms when he noticed her discomfort. "Here," he pulled her to his side placing his arms around her, "It's a bit cold but this should help."

Apprehension knotted in Nicole's stomach when Slade pulled her tight to him but the warmth radiating from his body quickly chased away the anxiety and had her forgetting about the cold nipping at her skin. "Thank you," she whispered as a new warmth started to form in her belly. Slade's masculine scent drew Nicole in as she sat wrapped in his arms. She felt the pull to lay her head against his chest and let herself enjoy the closeness and security of his arms but a tugging in her heart made her keep her distance.

Slade traced small circles on her arm with his thumb as he held her, "Can I ask you something?"

Nicole nodded but kept her eyes on the glowing night sky as she waited, afraid that looking into his ghostly blue eyes would be too much for her.

"When you say 'your people' do you mean the fae?"

The caress of his breath on her neck sent a new

course of chills down her body but she tried keep it from showing, "Both fae and warriors of course." She could feel his body stiffen slightly when she spoke so she turned to look at him, "Slade, I'm both so you cannot expect me to turn my back on one."

Slade weighed his words before he spoke as he looking into her eyes, "You can't save both, love. This war runs too deep so there's no way of knowing who the good guys among the warriors truly are."

Nicole's brows crumpled together as she processed his words, "Are you saying I should wipe out the entire warrior race just because of a few bad seeds?" She pulled away from his embrace and stood up. "That is the craziest thing I've ever heard."

"Nicole, it simply can't be done. Look at your warriors. They are hot tempered and violent where the fae race is a peaceful one unless they are pushed into fighting. Why would you want to let a bloodline like that continue to haunt this world," he stood with his arms wide and his eyes cold and hard on her. "Would you think about all that Loch has done to you and your family for just a moment," he pleaded as he grabbed her face and forced her to look him in the eyes. "Do you want your father hurt again? How about your friend Kat?"

Nicole jerked her face from his hands and took a step back from him, "That's the work of one man, Slade, not all warriors," she hissed. She could feel her body start to shake as the anger replaced the warmth for the man standing in front of her. "Just when I think you're a great guy you go and show your true side," she said throwing up her hands.

Slade let out a deep laugh, "I am a good guy, Nicole. I'm just trying to help you see the light in this dark world. Everything isn't as simple as you have it laid out in your head, love." He reached out and stopped her from backing away from him. He pulled her hands up to his chest and wrapped his arm around her small waist, "I'm being the man you need, the one who will be honest and help guide you in a realm you know nothing about. You are just too damn pigheaded to see what's best for you."

Nicole pushed against his chest trying to free herself from his grasp but before she could escape his full lips crushed down on hers, fervor and desire radiating from every press of his mouth. Nicole struggled to pull from his embrace as he tried to deepen the kiss. She could feel her body starting to warm to him. Her passion was building inside and a fire igniting though she tried to fight it. She began to panic; she was torn between the man she had glimpsed in Slade and the warrior she carried in her heart. Her hands ignited in a red glow as her panic overflowed and she shoved again sending Slade staggering backwards as she gasped for breath. "Don't ever touch me again!"

Suddenly a pull she knew without doubt tugged at her senses and she turned to see Luke barreling forward. He tackled the stunned Slade to the ground and they went rolling. Thumping of fists and grunts sounded as the two men tore into each other. Slade flipped Luke off of him and gained his footing just as Luke dove for him again.

"Stop this," shouted Nicole but the two men continued to bash into each other. Luke grabbed Slade around the waist and with a twist of his body he threw him into a tree thirty feet away causing leaves to rain down in twinkles of green light.

"It's time you learn to keep your hands off Nicole. She has made it quite clear that she doesn't want you!"

Slade stood up slowly dusting the dirt from his clothes, "Why? Because you think she will choose you," he laughed darkly. "She can see what a violent man you are," he looked past Luke to Nicole with a nod. "All warriors are like this Nicole," he pleaded with coldness in his eyes.

"I'm doing what needs to be done to protect her from people like you," Luke darted forward in a blur to where Slade was standing near the shaking tree but before he could touch him a wall of raging wind swept in between the two men. Luke skidded to a halt as Slade was blocked from his view.

"Stop this right now," shouted Nicole as she held her hands out in front of her. "I won't be fought over." Her heart was pounding in her chest as she struggled to keep her composure. She was worried about Slade, though he was trying hard to hold his own in the fight he was without his powers so he was much weaker than Luke. She felt the presence of eyes on her so she was sure the thundering booms of Luke's power had drawn a crowd behind her. "Luke," she demanded, "I want you here beside me right now."

Luke didn't hesitate. He turned on his heels and darted to Nicole in a flash. His chest was heaving from the fight and he had dried blood on his cheek from where a wound had been only moments ago. He nodded to Nicole as he took his place beside her, "As you wish."

With a deep sigh she let her wall down revealing a smug Slade with his arms crossed over his chest, "So this is your choice?" he nodded toward Luke standing at her side.

Nicole took a step forward with her head held high, "Don't you see, Slade? There doesn't have to be a choice. I can save both," she pleaded for him to understand. "It's not a choice between fae and warriors that I'm here to make nor does it boil down to a choice between having you or Luke fighting beside me. I need you both with me to make this work."

Slade's hard face softened slightly as he listened to her words then abruptly, his attention was drawn to the crowd. He nodded as if someone had spoken to him then turned away from Nicole giving one last cold glance to Luke before he disappeared into the garden.

Nicole watched him leave. She wanted to run to him and stop him from going but a familiar voice froze her. "Dad," she whispered desperately. She turned her eyes on the group of people murmuring behind her for the first time. Queen Teya and General Moyer stood in the front looking down at her but they quickly faded into the background when James' familiar, lined face and salt and pepper colored hair stepped out from the crowd. He looked thin and pail compared to the man she remembered leaving behind in Alabama. His polo shirt hung loose from his frame as he moved but his body language was still that of a strong man half his age as he smiled at her shocked face.

"Hey baby," he took his daughter into his arms hugging her tightly. "I've been so worried about you," he whispered into her hair as he kissed the top of her head.

Nicole looked up into his face with tears in her eyes, "How did you get here?"

James nodded toward Luke, "Luke came for us. He said you were having a hard time being separated from your family and thought us being here with you would help you figure out what you needed to do." He leaned in to whisper in her ear, "I think he's worried about you."

Nicole smiled at her dad, "You have always been on his side." She rolled her eyes when her dad gave her a sly wink, just as he always did when he brought up Luke. James was never shy about telling Nicole she should give Luke a chance, even before anyone knew that Luke was a warrior. He had said that Luke was the catch that she shouldn't let get away.

Nicole glanced to the side taking in Luke's poorly concealed smile as he stared at the ground around his feet. She knew he was hearing everything her dad whispered and loved the way it was making her squirm. This had been a fun game that he and James liked to play as they tried to wear Nicole's emotional walls down.

"Wait," Nicole looked back into her dad's face, "You said 'we' didn't you?" Does that mean–" Before she could finish she was wrapped in another pair of long, thin arms as a squeal pierced her eardrums.

"Nicole! I've been so damn worried about you."

Nicole let loose of her dad to hug her best friend as tears streamed down her face, "I've missed you too, Kat." She embraced her friend then stepped back. Kat's long black hair was just as lustrous as she remembered and her model thin frame was covered in a white Chanel dress with knee length, black leather boots. The height of fashion as always but when Nicole took in her friend's large brown eyes something was different. A bit of the fire that had always kept Kat listed as Nicole's wild and fun loving friend was gone. "How have you been?"

"I'm good now, thanks to you. You saved me that day and never gave me the chance to tell you how grateful I am." She hugged Nicole again.

Nicole remembered that day like no other in her life. Kat had been kidnapped by a sadistic detective and held as bait to draw Nicole to Loch. Kat had been drugged, beaten for days, along with other forms of torture that broke Nicole's heart to even imagine. Then in a stand-off at the airfield she was shot by the detective. Nicole was able to use her powers to heal the physical wounds and save her friend's life but she could tell the scars ran deep into her Kat's soul, changing her forever and robbing her of the spark for life she once had. She hugged Kat tight then stepped back wiping the tears away with her fingers, "I'm so happy to see you both."

"Hey, what aboot me?" came a thick Irish accent from behind Nicole.

Rhys picked Nicole up in a hug, squeezing her tightly against his bare chest with a laugh. Nicole giggled as he placed her back on her feet. Though he was without a shirt and bare footed he was wearing black designer slacks instead of his usual kilt. Nicole studied his smiling face as she regained her balance, "I'm glad to see you too Rhys."

"Ah, I knew the princess would be missing me," he beamed with a sexy wink then, to Nicole's surprise, he wrapped his arms around Kat's waist and she melted back against him.

Nicole's eyebrows shot up into her hair line, "Seems we have a lot of catching up to do, Kat."

Kat nodded as she tenderly patted Rhys' arms, "Yes we do," she laughed.

Chapter 16

The clock on her nightstand glowed three twenty in the morning when Nicole finally gave up on sleep. She flung the covers back and walked out to the balcony. The night air was warm but it still gave her bare arms goosebumps as it danced across her skin and seeped its way through her white, silk gown.

The town below was quiet and the streets were empty. The whole world seemed to be asleep except for her. The excitement of the night wouldn't allow her to rest. She had spent the rest of the evening dancing with her Dad and even Luke during the remainder of the ball along with laughing as Kat told stories about how she and Rhys had become the most unusual but blissfully in love couple that they were now.

The evening had made her so happy but at the same time she felt like a piece of her was still missing. Sage nor Slade made an appearance that night and she was worried about both. She knew that Slade was mad at her so she guessed that was his reason for staying away but what about Sage? What could be so important that she would leave without a word?

A pull in her mind tugged her way from her worries. She could feel Luke moving around the castle thanks to their bond. She could also sense faint pin points in her mind that were other warriors inside the castle but Luke's had his own signature: like it was made just for him and she could tell he was making his way in her direction.

You can't sleep either? she whispered telepathically to him as she grabbed her robe then unlocked the door to her room.

No and I could feel that you were up so I thought we would talk, if that's okay with you, Luke responded back through their mental connection.

Sure, the door is open. She slid her arms into her robe and tied it around her waist just before the door opened.

His dark blond hair was tousled from his restless attempt at sleep but it only added to the mysteriousness that Nicole liked about him. He wore black drawstring pants and a plain white t-shirt that fit snug around the defined muscles of his arms and chest. Nicole felt her eyes lingering too long on him so she cleared her throat and turned back to the balcony, "I was enjoying the night air. You want to join me out there?"

Nodding he followed her out the doors. He leaned against the railing as Nicole gazed out at the night but he never took his eyes off of her, "Why can't you sleep?"

She shrugged her shoulders, "I don't know, maybe the threat of war has me a bit on edge." She said sarcastically trying to hide her unease with being alone with him.

"I was hoping that having your dad and Kat here would help you rest a little easier."

She smiled at him, meeting his eyes for the first time, "I never said thank you for that. It is a wonderful feeling to have them with me again."

"But you're still worried?"

She nodded, "Yes, I...don't know what the hell I'm doing, Luke." Nicole found herself surprised by her own confession but not knowing what to do or how to end the war was really the root of her problems. She was worried about failing everyone. "What if I can't put an end to this war? What if people die because I'm not strong enough?"

Luke pulled her into his arms laying his cheek against the top of her head, "Calm down. You're stronger than anyone I've ever known and that's saying a lot since I've been around for hundreds of years."

Nicole relaxed into his arms, "I don't feel very strong."

Luke leaned back to look into her face, "Well, tomorrow we start training again. General Moyer is calling in his best troops from the field and has asked me to oversee your preparation. Even he was amazed by the power you displayed tonight."

The mention of tonight's fireworks between Luke and Slade made Nicole's heart ache. She gently pulled out of Luke's embrace and leaned her back against the railing, "Thanks, I really do need to get refocused on the job at hand. Training is just what I need."

Luke tilted his head studying her face, "Is it what you need to get ready or is it what you need to distract your mind from something else?"

Nicole refused to meet his eyes. She turned her

back to him and looked out across the moonlit town. She could feel him move closer to her though he didn't say a word. He stood behind her, his body heat caressing her back, and then slowly he slid her long curls away from her neck with one finger letting the night air touch the once hidden skin.

Without thinking she tilted her head, enjoying the simplest kind of touch. Her heart thumped hard in her chest as the warmth of his breath slid across her earlobe. Luke tenderly kissed the place where her shoulder met her neck causing a breathless moan to escape Nicole's lips, "Tell me you want only me," he whispered as he kissed her neck again. "Tell me that there has never been another man you wanted more than me."

Nicole took a shaky breath but before she could speak Luke slid her robe off one shoulder, tracing each new inch of skin with his lips. Her body was becoming weak as she fought to remain in control. She needed to stop this before it went too far, "Luke." She turned around to face him but before she could say another word his lips covered her own. Heated and needy he held her face in his hands as he kissed her again. Nicole tried to pull away but the fire was too much. The desire had been held a bay for far too long. Wrapping her arms around him she returned his kiss with the passion of a woman who had been without water for weeks and Luke eagerly presented what she had been missing.

Luke pulled away to look at Nicole, "Tell me you want me." He demanded with a faint glow of red circling his hazel eyes. He was having trouble containing himself but needed to hear her speak the words he had waited to hear for so long.

Nicole could see her own glow of red reflecting off Luke's tan skin but she didn't care. She was tired of having to pretend like she was someone else. With Luke she could be who she was, never having to second guess. He was the one. "I want you," she breathed then wrapped her fingers into his hair deepening their kiss with a slide of her tongue.

Luke pulled her up into his arms and carried her back into the room to lay her across the bed. He trailed his lips down the center of her neck as he worked to untie her robe. Nicole eagerly pulled his shirt over his head then traced the muscles of his chest with her fingers greedily.

Her back arched as her desire built. She quickly slid out of the robe and let Luke pull the gown from her body. He stared down at her bare skin as he slowly traced a line from her collar bone down the center of her breast with a single finger ending the path by sliding just inside the waist band of her white lace panties.

"You're so beautiful," he whispered in a husky voice.

In a flash of warrior speed Nicole was standing in front of Luke removing his pants then pushing him back onto the bed. She straddled his hips pressing her body against his hardness causing Luke to let out a deep moan. He grabbed at her hips pulling her harder against him as she leaned down to kiss his smooth chest, "Tell me you want me," she purred, reversing their roles with a sly smirk.

His hands glided up her sides and around to cup her breast but she grabbed him by the wrist and pined his hands above his head, "Tell me," she breathed as her long hair created a curtain round their faces. She ran her tongue along his lips and watched as Luke's eyes changed from a faint red to a fiery crimson.

The edge of his lips turned up into a lopsided grin showing a sexy dimple in his cheek just before he flipped

Nicole over on her back pinning her arms above her head. He pressed his body against hers so she could feel the effect she was having on him, "I want you right now," he pressed his lips to hers until they were both breathless then released the hold on her arms so he could cup her face, "I want you forever."

~*~**

The rising sun cast an orange glow across the room causing Nicole to blink as she opened her eyes. The birds sang their song outside the open doors leading to the balcony in a joyful way that Nicole had never heard before or maybe she had never cared to listen. Everything was so vibrant and new like the whole world was hers for the taking. She listened to the rhythm of Luke's heartbeat as her head lay on his bare chest. "Awake already?" Luke asked as he kissed her head.

She smiled up at him, "Yes, why?"

"I've waited so long to watch you sleep in my arms that I didn't want it to end," he rubbed her back gently as she placed her head on his shoulder.

Nicole smiled to herself while she thought about the night they had spent together. They shared a passion that ran deep into her soul and ignited every sense in her body. There were moments as they made love the air around them cracked with red and blue energy as their bodies became one. It was like no other experience Nicole had ever felt before.

"I wish we could stay like this forever," She looked up into his eyes and for the first time since they had been reunited she could see genuine happiness in Luke's smile.

"We have forever, Nicole."

She stretched up to kiss his lips softly but a singed smell reached her nose as the covers moved, "Do you smell something burning?"

Luke laughed a full, husky laugh pulling her lips back to his kissing her passionately, "That would be the smell of our bed thanks to you, my dear."

Nicole jumped up and flipped the covers back to see two large charcoal holes burnt in the sheets. She blushed brightly as she recalled knotting her hands in the red sheet while Luke sent her over the edge. "Wow, so...are we training today?" Nicole giggled at her lame attempt to change the subject.

"Well, I'm thinking that if we want to keep you from literally setting the bed on fire next time then yes, we must get you trained," he winked at her then stood to pull on his boxers.

Nicole put on her robe reluctantly as she admired Luke's lean, muscular body while he dressed. She longed to have his strong arms around her and his lips on her skin again but with a groan she walked to her vanity to brush out her hair. He was right; it was time to prepare for the task that lay ahead of them. She wouldn't be any good to anyone if all she could do is set some sheets on fire.

When she grabbed the brush from the tray a gold tube of lipstick rolled to the floor. Nicole picked it up and opened it, admiring the deep crimson color that only Sage could dare ware. As she studied the color her mind began to spin, "Luke?"

"Hmm," he mumbled as he searched for his t-shirt under the bed.

"What kind of mission do you think Sage was sent off on?"

Luke stood up with his retrieved treasure in his hand, "What do you mean?"

"The Queen said Sage had some unexpected business to attend to," Nicole mimicked Teya's proper voice as close as she could as she rolled her eyes.

Luke's brow creased as he thought, "It isn't unusual for us to be given assignments without notice but usually the Queen has no part in them."

"So why did she know that Sage was gone?"

Luke shrugged his shoulder then slid his shirt over his head cutting off the view that Nicole was still secretly enjoying, "Maybe General Moyer told her. He's who usually oversees matters like that."

Nicole dropped her eyes back to the lipstick for a moment then recapped it, "Maybe." She agreed but something was telling her that this was wrong on a much deeper level.

Luke stepped up behind where she sat and took the brush from the table. He glided the bristles through her hair slowly. Nicole melted back into her chair as the soothing rhythm of Luke stoking her long hair relaxed away a bit of her anxiety. "I need to see Moyer this morning about your training. If it will make you feel better I will ask him about Sage. Keep in mind he won't tell me any details but at least you will know the truth."

Beaming a bright smile up at him Nicole stood and wrapped her arms around his neck, "You're the best."

He laughed and kissed her on the nose, "You just remember that when Slade starts snooping around your room again."

A bit of Nicole's energy seeped away when she thought about Slade. She wondered if he was still mad at her. Having him on her side would be wonderful and she was sure there were things he could teach her during her training but his and Luke's constant bickering was going to have to be fixed.

"Luke, don't you think you could try to be nicer to Slade. After all he did help us escape from Loch."

"I'll be nice to him when he stops trying to steal you away from me."

Nicole's couldn't believe his words, "Steal me away from you?" She stepped back from his arms, "Since when do I belong to anyone? No one can own me or choose my life for me—not you, not Slade, not Loch or anyone else."

Luke rubbed the back of his neck, "Nicole, I just mean that I want you to be with me and only me. I've always wanted it to be us," he pleaded.

"Then don't start acting like a possessive jerk. Slade may be a little pushy but he can help us stop this war."

Luke threw his hands up in the air as he walked to the door, "You can't really say you trust him after all he has done to you. He's the one that had you locked up for Loch. He deceived you for his own gains, Nicole."

Nicole stood her ground; her chin held high, "He's not that person, Luke. He's on our side."

Laughing darkly Luke opened the door to walk out. He stopped in the doorway and then turned back, "Tell me one thing."

"What," she crossed her arms over her chest. Her anger was starting to give way to fear of losing Luke again. She had just gotten him back, the real Luke, the one that she had back in Alabama and she didn't want to let him go.

"Did you really hate it when he kissed you that

night? The night he was drunk and pinned you against the glass of your balcony door?" His jaws were flexing with tension as he spoke, "I watched you kiss him back. Slade knew I was there and that I couldn't reach you so he let me watch as you went weak in his arms."

"I..." Nicole's voice trailed off as she tried to find the right words. Her heart was thumping in her chest and her throat was closing on her. Maybe she did enjoy Slade's company more than she wanted to admit to anyone, including herself.

Luke turned his back on her as he ran his hand across his face, "Save the excuses, Nicole. Just know this, you can't have both worlds, you will have to choose." He slammed the door behind him when he left.

Nicole sank down onto her bed, the bed she had just shared with Luke, and stared down at the rumpled sheets. "Damn it, Luke."

Chapter 17

The pain was gone in Sage's arms and replaced by an unsettling numbness after countless hours of hanging from her wrists. Her head lulled back heavily leaving her staring up into the chains that looped over a wooden beam. Aimlessly her mind drifted, wondering how many thousands of years these shackles had been used to hold prisoners until the moment of their judgment.

Laughing at her train of thought she reached back into her memories for the last time she was wrapped up inside her own head. She was trapped now, unable to reach outside of this room into another mind, by the charm that enclosed the dungeon. This must be the first time since her mind reading ability surfaced that she was truly alone with her own thoughts. *Such a boring place inside my head*, she thought. She was always in the know before anyone spoke, ahead of the crowd and a seer of dark secrets. *Maybe that's why I'm really here. Not just because I wouldn't send Nicole away but because I know too much.* Her mind kept bouncing around ideas as to how things got this bad but they all came back to two people: Teya and Loch. They were both greedy and power hungry in Sage's mind.

But what could she do now as she hung from chains? This was a situation that she had seen end exactly the same way each and every time—death. There was no swaying the Queen once she had you imprisoned. Teya's mind was made up the second she ordered those cold cuffs to be wrapped around her wrists.

A dry laugh escaped Sage's lips, "Bring on the judgment, I'll die with my honor before I betray this kingdom." She yelled out finding strength in her own words. Sage was prepared to die today because in her heart she knew she was doing the right thing not only for Nicole but also for the future of her people. Nicole could change things if she could find the belief in herself. Sage knew it in her heart that Nicole could rule this kingdom and put a stop to this war if she could only keep her safe for a little while longer.

The sliding of a metal plate in the door drew Sage's attention to eyes peering through the hole. Normally that would be all the opportunity she needed. Just a split moment of direct eye contact would let Sage drill into her target's mind making him a puppet, but her powers were as useless as her numb arms that were allowing the tips of her toes to scrape the surface of the dirt floor.

"Quiet in there," demanded the guard.

"Or what? You're going to string me up," Sage taunted. "I don't think it can get much worse for me," she mumbled.

Instead of the guard sliding the plate close again he turned his attention down the hall. Sage could hear the approaching footsteps just before the door opened.

"Sage, my dear, you look dreadful," crooned the queen as she gathered her long, eloquent dress up in her hands so it hovered above her ankles before her shoes hit the floor. Her nose wrinkled from the putrid stench of old blood and rotting flesh that lived in the walls and in the soil floor of the dungeon. "I really wish you hadn't pushed me into this. You are too valuable to this kingdom to waste away in this horrid place."

Sage glared at the queen, "I'm enjoying the peace and quiet."

Teya looked back at the guard, "Leave us."

When the door closed Teya stepped closer to Sage, taking in every inch of the confined woman's hardened face, "You have such a strong spirit. So loyal. Believe it or not I do find that a wonderful trait."

"It seems to be a trait you are lacking in," spat Sage.

"Ah, my dear, don't you see? I am very loyal but my loyalty is not wasted on a silly girl who dreams of playing queen. My goal is to protect our kingdom's future."

"By getting rid of the true queen so you can keep the throne? Sounds a little bit like you have some self-serving goals, sweetheart." Sage shifted slightly trying to watch Teya as she circled her slowly but all she could manage was a glimpse in her peripheral.

"I guess it might seem that way to you. Maybe I give you too much credit." Teya stepped forward putting her face within inches of Sage's. A dark grin bared her perfectly white teeth as her eyes narrowed, "How about I give you one last chance to make things right for your people? You wipe Nicole's mind and I'll forget all about you being a traitor to the kingdom."

Sage spit like a venomous snake in Teya's eyes causing the queen to take a step back, "You make me look however you want to. I will not betray Nicole."

Teya wiped the wetness from her face with the back of her hand, then without hesitation, she slapped Sage across the cheek causing her body to sway from the chains like a helpless punching bag.

After a moment Sage trained her cold eyes back on Teya, "Is that the best you've got?"

A dry laugh cut through the space between them. Teya raised her hand as she continued to laugh sending a single, dark thread of power rushing to Sage, "I've only begun."

Sage shook and swayed trying to put some distance between the snake-like darkness and herself but it was no use. It wrapped around her bare ankle causing a gasp to escape Sages' lungs from the contact. A chill as cold as a December's wind danced underneath every spot where the evil power touched her. But, unlike last time, it was not hurried or rushed to confine and subdue her. Now it moved slowly and calculating as it curled its way inch by inch up her legs.

"Do you really want it to end this way, Sage? All you have to do is say you will send Nicole back to her life in Alabama. You know it is what she wants."

Kicking her leg in attempt to dislodge the coiling black mass had no effect so Sage let out a frustrated scream, "Fuck you!"

The door to the dungeon swung open, "My queen, is everything alright?" The guard who had let Teya in passed a confused look between the queen and Sage.

Teya waved a hand at him dismissively, "Go back to your post. I'll summon you when I'm ready to leave."

"But your majesty—"

"Go!" Teya's voice echoed off the stone walls. The guard quickly closed the door. Teya turned her hard eyes back on Sage. "Really? Is that how you address your Queen?" Teya gave another flick of her fingers and the power sped up its ascent, wrapping around Sage's waist then becoming as thin as a worm to shoot two threads up above her hands and lock onto the cuffs that held her.

"You're a coward and they will see that. You're lucky that you're the only one who can use powers in this room or I would make you my lap dog after I beat the hell out of you." A wide grin lit Sage's face but her eyes stayed cold and dark. "I would make you like it too. Convince you that you enjoy licking the dirt from my feet."

"Such a powerful woman," teased Teya, "Too bad in here you are no better than your useless brother." Teya took in a deep breath as she tapped her chin with a finger, "But I am a fair Queen so I'll grant you that one last request."

Before Sage understood what was happening she hit the floor. The black power had released her bonds then retreated back to its master leaving Sage to try to pull herself together before the Queen attacked. She had to buy some time because she couldn't feel her arms yet, "What are you doing?"

"You wanted a chance to, oh how did you so delicately put it? Oh, yes, *beat the hell out of me*, so I'm giving it to you." Teya took a step back leaving about ten feet between them then gave a taunting curtsy. "Now is your chance to have what you want, dear. Don't waste it by sitting on the floor like the fae trash you are."

"What's the point? You'll use your magic to kill me before I can reach you." Teya was pushing her too fast. Sage could see the calculating look building behind the queen's eyes but her arms were just starting to tingle as the blood rushed back into her limbs. She rubbed the chafed spots around her wrist then held them up, "This isn't a fair fight either way. I'm wounded and weak from hanging for almost two days."

"Are you afraid you will lose? This is the chance you wanted Sage and I'll even sweeten the deal for you." Teya pulled her long hair back and started working it into a braid as she talked, "You beat me and you go free. As far as everyone outside of this room knows you are away on a mission so no one ever has to hear what happened. You'll be able to go back to life as usual."

Sage could hear the deceit behind Teya's words but knew the alternative would not be much better, "If I don't win? Then what?"

Teya shrugged her shoulders as she released her hair into a long white braid down her back, "Then no more fighting me. You do what I ask and remain my loyal servant for all of eternity."

Sage pushed herself to her feet dusting off her dirt covered hands on her sweat stained yoga pants, "And I can assume your first command when I'm your servant will be to wipe Nicole's mind?"

No answer came from Teya. A grin turned up the edge of her lips as she motioned for Sage to make her move. She knew Sage wouldn't walk away from this gamble for revenge no matter how high the stakes were. She had her right where she wanted her.

Circling to the right, Sage kept her eyes on Teya while she tried to figure out what to do. She needed to end this fast before the queen had a chance to take advantage of her weakened body and lack of powers. Sage studied the walls behind Teya as they continued their dance, looking for a weapon or an escape, but before she could spin out an idea Teya dashed forward, leaping up into the air and coming down with her elbow with precision. Sage managed to keep the blow from hitting her in the face with a quick lunge but still took a hard hit on the shoulder.

Sage fell to one knee but pushed herself back up with as much speed as her drained body would allow.

"Come on, Sage. You're holding out on me." said Teya as she took a step back giving Sage room to recover.

Turning to face the queen as she struggled to regain her balance she laughed, "Let's take this to the training field so it's fair."

Teya went for Sage again but this time with a sweep of her legs knocking Sage into the dirt, "You will fight me here or you can cuff yourself back into those chains right now," she growled then kicked at Sage's ribs.

With surprising speed Sage caught Teya's leg and yanked her down into the dirt. A cloud of dust swirled around them as Teya struggled to regain control but Sage swung her arms as fast as they would obey and hit the queen in the face sending deep red blood trickling down from her nose. She swung again but Teya shoved using her power to send Sage across the room to land under the chains that had been holding her.

"You've had your fun now it's time to admit defeat. You can't win." Teya appeared in front of Sage as fast as a breeze. She wiped the blood from her face with a shaking hand.

The fear in Teya was easy for Sage to see though the queen was trying to hide it. She knew the queen was done with fighting fair so she had to think fast. She reached up and held a cuff in her hand, "I would rather rot in these chains."

"Have it your way!"

Teya swung her fist toward Sage's face but right before impact Sage dodged letting Teya's momentum carry her forward then she wrapped her arm around Teya's neck and clamped the shackle she held onto the queen's wrist.

"I will have it my way," shouted Sage as she released her hold on Teya to leave the surprised queen staring at the cuff. Sage knew the bounds wouldn't hold long so she swung an uppercut hitting Teya on the chin. She could see the fairy's eyes glaze over as she started to pass out from the blow that would have made any boxer proud but just as her knees started to buckle the black power began to seep from its master's hands and wrap around Teya. The dark mass cocooned the queen from head to toe, leaving only her closed eyes exposed.

Turning, Sage started for the door. She knew this couldn't end well so she needed to get out of this room. She needed her powers back to finish this fight and the only way to do that was to get past that closed door. Two steps and she was at the bottom of the small stair case leading up to the door but then she felt it, the all too familiar coldness seeping into her skin as the dark mass wrapped around her waist and mouth, cutting off the scream that was on the tip of her tongue.

In one rough jerk she was pulled backwards. Sage's feet left trails in the packed dirt as she tried to fight. The mass spun her around to face the wide open, dark pools of evil now staring back at her from the still cocooned face of Teya. The sight was overwhelming, making Sage struggle harder to break free. The coldness and evil that radiated from the queen was sucking the life and soul straight from Sage. Bleakness and despair replaced any hope that lived inside of Sage with each inch closer her body got to the puppet-like figure.

"Did you really think I would let you win?" The queen's voice echoed in an unnatural way, like a second, deeper voice was talking in unison with her. She shook the one arm that was still hanging from the chain, "Did you think this through?" She winked, "Because I did." With a whip of her free hand Teya commanded the blackness to feed into Sage's nose and mouth. The darkness consumed the fairy as she fought to break free.

Sage clawed at her neck. An ice cold, thick tar filled her throat, blocking any air from entering her burning lungs. With each ticking second her panic grew stronger, her heart thumped harder and her vision became spotted as her body begged for that life force that no fairy could live without. She could live for thousands of years and heal from the most severe of wounds but cut the air off and all those powers and years of experience meant nothing.

The spots dancing across her vision began to pulse larger and larger as the world around Sage tilted. She gave up trying to pull the dark mass from her because she didn't have the energy to fight any more. Calm overtook her. A sense of peace, happiness and acceptance all balled into one filled her mind just as the darkness took her under.

After a few moments of silence Teya pulled the power back inside of herself then stood staring down at Sage's still body, "Such a stupid girl."

"Guard!" Teya called out in a desperate voice. Within seconds the door opened and the guard she had dismissed earlier came bounding down the steps. He stopped as soon as his eyes spotted Sage on the floor.

"You idiot, don't just sand there. Get me out of this awful thing."

"I don't understand. What could have possibly

happened to cause all of this?" The guard stammered as he hurried to the Queen's side.

"It would seem the prisoner was immune to the dungeon's power shields. She tricked me into getting close then she attacked me, locking me in these chains and even hitting me." She gritted her teeth as if the pain of admitting getting tricked, even if it was a lie, hurt her to speak of. "I had to defend myself."

The guard went to work on the cuff, "I'll call a healer for the both of you."

"No, there's no time and, well, she is a traitor so death was coming for her soon enough. Just return to your post until I come back. Don't let anyone in and tell no one of what you've seen."

The guard nodded obediently as he followed the queen up the steps. He was well trained and knew his place. Don't ever speak of what you see and never question any order. Following command was drilled into warriors from day one of training as the ultimate trait. Obey without questions because your commander, or in this case the queen, knows what is best for everyone even if the warrior cannot see it at the time but it didn't stop him from taking one worried glance back at Sage before he locked the door behind him.

Chapter 18

Nicole stood in the center of a green field with the sun on her back. She turned in a circle, watching her footing, keeping her hands up in front of her and probed with her mind for any slip. Eyes glowed back at her in red, blue and yellow from each different face—all piercing and determined, waiting for her to let her guard down so they could prove how worthless she was.

A bead of sweat dropped from her hairline and rolled down her neck like it was a small insect crawling along. That was all the distraction it took. A lunge to her left had her spinning quickly to intercept the large, gorilla sized man who was inches from her in under a second. His rotund build would lull anyone into a fake sense of security but as Nicole flipped backward narrowly escaping his sledge hammer fist she realized that looks were very deceiving here.

As she landed on her feet a blue glow pulled her eyes up. A tall, sharp featured woman held her hands above her head calling a massive ball of water into an orb above her. Nicole bolted forward seeing her opening while the warrior was collecting her energy. Half way to her goal a red glow to her side caught her attention. It was Luke. He was running parallel with her across the field.

With a hard look he released the fire at her. Tossing her hand up, she sent an identical ball of fire knocking into his, sending it off course. Two more were right behind it so she prepared to release another as she ran but gorilla guy bolted in front of her making her stagger and trip as she tried to correct her path. Without a second thought she sent a blast of wind at the approaching orbs slapping them to the ground.

Struggling to pull herself from the ground she rolled to her stomach to try to get an eye on all her attackers. She caught a fleeting glimpse of Luke just before he released flames like a dragon's breath from his palms. Nicole froze unsure of what to do. She tried to right herself on her feet but the flames were getting close fast. There was no time to flee so she called wind to herself and created a shield around her body. The raging winds cut off her view of the world outside but she felt the heat of the flames as they tasted each inch of her barrier, dancing up one side and over the top casting an orange glow on the dirty gray walls around her. Just when she thought her idea was going to fail and that she was going to suffocate in the inferno it stopped. It was over.

With a relieved sigh Nicole set the winds free with a dismissive flick of her wrist. She pulled herself up on her knees and studied the area around her as the dust started to settle. The grass that had been inside of her protective ring was still vibrant and green but the area around her was black. Red embers glowed as small fires spread slowly across the field filling the air with gray smoke.

"What the hell was that," screamed Nicole as Luke walked towards her.

He cocked one eyebrow giving a smug look, "Training."

Nicole stood up dusting the dirt from her jeans and t-shirt, "You were trying to kill me! That was excessive."

"Do you think anyone is going to go easy on you in a real battle?"

"I don't think I'll have three people attacking me at once," she retorted.

"Three?" Luke laughed drily. "You couldn't handle three people attacking you."

"What is that supposed to mean?" Nicole asked placing her hands on her hips.

Luke took a step back with a smug smile stretching his lips. He pointed one finger up causing Nicole to look into the air just in time to see the giant orb of water floating above her head. She gasped as it opened up and dumped a waterfall of cold water over her, drenching her completely and, at the same time, putting out the remaining fires.

Luke's face twisted as he tried not to laugh but he couldn't contain it. He doubled over with amusement over Nicole's shocked face.

Nicole watched him enjoying her frustration until she had enough. While his eyes were on the ground she raked her hands through the air then lifted them above her head. Within seconds the water had beckoned to her call and a huge blue ball dangled dangerously close to Luke's head, "Hey tough guy," she purred in her sweetest voice grabbing Luke's attention.

Luke was still trying to contain his laughter when his

face took on a stoic look, knowing that he had asked for what was coming, "Damn it," was all he muttered when the first drop of water hit him. The downpour drenched him to his skin and left him dripping.

Laughter erupted from behind them as the other two warriors came to stand beside Nicole.

"It would seem you have your hands full with this one, Luke," chuckled the bear like man as he patted Nicole on the back. "My name is Braden"

Nicole shook his hand then turned to receive a warm hug from the tall, slender woman, "I'm Harlo. Sorry about the bath but you looked like you could use something to cool you off," she joked.

Nicole looked down at her wet clothes then back a Harlo with a smile, "Next time a glass of tea will work just fine."

Luke chuckled as he leaned his head back and closed his eyes, "You still have so much to learn." The air around him heated and steam started to rise from his clothes. He was using his fire like a dryer to evaporate the water from his body.

Nicole narrowed her eyes, "I can do that." Mimicking Luke's actions Nicole was happy to hear the hiss of water evaporating off her. After a moment she opened her eyes rubbing her hands along her clothes, "See, all dry." She gave Luke a smug wink.

"Only one little problem," retorted Luke. "You're shoes are on fire." He smiled and turned away.

"Oh crap!" Nicole danced out of her shoes then patted out the small flames that were working their way around the strings of her tennis shoes.

"When you're done playing we will get back to training," Luke called over his shoulder.

"Asshole," mumbled Nicole under her breath.

Luke turned on her, "You know if you'd keep your mind on the training this would go a lot smoother."

"My mind is on the training"

"To hell it is. When you're focused on defending yourself you let the guard down inside your head so all those thoughts of yours flow out for all hear. You're broadcasting your next move so loud you might as well give everyone a hand-out."

"This isn't easy, Luke." Nicole stepped up to him, toe to toe. "You don't know how hard it is to control this many abilities," she poked a finger against his chest as her temper started to reach its peak.

Grabbing her hand he leaned down to whisper in her ear, "It seems to me that you're worried about Slade. Lots of nice images of him keep popping up too." His words seeped with venom.

She yanked her hand back and didn't try to keep her voice low, "If you bothered to snoop long enough you would see that I'm worried about him and Sage. If you haven't noticed both of my *friends* have disappeared. You're jealousy is blinding you, Luke," she hissed

Without hesitation Luke pulled her into his arms and crushed his lips against hers. She pressed against him roughly at first then as the seconds ticked by her anger melted into desire. The tension had been too much to bear for both of them.

Luke ended the kiss leaving her breathless. He leaned his head against her forehead, "I'm sorry I'm such a fool but it's your fault."

Nicole's eyed him confused, "My fault?"

He smiled her favorite one sided smirk, "Loving you

has made me this way."

Nicole giggled, "Maybe you should find a good therapist." She wrapped her arms around his neck as he hugged her tight.

"Nope, all I need is you." He kissed her lips again but this time it was soft and tender.

Nicole's heart felt full to the point of bursting while she was wrapped in Luke's strong arms. She wanted to stay like this forever but just as the thought drifted through her dreamy haze Luke's muscles went stiff where her arms were wrapped around his neck.

"Nicole, can I talk to you?"

Nicole spun around to see Slade standing at the edge of the field. His face was hard and his forehead lined as he glared past her to Luke, "Slade," She gasped in surprise as she walked over to where he stood. When his eyes met hers she could see genuine worry in his features, "What's wrong?"

"Have you seen Sage?"

Nicole's heart sank, "Not since before the ball, why?"

He ran a hand across the back of his neck, "I heard that she was sent out on a mission but..." his voice trailed off.

"But what?"

"I asked Moyer when she would be returning and he didn't know she was gone."

Nicole's brows crumpled together, "What does that mean?"

Luke walked up placing a hand on Nicole's shoulder, "I wanted to tell you after today's training but it's true, Moyer told me the same thing when I asked."

She shrugged off his hand and stepped away from him, "You knew and didn't tell me? Why would you do that?"

"You have enough on you already and very little time to focus on your training, Nicole. Plus it could be the truth that the queen sent her on a mission."

Slade snorted, "I doubt that. She doesn't dirty her hands with things outside of this realm." He turned to Nicole, "Can you reach her mind?"

"No, I tried already." Her heart was pounding, "What does that mean?"

Slade shook his head, "Only two things, either she's locked in the dungeon or—" his emotions choked off his words. He took a deep breath, "Let's just try to find her before we let our minds jump to anything else."

"Where do we start," asked Nicole.

"We go down to the dungeon of the castle and have a look."

"It's not that simple," whispered Luke as he looked back toward Harlo and Braden who had taken a seat under the shade of a tree at the far end of the field. "The dungeon is guarded."

Slade started walking away with Nicole on his heels, "You managed to help your dear ol' dad out of there once so I'm sure that getting us inside should be easy for you."

Nicole turned back in time to see Luke's concerned scowl turn into a pained grimace thanks to Slade's reminder that he had set Loch loose from that same prison years ago. He had suffered both mental and physical torment due to that one mislead act of family loyalty. Nicole thought about the jagged scars that covered Luke's back. He had been whipped continuously for days in an attempt to lure Loch back but it turned out that Loch wasn't as loyal to his son as Luke had been to him. He didn't return and if Queen Titania hadn't come out from hiding when she did he would have been killed.

Nicole shook the heartbreaking thoughts from her mind then reached for Luke's hand, "Please, Luke. Do it for Sage."

He pulled her fingers to his lips and kissed her knuckles, "I'll do it for you."

~**~**

The group entered through the kitchen of the castle. The modern day stainless steel appliances and bustling staff of cooks seemed out of place to Nicole compared to the ancient and magical world portrayed by the outward appearance of the fairy realm. She wondered if the need for technology was due to the thinning powers of the race or if it was just to fill a want for the queen.

Nicole followed Luke and Slade through the large, busy kitchen without much more than a glance being passed between them and the cooks preparing lunch. They took a right when they emerged into the hallway and tried to walk casually down the passage.

A knot was forming in Nicole's stomach with each step deeper into the castle. A mixture of anxiety from not knowing what would be waiting for them when they made it to the dungeon and guilt for not trying to find Sage sooner was eating away at her, "What's the plan?"

Luke placed his hand on the small of her back urging her to keep moving, "We keep acting like nothing is up—after all, we do belong in this place, then we talk to the guard."

"Wow, you just made that sound really simple. Why didn't I think of this plan," Nicole rolled her eyes but kept her pace with Luke. "But how do we get past the guard?"

"For once would you please trust me?"

A strength and confidence radiated from him in a way that Nicole hadn't seen since the night they were fighting to save Kat's life at the airfield. Sometimes she let herself forget that he lived for moments like this. Now she understood why her great grandmother had chosen Luke to guard her bloodline. He was unwavering and unfazed in the face of danger in the way that true warrior should be.

Nicole nodded then fell in behind him as the hallway started to descend down a staircase. The walls were the original cold stone on this level and there weren't any touches of remodeling that Nicole could see outside of the long, florescent light fixtures that were dotted along the ceiling. She could feel the growing pin dot in her head that told her a warrior was not far ahead.

Luke held out a hand signaling Slade and Nicole to stop, "I need a minute. Wait here until I call."

"But--" Nicole started to protest but Slade took her hand so she stopped where she was.

Slade gave her hand a gentle squeeze, "Let him go. He knows what he's doing."

Luke glanced back at Slade and Nicole's intertwined fingers then gave Slade a nod, "Keep her close."

When Luke disappeared around the corner Nicole leaned back against the wall and closed her eyes. Her heart felt as though it had taken up residence in her throat causing her to swallow hard. Her anxiety was tripled by the fact that she was left hand in hand with

Slade who had tried to kiss her the last time they were left alone.

"Nicole," Slade whispered.

She could feel the heat of his breath on her neck but she kept her eyes closed, "What?"

"You're breaking my fingers," he chuckled.

"Oh," she let him pull his hand away and watched as he rubbed along each finger to ease the pain. "Sorry."

"Don't forget," he pulled out the large silver medallion from inside his shirt, "with this thing on I'm only as strong as a human. Even my immortality is forfeited if I was to be severally wounded." His words were soft but serious.

"It must be hard on you to not have your power while you're here. I know it almost drove me insane when you held mine away from me."

A small regretful smile touched his face, "I should have never done that to you but I hope you understand it was only for my undercover persona, not because I truly wanted to hurt you."

Nicole took a deep breath and let it out. She found herself wondering who was the real Slade but his apology had lifted a small amount of the weight from her shoulders. She gave him a warm smile then leaned her head back to listen for Luke. She let her mind stretch out to the pull that was uniquely his in her mind. He was still and she could hear his mind spinning ideas of what to implant in the warrior's head as he got closer to his destination.

"So that's his plan," she laughed.

"Hey, Luke's fine but us on the other hand," Slade looked back down the hall in the direction they had just come. "Why don't you scan the castle and see if anyone is onto us."

Nicole closed her eyes again and began to urge her power farther out. With each growing wave she picked up more and more minds. Thoughts of working staff reached her loudly. One was worried about dusting the massive chandelier in the throne room while another was half thinking about the bed she was making while she dreamed of a young man who lived next to her family.

She ran along some warriors as she pulsed outward, most were focused on making their rounds along the perimeter walls of the castle while a few where thinking normal guy stuff like projects around the house and getting home to his family. The thoughts made her shake her head. For a magical kingdom, it seem very much normal, almost like home. It was filled with people just like her small Alabama town was, all trying to carve out a living for themselves and their families.

The thought of family had a sudden plan come to her mind. She needed to get Kat and James away from this realm right now. Everything felt wrong. As if the kingdom wasn't safe for her let alone her dad and best friend. She pressed out searching for the mind of Rhys because she knew he wouldn't hesitate to protect them. After a moment his mind became clear as he was consumed with a thought about how beautiful Kat was.

For the first time Nicole actually felt herself blushing from hearing the private thoughts of someone. She noticed Slade was watching her curiously, "Ummm, I've got a plan to get Dad and Kat out of here. Give me a second." She waved him off and stepped back down the hall a few feet so she could concentrate. *Rhys, can you hear me,* she called out inside her own mind.

Ey, I can princess, His old Irish accent was thick even

in the voice of his thoughts.

I need you to sneak Kat and Dad out of this realm. It's not safe for them here.

What do I tell ye father?

Tell him...I love him. That was all she could think to say. There were no guaranties that she would be coming home, no promise of a reunion in a few days nor was there another way. They had to leave without her. *I'm depending on you to keep them safe, Rhys. Don't fail me*

Ey, princess.

With that, she closed the connection between them just in time to hear Luke, *It's clear. Come on.*

"Let's go," She fell in behind Slade as they made their way down the musky, dim corridor. When she made the turn she stopped gaping at the guard laying in the floor, "What did you do to him?"

Luke was blocking a door open with a metal folding chair, "I needed the chair so I told him to take a nap on the floor."

"Okay," she stared down at the man snoring on the floor then back at Luke. "Is Sage in there?"

"Yes but the dungeon is charmed just like Slade's necklace so powers are useless inside there."

Nicole started past the door without a second thought. Sage was inside and that's all that mattered, powers or not, she was getting her out.

"Hey," Luke stopped her, "One of us needs to stand guard."

"I'll do it," said Slade.

"No offense, but you're already powerless so it has to be me." Luke kissed Nicole's cheek, "Be fast, no matter what kind of shape she's in, you have to be fast."

Chills danced up Nicole's spine. The sense of urgency was clear in Luke's words. She could tell there was something he wasn't saying but there wasn't time to talk now.

"In and out, gotcha." She walked past the threshold of the doorway and immediately felt her powers drain away like her very soul was being pulled from her body but she pressed on down the small set of stairs that ended on a dirt covered floor.

The room was dimly lit by small rays of sunlight creeping through one long, narrow window near the ceiling. The stench of the room assaulted Nicole's nose with a smell that intensified with each disturbed grain of dirt beneath her shoes. A few steps in and her eyes fell on a heap under dangling chains.

"Sage," she whispered as her feet froze and refused to move forward. Slade rushed past Nicole and dropped to his knees by his sister's side. He attentively brushed strands of her black hair off her forehead. Nicole could hear him whispering his sister's name again and again building in desperation with each attempt to rouse her from slumber. He didn't have to say the words for Nicole to understand. Sage was dead.

Chapter 19

Shaking her head in denial Nicole shouted, "Help me, *fast*!" If she could just get Sage outside of this room she could help her. "I can save her." She spoke to Slade but he didn't acknowledge her. He sat staring down at his sister, motionless.

Nicole dropped to her knees beside him, "Help me get her out of here so I can help her." Slade shook his head in response but still didn't look up from his sister's face. Panic fills Nicole when she saw Slade wasn't moving, "Don't you want to save her?" The question came out in a scream before Nicole realized the panic flowing into her voice.

"It's too late," Slade's tone was one of numbness. He kissed Sage's cheek then stood. "Her spirit is gone and there's no bringing that back."

"But it worked on Kat. You have to let me try," Nicole pleaded. "Help me carry her." Nicole raised Sage's head into her lap and for the first time felt how cold her friend's body was. There was no pink glow left to her translucent skin. Only a small trace of red lipstick remained to add any color to her face at all. That's when reality hit Nicole. The life had gone from Sage and left an empty shell behind. Her mind screamed *this can't be happening* but her heart was heavy and splitting in two. "Why?" Was all she could whisper as her tears started to flow silently down her cheeks.

"I think Luke may be able to answer that for us." Slade placed a comforting hand on Nicole's shoulder. "We need to go."

"Go? How can you be so calm about this, Slade?" Nicole's voice cracked as she tried to speak. This makes no sense. How could he be so at ease when she is falling to pieces? Did he not care for her? Didn't he love her like a brother should love his sister? She wanted to shake him until he showed some emotions. A single tear or a fist into a wall—anything to prove he cared half as much as she did for Sage. Sage *deserves* that much.

"I'm doing what I do best—bottling up my anger until the time is right." He reached out his hand to Nicole and pulled her to her feet then took one last look at Sage. "Someone will pay for this."

Just as Nicole was about to follow Slade a gleam caught her eye. Next to Sage's body was a necklace with a beautiful emerald stone dangling from it. She picked up the stone and found that the end of the chain was tucked inside of Sage's waistband. "Who were you hiding this from?" she asked even though she knew she would never have the answer from the voice she wanted to hear. Nicole tucked the necklace into her pocket.

Outside the door Luke was waiting with a miserable gaze. Nicole could tell that he knew what they were going to find inside but now she needed to know everything. "What do you know?"

"Just what I saw in the guard's mind. There were images of Teya tormenting Sage and then of the queen cuffed in the dungeon while Sage lay at her feet dying."

"I don't understand why she would do this. What could Teya gain by killing Sage?" asked Slade.

Luke stood in silence. A torn look creased his face and remained there as he spoke, "Sage had to choose between saving herself or Nicole."

Nicole's world started to spin. She had caused Sage to die. She had stood by without doing anything and probably would still be out there in the training field right now if Slade hadn't gotten worried. What kind of friend had she been? How could she be worth a life? Her chest tightened as she tried to focus on Luke's words.

His face hardened as he continued, "Then there was Teya standing in this hallway telling the guard not to leave his post. She called for another warrior to escort her to the gateway. She was going to meet someone that could help with her problem."

"Her problem?" asked Slade. "What is that supposed to mean?"

"Those were the exact words she used but I'm guessing—"

"I'm her problem." Nicole finished his thought. Her self-hate was quickly being replaced with a burning desire to avenge her friend. To make Teya suffer like Sage had suffered but one questions still lingered in her mind, "What do you know about this?" Nicole pulled the necklace from her pocket and held it out for them to see.

"Where did it come from?" asked Luke. Nicole explained where she had found it and only received puzzled looks.

Finally Slade broke the silence, "You said that the last time you talked to my sister was the night of the ball, right?" Nicole nodded in agreement trying to follow his train of thought. "Well, it is the exact color of the dress you wore so maybe she intended on you wearing it."

Nicole studied the jewel as she spoke, "Maybe. But why would she be carrying it in her waistband like she was hiding it?"

"That may be a question we never know the answer to, Nicole, but either way it was Sage's." Luke took the necklace and opened the clasp, "I'm sure she would want you to have it."

Nicole moved her hair out of the way so Luke could put the necklace on her and at the very moment that the clasp closed Nicole let out a gasp, "Get it off." Her power was gone but not only that but her desire to move. The necklace was weighing her down so she felt weak—too weak to even try to remove it. It was ten times worse than being in the dungeon. The power the necklace was emitting was more like it was sucking the very life from her body, taking away her will to live.

Luke quickly removed the necklace leaving Nicole staring in disbelief, "It was like I was dying...slowly." She shook her head trying to clear the cloudiness from her mind. "Is that what it feels like for you, Slade?"

"No. Mine just takes away my power. That's all. That thing is something different," he studied the necklace with a strange fascination. "That was meant for a much darker purpose than containing power."

Nicole nodded, "It took away my will to live. Death wasn't scary anymore, I wanted it and I needed it to escape the darkness that was consuming me."

Suddenly Luke's words clicked into Nicole's head

like she had just heard them for the first time. Recognition of a grave mistake. "I sent Kat, Dad and Rhys to the gateway."

Nicole and Luke were blurring through the hall of the castle and out the doors in no time. "What about Slade?" Nicole asked. Even if he was allowed his powers he couldn't keep up with Luke and Nicole.

"He'll have to catch up." Nicole nodded her agreement as they darted out the front gate of the castle and down the cobblestone street that ran through the center of the town. Nicole tried to reach out to Rhys but came up empty. Maybe they had made it out already. They could have beat Teya to the gateway and be safely back in Alabama by now, sipping sweet tea on her dad's back patio. That's what she hoped as they made the turn that would take them up to the gateway in the woods where they had entered days ago. That's when she felt it but it was too late to stop. A dozen warriors appeared where before there had only been two on her mind's map. Someone had just let them in the gateway and she had a good guess whom it was before Luke pulled her to a stop just out of sight of the great willow.

"Did you feel that?" he asked.

"Yes. There was only two then there were twelve more." Nicole debated for a moment as she searched the minds she could reach. Most of them were closed off to her so they must know about her abilities but then she reached a familiar one, "Kat's there."

"Let me go in and try to get her out."

"But where's Dad and Rhys?"

"Maybe they made it over before Teya got there," said Luke but the doubt was heavy in his voice. He knew just as well as Nicole did that they would never let Kat be the last one through the gateway. Rhys loved her and so did James so they would have been protecting her.

Just as Nicole was going to speak a voice echoed in her head and she could tell by the sudden stiffness in Luke's shoulders that he was hearing it too. "Come join us. I'm sure we can make a trade," demanded a deep voice that hunted her nightmares. It was Loch.

~**~**

Nicole's skin crawled knowing what was waiting for her but Kat was there also so she moved without hesitation. Luke took her hand and they topped the crest of the hill together. Luke was confronting his father who had used him then left him for dead and Nicole was about to face the man who had put this chain of events into motion years ago on a Florida beach.

A line of warriors in black military fatigues flanked each side of a tall, dark haired man with a full beard and eyes as black as night. He stood with his hands laced in front of him as if he didn't have a care in the world. Nicole and Luke stopped a safe distance away from them. A smile turned up the edge of his lips as he stared at their interlaced hands, "It's seems you are making some wise choices for yourself, my son."

"My choices aren't your concern," said Luke coldly.

Loch nodded his head as if to say he understood but wasn't concerned about Luke's brashness. Then he motioned to the line of troops to his right. The formation parted revealing a scene that had been concealed from them. James and Rhys lay unconscious on the ground and Teya stood beside them with a wide grin on her face. A guard held Kat by the arm. "That may be true son, but I'm afraid the choices Nicole makes do concern me along with all these *innocent* people."

The way the word “innocent” rolled off Loch's tongue made the threat in his words clear. Rage and hatred pounded in Nicole's heart. She wanted to spill Teya's blood more than anything she had ever wanted in her entire life. For Sage, for her unconscious father and friend and even for her own satisfaction, but she stood her ground. "Why are you here," Nicole asked Loch.

"I was invited by your sweet Queen."

"She is no queen of mine." spat Nicole.

Loch released a dark, cold laugh, "I've always enjoyed your bluntness, princess. I'm actually very surprised you've not killed this poor imitation of a queen yourself." He looked over at Teya who was holding Nicole's gaze with surprising confidence. "She is quite despicable but," he let out a sigh, " She has been useful in putting us together.”

"Despicable?" Teya turned her hard eyes onto Loch, "Don't forget whose home you are in."

A ring of red outlined Loch's dark eyes and Nicole realized that things were about to turn destructive fast if she didn't act. She was through with losing people. Sage was gone, her dad and Rhys lay on the ground and her best friend was being held hostage. "Don't worry. She will be taken care of soon enough. I'll make sure of it....For Sage." Nicole caught the twitch of surprise in Teya's face before she turned her attention back to Loch, "I'll ask again, why are you here?"

Loch nodded a warrior toward Nicole which made Luke step in front of her, "Back off!"

"But she's part of the deal, son. Nicole and I have a lot to talk about and Teya has agreed to turn her over to me if I will leave her to rule this kingdom."

"You're not taking her anywhere."

Loch leaned his head back just as invisible energy swept out like a small atomic blast sending everyone stumbling backwards. Loch's eyes were consumed in crimson when he opened them again. He stepped forward and another wave shock sent everyone to their knees. Nicole covered her ears just as the ringing started. This was all too familiar to her. The pain, the crippling effect, the drilling inside of her head—all of it she had felt before when he triggered her hidden power years ago.

Just as she the pain became unbearable and a scream hovered at the back of her throat it stopped. All of the agony was gone and she was being pulled to her feet. Once her eyes focused she realized that Slade stood at her side holding her steady. His medallion was dangling between his fingers. Slade had leveled the playing field in one move.

"Slade, so nice to see you again," smiled Loch. Before anyone could understand what was happening the guard who had been retrieving Nicole punched Slade solid in the face and he crumpled into a heap.

Nicole could feel her power rushing back into her body but she knew the same thing was happening to Loch, "Stop! You let them go and I'll come without a fight." All the work they had put into wiping Morena's mind so Slade would look like a victim was wasted by his one noble move. He would be at the mercy of Loch if she didn't work fast to draw the attention back to herself.

Loch considered her words as he took in the scene. He seemed to be taking great interest in the move Slade had just made. Then he waved his hand at the guard holding Kat, "Release them."

Nicole held her head up high as Kat was released. She tried to rush to Nicole but she stopped her, "You've got to hurry, Kat. Get Rhys and dad up." Nicole kept her eyes trained on Loch. She watched for any objection to what she had said but instead he just scrutinized the scene like a chess player studying his next move. When Kat had the two men roused she reached her hand out taking Luke's. To anyone watching them it would look like Nicole was saying goodbye but she stealthy dropped the charmed emerald necklace into Luke's palm. *Use it on Teya. You rule this kingdom by using her as your puppet. Prepare for war.* Nicole sent her words into Luke's mind. Their silent exchange would change everything.

Luke shook his head, "I can't let you go." Desperation was etched into the lines of his face as he searched for another way out of this.

Nicole kissed his lips softly then stepped back, "There's no other way." Before she could say more a firm hand tugged at her arm. She stepped into the group of warriors and followed Loch out the gateway.

Chapter 20

Not a prison to keep her locked away. No shackles to hold her tight. Not a mildew filled and sun-poor room deep underground. Nicole sat on a plush sofa staring blankly at the wall in front of her. The sitting area of the room was large enough to be considered a living room in most homes. The room...*her* room was well lit and inviting. All the comforts of home if you didn't notice the guard that stood on her balcony and the one outside her bedroom door—both holding semi-automatic rifles.

No one had made any demands on her. There had been no interrogations, no test of her powers and no push for her loyalty since she arrived at Loch's estate. A guard had escorted her into this room almost a full forty eight hours ago and left. There had been trays of food brought in at the correct time for each meal but Nicole hadn't eaten. She only waited, wondered, and worried. Nicole waited for what was to come, wondered if Luke would have time to prepare before his father staged an attack on the kingdom and worried; lots of worries ate away at her mind.

War was coming. She made the call herself. In those moments staring into Loch's and Teya's eyes she knew there was no way around it. Teya wanted power and control just like Loch. She didn't care if her people were wilting away, growing weaker and weaker until there wouldn't be a fae race left. She would sit by and let the race drift away and, in the end, it would be the same end result. Loch would have his genocide. The entire fairy race would be wiped out.

How could she fix this when it seemed the leaders of both sides were working toward the same goal? Nicole kept wrapping her mind around it again and again, trying to see the whole story but something felt off. A large piece of the map was missing and she needed to find it to reach the correct point.

The door to her room opened but she didn’t rise or look up. Nicole continued to stare at the same spot on the wall uncaring about her visitor.

"Why are you refusing to eat?" Loch sat in a chair across from her.

"What does it matter? I'm immortal so I won't starve."

"True. But it will make you weak." He was right. With each passing hour her limbs became heavier and her mind became cloudier. Even now, if the opportunity presented itself she knew that she couldn't effectively attack Loch. Maybe she could get a small ball of fire or a wisp of wind to form but it would only fall flat before it could do any damage.

Nicole didn't respond so Loch continued, "Do you not appreciate the living accommodations?"

"It's just another prison."

"I guess you would see it that way." Loch stood cutting off her view to the spot that had been her escape. "Did you ever ask yourself why the warrior leader lives here in your world?"

Nicole had wondered that when she had been held in the basement of his estate. She had expected the warriors to have their own kingdom or fortress just like the fae but Instead they live in the same world as humans. She thought it was their choice since they could blend in with humans so easily but maybe she was wrong.

"Fae and warriors used to live in the same kingdom. The castle you just left was also shared by the King of the warriors. We protected the fae so it only made sense to stay close. Our races shared everything. But as time passed the fairy race stopped looking at warriors as their equals. We went from being the strong protectors of the fae to being no more than servants. Then when your grandmother Titania fell in love with her warrior she tried to change that way of thinking. She wanted that equality to come back but it was for her own self-serving interest not her love of the warrior race."

"What does that matter? Your people would have had their place back," snapped Nicole. She could not tolerate the picture he was trying to paint of her grandmother. Titania was the only person, even if in spirit, that had been her constant guide. And she was family.

A ring of red brightened Loch's eyes. He was not one to be questioned and it was clear he would not tolerate it long. "Her idea of a union would lead to a mixed race. A race like you. No one wants that." He stared at her like she was diseased.

"So kill me and put an end to it!" Nicole stared fearlessly into his eyes. Death would be the way to end it all then. No mixed blood would remain so there would be no need for war.

A dark laugh came from inside Loch; taunting and knowing. "You're death will not end this." His laughter shut off as fast as it appeared, Loch's very presence was pressing down on Nicole. Drilling deeper into her head with each second his eyes met hers. "But deaths by your hand will. The fae kingdom will be mine because everyone will see that the Princess herself is loyal to her warrior blood. That means more than any amount of pain I could inflict under my own command."

"But you made a deal with Teya. You said that you would leave the kingdom alone if she gave me to you."

"And why would I consider keeping my word to her?" A smile crossed his lips, "Did you know Teya locked the gateway to the Fairy burial grounds?" He chuckled, "I'm guessing by the confused look on your face that you didn't. It's actually very clever of her. She locks away the power so that there will never be a fae born stronger than she is. It insures that she keeps the throne. Well, that is unless you had decided to take it from her."

Nicole was reeling on the inside though she kept her face slated. Every last word about Teya made sense. The way she belittled her in front of people, the way she made her feel like an outsider—all of it was Teya's way of keeping Nicole from thinking about wanting the throne for herself. She had done it too, and so easily. Made Nicole seem like a child who couldn't take care of herself and Nicole had fell right into her role like a fool. Inwardly Nicole groaned as the pieces fell into place.

"Now, it's time for you to play your part. You *will* lead my troops into war. You will be their general and I will have what's mine," Loch's voice was confident and commanding.

Nicole stared at him then after a moment right through him. She was done listening. She would not fight on his behalf. All her time had been spent trying to find a way to avoid this war so she wouldn't allow herself to end up fighting on Loch's side of the battlefield.

Loch walked to the door, "If you refuse to fight I will kill them all. All, as in that whole pathetic town you call your home back in Alabama, including your father. I'm done playing games."

~**~**

Sleep came to Nicole in fitful bursts. A single nightmare repeated again and again each time the darkness took her.

She was standing in the middle of a battlefield, explosions and gun fire all around her, but she was frozen. Frozen by fear and confusion. Frozen by not knowing who the enemy was as bodies blurred around her: warrior and fae alike. The fog cleared a little allowing her to move but she refuses to fight anyone, dodging attacks, ducking bullets until she falls to the ground. When she tried to crawl forward she was suddenly staring into the lifeless eyes of Slade. His body was charred by fire but his face remained for her to bear witness to what her decisions instigated.

Digging her fingers into the ground she crawled closer to Slade but just as she reached out to close his haunting eyes a boot met the back of her head smashing her face down into the blood spattered dirt. Just when she thought she was going to suffocate the pressure released and allowed her to roll over only to meet the blue glow of Luke's palm. She could see his face behind the power, glaring at her with cold black orbs. "You should have chosen me sooner," He hissed as a burst of power escaped his hands.

Nicole awoke gripping her chest where she was sure the fire had drilled a hole into her skin. Tears rolled down her face while she struggled to catch her breath. Her eyes darted around in confusion before she realized that she was still in Loch's estate. A fate just as bad as the nightmare.

Sleep did not return to her that night and dawn brought no singing birds or happy thoughts. Nicole sat in a straight back chair watching the bedroom door. She was dressed and ready just as she was instructed the night before. A black military uniform was brought to wear so that she matched the rest of the warrior army. She pulled her hair back into a simple braid before taking her seat to wait for her "training". Once again she would be trained by the warriors. Only this time it would be Loch's warriors so she could lead them into battle against the fae.

After the fitful night without rest only one conclusion felt real: she would be a fool to pass up learning what Loch's army had to offer. She would contribute on the battlefield by learning the weaknesses of her enemy and using that knowledge to burn them down. Loch could try to control her but she would always try be one step ahead. "Smarts will win over brute force in this war," she told herself.

Chapter 21

"You've got to be kidding me," hissed Nicole when she walked inside the training arena. Obstacles courses, target dummies, weights, and various mats were placed around a building the size of a football field. All were occupied by warriors honing their skills which, from Nicole's vantage point, looked perfectly polished already. She only had a few moments to take in the spectacle before all attention turned on her. Fighting the pressing feeling she should run, Nicole lifted her head and walked out into the center of the floor.

Nicole's eyes were drawn to a window high above where Loch and Mr. Casey, the man she had met at Slade's cocktail party, sat watching the show below. Within seconds the crowd descended, surrounding her. The tension pressed in on Nicole but she held her ground.

"Hey there, sweetheart," taunts came from a broad but slender warrior with a scar running from the edge of his lip in an arch up to his ear like a half smile. "I've been looking forward to our playtime." He skillfully spun a small silver throwing knife in his hand. Before Nicole could react he buried it in the mat between her feet.

Without hesitation Nicole yanked the knife from the floor and sent a streak of silver through the air. The blade cut a red trail across the warrior's unscarred cheek before he knew what hit him. "That was your warning. Next time I'll make sure it's deep enough to have you wearing a permanent smile all the way across that ugly face."

The man wiped the blood from his cheek with the back of his hand then lunged forward smashing into a body that wasn't there seconds ago. "Brien, her warning was clear," Claude commanded the room with his strong voice. Nicole was taken aback by the authority that resonated off the man she had once thought to be no more than Slade's driver and body guard. The black uniform suited him, like he had donned this role for years. The crowd backed away silently but the message was clear: Nicole wasn't welcome here.

Claude turned his head toward Loch who was watching the scene play out with eager attention. He gave Claude a nod then walked away from his seat in front of the window.

"Shall we begin?" Claude motioned to a balance beam that hovered a few inches off the ground. "One rule: No using your fire power. You are allowed your speed and strength but that is all. We have a special area we use to train those more...explosive abilities." He waved a hand towards a tall woman who was positioning herself on the far end of the beam, "Shala will be your sparring partner for this exercise."

Shala was the embodiment of intimidation. Her slender but solid frame screamed discipline. The composed stance she took with a wooden staff in her hand did not project arrogance, it screamed confidence and strength. Nicole would have guessed her young enough to be in college except the hardness of her eyes said she was much older and wiser than a woman in her early twenties.

With a deep breath Nicole pushed away the intimidation and planted her feet on the narrow beam, quickly finding her center. She took the cold, wooden staff that was offered to her. It felt bulky and awkward compared to the baton she had trained with in the police academy, but there was no time for test swings. Shala lunged forward slamming her staff into Nicole's with a loud bang. Nicole pushed hard shoving the warrior back a step but Shala immediately swung the staff low sweeping Nicole's legs from underneath her. Nicole landed with a thud on the beam but didn't fall off.

The hoots and cheers for Shala by the warriors barely registered in Nicole's ears. She lurched to her feet and balanced on the narrow piece of wood again. Giving Shala a confident smirk, she drove forward in a blast of warrior speed. Shala managed to block the swing of Nicole's staff but not the head butt that followed. Seeing her move had stunned her opponent Nicole swept her leg out knocking the warrior's feet off the beam and sending her backwards to the mat below.

Shala's eyes glowed bright red as she stared up at Nicole. The woman was struggling to contain her anger as the faint glow of crimson pooled in her palms. Fire roared to life in Nicole's hands just as Shala slammed her fist against the floor then pushed to her feet. The fire was gone from her extended hand. Nicole stared at the woman confused at the sudden change. "Seems you may be able to teach me a thing or two, freak." Shala gave a small smile that bordered on friendly.

Nicole let the warrior shake her hand...well, it was more like her wrist because that's where she placed her hand on Nicole's arm giving it one strong shake before she took a step back.

Claude nodded his approval then pointed Nicole to the next section of her training. A large obstacle course containing a track of barbed wire inches above the ground, two story tall walls and a long rope bridge but that wasn't the worst of it. All along the path were warriors of all shapes and sizes who intended on blocking her path and the last one she would face on the bridge would be her favorite scar wearing warrior, Brien.

Claude explained the route to her then stepped back. "Don't let them get to you," he whispered. If they see your fear they will kill you. You don't belong here and they want you gone."

"Well the jokes on them because I don't belong anywhere," Nicole shrugged her shoulders flashing a cocky grin. "Let's do this."

Claude gave a quick nod, "Begin!"

Nicole had been through the academy and seen enough military movies to know what she needed to do. She dove below the barbed wire and slithered on her stomach, expertly keeping her body from touching the spikes. Just as she neared the far side gunfire erupted around her.

Blanks, she instinctively thought just before a burning sensation ripped through her calf. There wasn't time to check the wound and really no point. She knew by the warmth of the blood and the heat of her leg a bullet had struck her but she lunged forward again using her arms as much as she could.

Jumping to her feet she blurred to the climbing wall hoping for shelter from the shower of gunfire. The shots kept ricocheting off the concrete floor and even embedding into the wooden wall she was expected to climb. Grabbing the rope she started to hoist herself up when another bullet grazed her tricep. "Sitting duck," she mumbled. Claude was right, so far they were giving her minor injuries but if she left herself open for too long they would try to kill her. *Was this Loch's Plan? Would he let her die in a training scenario?* She didn't think so. This felt like pure hate by the warriors that had been told to follow her. Egos and pride were being bruised and she was at their mercy....unless.

Images of training with Luke flashed in her head. She called wind to her, creating a shield that wrapped from her left side, around her back, and ended at their right side. With a smile she grabbed the rope again and started to climb. She wasn't in the mood to test the limit of her immortality today. After all, there did have to be a limit or neither fae nor warrior would fear war. Immortal doesn't equal invincible.

The wind roared around her making it almost impossible to hear anything but the clink of bullets as they tried to penetrate the barrier. At first her footing was difficult because of the blood that had dripped from her leg down to her boots. But after the first few steps the slickness wiped from her soles leaving a trail of red shoe prints behind.

As she pulled herself over the top a silver knife dug into the wood between her fingers. Scarface, the nickname she had given Brien, wasn't wasting any time. Positioned halfway across the rope bridge he slung knives with every step. Nicole could still see the streaks of dried blood from the wound she had inflicted though it had already healed but what really caught her attention was the look of pure hatred that came from him. He wanted her dead.

The wind shield wouldn't allow her to see where she was walking so she dropped it just as Brien reached to pull another knife from his waist. She discreetly drew the knife from the wood as she stood keeping it tucked inside her palm. Running forward she side stepped when he threw another knife narrowly avoiding being stuck in the eye. She hit the rope bridge hard causing it to sway wildly so Brien was forced to hold on then she rolled forward and sprung straight into Brien landing hard on top of him. "Don't move!" Nicole held the blade against his neck cutting a small crimson line to get his attention.

Brien's nostrils flared and his eyes were glowing red but he remained still as she stepped over him to the other side of the bridge. Nicole turned to run but just as she reached the edge of the platform she heard it—the roar of fire.

Slammed forward by the force of the flaming ball Nicole landed on her stomach sending all the air rushing from her lungs. The lick of the flame didn't completely devour the fire retardant military fatigues but she could still smell the stench of burning cloth as she rolled to her back. Shouts were echoing around her then hands were rolling her back to her chest.

"I'll put it out." Shala covered Nicole with a jacket and began patting frantically. A few moments later she removed the cloth and gave a satisfied grunt, "All good."

"Thanks," replied Nicole.

Shala held out a hand pulling Nicole to her feet just in time to see Brien jumping to the floor below. He bounded into a group of warriors laughing and exchanging high fives until Claude's voice echoed off the walls. The barrage of profanities that flowed from Claude seemed to wick the joy from Scarface. "Sucks to be you." Shala said dryly to Nicole.

"That's an understatement," joked Nicole as she

accessed the damage. Her uniform shirt was crisp and flaky as she pulled it off but the t-shirt underneath was untouched.

"Well, at least the fire didn't do much damage. Why didn't you fire back?"

"I think death is senseless."

"But he tried to kill you. The fact that you're still alive is amazing because Brien never misses. That's his gift and it's a deadly one."

"Doesn't change my stance on this war and really that's all this is about. The fae want me to see how destructive warriors are and the warriors want me to see the evil in the fae. In turn the majority of both sides seem to hate me." Nicole started rolling up her pants leg to see how bad the bullet wound was.

"You're in a very hard place, that's for sure. Maybe you should just wipe us all out." Nicole's eyebrows shot up at the boldness of Shala's statement but Shala lowered her voice and continued, "Has either side really been pure good?"

"Is anyone pure?" Nicole let the question hang in the air, turning her attention back to her leg. She took the sleeve of her ruined shirt and wiped at the blood. The longer she wiped the more her brows crumpled together, "Do you see this?" Pink flesh as smooth as a baby's butt was hidden under the crimson fluid. There was ,lood that hadn't had time to dry.

"I see." replied Shala with a hint of annoyance, "A normal warrior's body would have taken hours to heal from that."

"Another perk of being a freak." Nicole joked. The shine of silver caught Nicole's eye. Sticking a finger just inside her boot she pulled out the slug that had been in her leg only moments ago. "Hey, Brien!" She tossed the lead to him. "A souvenir from an event you will never get to relive."

Brien fisted the slug tightly but held back the remark she could see fighting to burst out. Nicole had a feeling this wasn't the end of butting heads with him. His hate ran too deep. Honestly, after today, the feeling was mutual.

~***~**

After a full day of training Nicole found herself back in her room. The guards had taken their places so it was back to business as usual—guards guarding and prisoner imprisoned. She lay across her bed her hair still wet from her recent shower. Her body was tired but still fueled by adrenaline from the day's events so she was restless. A day full of watching your back in a room where everyone wanted to kill you has that effect. Half the time she didn't know if the attack was real or part of the training. Confusion of that degree could have ended very bad.

One thing she did know was there were a few people high on her list to watch out for. Of course Scarface took the number one spot but there were also a couple of brutes that she had dubbed the twins. They didn't resemble in physical traits like family members would but instead it was their skills with the sword that peaked her interest. Nicole had watched them sparring from a distance at first but was drawn closer by the intensity of the two men. Each had an identical stance. Each swung the blade with such ease and never once did the other let the steal touch him. It was like a deadly dance, perfectly choreographed to hint at danger but never stirring it. The duel was eventually called a draw and left Nicole with a new respect for the swordsmen.

Strangely enough number four on the list was Shala. Nicole couldn't gauge the tough-as-nails woman. At times she bordered on friendly but there were those moments when calculation was clear in Shala's dark brown eyes. The look was of someone studying hard to figure something out but what exactly Nicole wasn't sure. Maybe she was just curious about the limits of Nicole's powers or maybe she was looking for Nicole's weakness. Either way there was no letting her guard down for anyone.

Rolling onto her back Nicole closed her eyes. She tried, as she had each night since her imprisonment, to reach out to Luke's mind. Her heart hoped for a response but her mind told her it was foolish to keep trying. True to logic no response came making her situation all the more unbearable. She wanted to know that they were preparing, she wanted to tell Luke what she had learned, but most of all she needed to hear his voice. Not knowing if he was safe, never feeling the tug of their warrior's connection and being left with an empty hole in her heart was weakening her spirit more and more with each passing hour.

At some point while deep in her thoughts sleep did pull her under and for the first time in a long while her spirit awoke in Titania's company. The graveyard, though over-ridden with weeds, was in full bloom. The willow's limbs were a bright green with opening buds and dandelions exploded into hundreds of cotton dancers pirouetting on the salty breeze. Even the small yellow flowers that marked her path in this magical place on her first visit were exceptionally vibrant.

"Spring is beautiful," whispered Titania staring out across the landscape.

"My favorite time of year," replied Nicole.

"Yes, mine too. After a hard, cold winter the world

needs spring. It reminds us that good things always return to our lives. It's a timeless formula that never fails to repeat."

"Do you really believe that? With all you've been through?"

"Yes." Titania said simply.

"But you're trapped in this limbo." Nicole waved her arms around the spiritual graveyard that had been her grandmother's prison. "You chose death over immortality so how can you tell me you believe things will get better?"

"My path, though it was hard, lead me here so I could guide you. If I had passed on to the other realm then I wouldn't be here for you now. Every trial has a greater reason behind it just as your journey is for a greater good."

Nicole fisted her hands at her sides, "Do you not realize that Kat and my dad almost died for this *greater good* and that the lives of both fae and warrior alike teeter on the outcome of this war. Sage died because of what you set in motion."

Titania's eyes remained soft despite Nicole's brashness, "This is a war that needed to be started. The outcome will create a world that is better for all of us."

"You don't know that," hissed Nicole.

"I have faith in you. You weren't created by accident my dear. Greatness is your destiny and through it you will unite mine and your great grandfather's people."

"How will war and death unite both sides? It doesn't make sense. Too many innocent people have already perished when only one person deserves to die and that's Loch. I will not kill anyone who doesn't deserve it."

Smiling, Titania kissed Nicole's forehead, "Sweet dreams my brilliant granddaughter."

Nicole stared confused into her grandmother's face as the world around her dissolved. She didn't understand. How would her not killing anyone solve this? This is war after all. Her eyes opened and she was back in her room staring up at the ceiling. The sun cast small columns of light across her bed but she didn't see them. An idea was spinning in her mind and it consumed her. "I will not kill anyone who doesn't deserve to die."

She sprung from her bed and bounded out to the balcony causing the guard to jump clutching his gun tightly. Nicole grabbed onto the rail and stared out at the sunrise in silence. The colors of the horizon were the most beautiful and vibrant she had ever witnessed. The orange blended into pink which in turn blended into blue creating an artist's canvas. "So beautiful," she whispered. The joy of having a plan gave everything a brand new light. The world up until that moment for her was covered in a gray haze that only hinted at the pristine picture living underneath but now it was as if she had new eyes. There had never been a way to stop this war, it had to happen. But it could be a tool to create a new beginning.

"It's a bit chilly for my liking," responded the guard who had been watching her from a safe distance.

"Back home we call the final cold snap just before spring the Blackberry winter. After those last couple of cold nights you know the world around you is about to change into something beautiful." Nicole smiled and walked back into her room. Training today would be in the field with fire so she had to prepare.

Chapter 22

"Do it again," commanded Luke. He joined the front line in the formation of warriors and fairies as they re-aligned themselves to run through the drill again. Each time the front line consisting of warriors would begin by pummeling the first line with fire. Then the fae's archery line would fire a spray of arrows raining down on the target dummies. After the first two lines passed blurs with blades, both warrior and fae would inundate the field. Some flung small knifes through the air with such skill that they flew straight into the necks and eyes of their opponents; while others brandished swords that glowed with a blue power. In one swing the blade decapitated the target. An electric hiss accompanied each swing of the unusual swords.

General Moyer stood above the group watching the action with a docile Queen Teya in a chair at his side. "They are perfect. You should be proud of your army."

"Yes, very proud," Teya mumbled. Her eyes lazily drifted around the field then she went back to staring at the tips of her long hair. The necklace Luke and Slade had forced onto her glowed green against her pale chest. It was doing its job. Teya had become complacent and easy to manipulate because she could care less about the world around her now. All goals of world domination were gone along with any desires she had of living life itself. She only sat staring into space until someone spoke to her.

General Moyer chuckled at the queen, "You were such a fool to treat Nicole that way. She should have killed you and taken the crown the day she arrived. You never deserved the throne."

"Yes, she should have killed me." Teya agreed as if she was commenting on the rising sun.

"Maybe she will when we go to the battlefield. We will let you stand in the middle like a trophy. The first one to kill you wins. How does that sound?"

Teya's attention was distracted by the action on the field as the army finished the last wave of the assault so Moyer didn't receive an answer to his taunting. Luke and Slade walked up to the platform where they sat. "How did it look to you, General?" asked Slade.

"Like a killing machine."

"Are you seeing any weakness?" asked Luke.

"Yes. Divide them up into two opposing groups then neutralize all powers, Slade. Have them go head to head. I'm sure that Loch is counting on you being there and possibly using this tactic so they will be skilled in hand to hand combat too. We should do the same."

Slade nodded then darted into the soldiers but Luke stayed behind. "What if Nicole is there?"

"You need to focus on winning, not her. If Loch has somehow managed to convince her the warrior race is superior then she is just another fly to be swatted down."

Luke kept his eyes on the army as he processed Moyer's words. "I know she won't turn on us."

"Our intel says otherwise. She's training side by side with them."

"There has to be a reason for what she's doing. I won't write her off that easy."

"You will forget the woman you knew or you will not lead this army out on that battle field. You can't go into war with conflicted feelings."

"I can lead this army," Luke shouted back at the General, upset that he was questioning his abilities.

Moyer stood staring with a face of stone, "She will be leading Loch's army into war. Do you really think you will be able to stand your ground when the woman you love becomes your enemy? You will write her off and remember what your duty is to this kingdom." His voice softened slightly, "If she is still on our side she will make it known."

Luke nodded then confidently walked back to the field to oversee the exercise but inside his head there was an explosion of anger. How could she be leading Loch's army? What could Loch possibly do to convince her to train with them? This was not right and there was no way he would allow himself to believe it. He would prepare for this war alongside his soldiers but when the time came he would do what was right. He belonged to Nicole. He was her warrior. Nothing was greater than him protecting her.

Another two hours of training without powers had everyone breathing heavy but much more aware of what this war would look like if Slade was forced to level the playing field. The warriors were great with hand to hand combat because of their natural strength but not having their speed made them clumsy at times. The fairies were weaker without their magic but most were at least skilled swordsmen and archers so that advantage remained. Over all Slade and Luke agreed that they still stood a chance on a powerless field.

"Do you believe it?" Asked Slade as the soldiers set up for another round of attacks.

"Believe what?"

"That Nicole is against us now?"

Luke shook his head. He peeled his sweat drench shirt from his body and threw it to the ground. "Not a chance in hell." He knew in his heart that Nicole wouldn't side with Loch. She of all people would be able to see through the lies he was sure Nicole was being fed by his father. If she was training with them there had to be a damn good reason. But it didn't matter. Nicole belonged to him. He didn't care how barbaric that sounded. She was his to love and protect no matter the cost and he wouldn't let anything or anyone, including General Moyer, stand in his way.

"Me either. She's too smart for Loch's games." Slade smiled a lopsided grin, "What's our plan?"

"My plan is to lead this army into war," smiled Luke. Slade could read him a little too well but it would be nice to have another person watching his back as he tried to get to Nicole. "But *our* plan will be slightly different once things start rolling."

Slade patted Luke on the back, "Let's get our girl back."

~**~**

A single fire ball fell at Nicole's feet when she stepped to the edge of the field. She knew without looking who slung it her way. Brien smiled broadly from his group of buddies in the center of the fire training area. Nicole didn't give him the satisfaction of a reaction but instead took in the setup of the arena. Over all it was a basic field close to three hundred yards long and a hundred yards wide with a wide pond running down either side. Large boulders, a few narrow walls with doorways and several large dirt mounds made up the inside of the area. Dotted around the edge were several seared and unstable looking building shells, some two stories tall. Nicole made quick notes of each area of safety she could find. Today her strategy would be much different. No more being the hopeless rabbit in a maze of blood thirsty warriors.

Claude tossed her a black jumpsuit and a red armband. "You're on team red. Team blue is your enemy. Only use red fire and shoot for the area covered by the suit."

"Guess you don't want me scorching any of your men's pretty faces?"

"The suit is fire resistant so yes it is much better for training purposes to avoid the face but the suit also marks your hit."

Nicole slid the jumper on and zipped it. "One hit and the person is out?"

"One hit in a fatal zone and you're out."

"How will I know if it was fatal?"

Claude pinched at the material on Nicole's sleeve. She could feel that the top layer was loose compared to the tightness of the liner when he tugged. "Under the fire resistant layer there are different color zones that will shine through when you're hit. If you see red...you're dead."

"Easy enough." Nicole made her way to the edge of the red squad and as usual she was ignored. Shala stepped to Nicole's side and started dancing her way into her own jumpsuit.

"What's the strategy Soldier Keenen?" A hush settled over the group as they all stared at Shala in disbelief. Shala stepped through the group until she was in the center. "She will be leading us into war so it's time to see what she's made of."

All eyes drilled into Nicole. Her heart jumped up into her throat making it impossible to speak. Mentally she started pulling a list together of her experience with war. *Battleship, ummm Call of Duty...I wonder if Contra counts?* Then she remembered one advantage in strategic planning that she had over them all. Telepathic ability. So far most of the warriors had been successful at keeping her blocked out but she had never bothered to challenge their barriers. After all there were times she was able to temporally overcome Slade's shield powers like when she opened the gateway the first time. "I hope this works," she mumbled under her breath just where Shala could hear her.

"Here's the plan." She stepped into the center of the group and lowered her voice. "You all must let me inside your heads. Stop blocking me so I can guide you."

"We don't need you to guide us. We all know where every warrior is just like you do thanks to our blood." One of the twins had managed to be thrown onto Nicole's team and he wasn't too friendly. He was the slightly leaner of the two skilled swordsmen with black hair and eyes that matched.

"Kade, give her a chance to prove herself," shouted Shala. Everyone, including Nicole was baffled by the support Shala was showing. Nicole couldn't help to wonder if this was just part of her game or if Shala really believed in her.

"We will go up the field in two teams. I'll fall back into the second team and issue the commands as we move forward. Trust me and I'll get you all through this safe." Nicole was surprised by the confidence in her own voice. She didn't realize until that moment how much she was depending on this plan to work. There was no other way. Not just for this training game but for her plan to win this war.

Though the reluctance was clear in their faces they all nodded and divided up into two teams. Nicole walked around the front team as Shala told her everyone's names. She tried to quickly associate each warrior's slightly unique pull with a name. When she felt that she had a good handle on the links she stepped back and talked to each warrior by name telepathically. She couldn't help but giggle at some of the shocked and startled expressions on the hardened warriors' faces when she spoke.

When both teams were ready she signaled Claude who was perched on a watch tower above. The enemy team would be coming from the opposite side of the field and though she could feel them there she couldn't see them. She didn't wait for the gun shot to signal game on—she pressed her power forward imagining it drilling into each mind on the far end of the field. It licked and swirled like invisible flames as it tried to taste each mind, dancing along every wall until it found a weakness. Most of the minds were simple to touch. They had grown accustomed to her not trying to break in so they weren't paying close attention but she knew the second she ran across Scarface's mind. It was locked up tight. Each time she pressed forward the shield blocking her pressed back.

Not wanting to test her luck she pulled back. The news that she could penetrate blocked minds was a little secret she wanted to keep to herself. Pushing too hard on Brien could give her away when he was making such an effort to conceal his thoughts.

Scanning the field one last time she turned her attention on the people around her. "Team one up the right. Team two will go left once the first shot is fired." Nicole nodded to both groups then added, "From here on out remain silent. Speak to me in your mind and listen for my orders. Stay hidden until I tell you to fire."

Kade grunted in Nicole's direction as he led the first group away. Nicole took the sound as agreement as she watched the unit move up the side of the field. *Send two into the first building.* Instantly, and to her relief, Kade signaled the two men flanking his lift side to split off into the building. The unit quickly moved out of Nicole's sight so she switched tactics and monitored the tugs in her mind that linked her to each warrior.

The blue team was approaching but cautiously. No burst of speed or showing off. They were playing everything just as they would in a real battle. The first troop of the blue team was about to reach Nicole's first hidden soldier, Terry. She was a small framed woman standing just over five foot who, aside from her skill with fire, looked very much normal. She had taken cover behind what used to be a complete building. But now it was no more than a two battered walls creating an 'L' shape with one broken window.

Terry, Nicole spoke via their connection, *on my count fire out the window. He's about to run past you to take out a bigger target.*

What? She huffed. *Like I'm not a threat.*

Three...Two....One...Now! Silence was all she heard

then a torrent of profanities broke the calm. A warrior walked out to the middle of the field and yelled, "I'm dead," then sat down shaking his head and mumbling under his breath.

Got him, announced Terry proudly to Nicole.

Great job. Now move to a safe area. Nicole motioned for her half of the team to follow her. Most of the enemy was moving toward the action on the right side of the field just as she expected. She led her team around the first dirt mound then signaled for Jake, Rain and a young man who looked like he should still be in high school named Scott over to the next building. *Scott upstairs, Rain take the bottom floor. Jake, post around back.*

Creeping through the next two sections Nicole and Shala took a spot behind two large boulders. *Kade, there's a pair coming up from behind—*

I feel them, he snapped back in her mind.

The urge to teach him a lesson was hard to pass up but instead she said, *They are going to knock the wall on top of you so you need to do it first.* Within seconds she heard the wall crashing to the ground and could see the rising plume of dust and smoke just a few hundred yards away. *Finish them before they can get free of the debris.* Two things happened in the next second. The tug that signaled Kade was approaching the downed targets told her that two more warriors were out of the game but in the same moment she felt the heat of fire. In her distraction she let Scarface slip in on her and Shala.

Before she could react Shala tugged her forward in a run, "It's not a fatal hit." The two blurred into the next building taking the stairs two a time to the second floor. The room was empty with scorched walls and the floor boards were worn thin. Once they stopped Nicole checked the burnt spot on her shoulder. Yellow cloth showed through the hole in her jumpsuit confirming Shala's non-lethal assessment. *Back to it.* Nicole spoke to Shala's mind with a small smile.

Do you feel that? asked Shala silently

Yes. Nicole could feel Scarface was approaching them quickly along with the other members still alive in his team. Something was off. The way he had shot her in the shoulder when he could have easily gotten a fatal hit didn't seem right. And how he kept his mind locked up like a steal trap. It all left a pit in her stomach as she rolled the facts around in her head. Then Shala's words from the first day of training replayed in her head, *Brien never misses. That's his gift.*

It's a trap. Nicole's mind wrapped around the thought just as the first fireball hit the bottom floor. He was going to set the building on fire with her and Shala in it. He wasn't playing by the rules any more.

"What is going on?" Shala blurted out loud as her eyes went wide.

Nicole bolted to the window. Studying the terrain below the shimmer of the brackish pond caught her eye. "Seems Brien is out for my head but don't worry, I've got a plan."

Smoke began to fill the room as the lower half of the building started to burn. The old, dry wood wouldn't take long to become an inferno so Nicole had to act fast. Focusing on the water she held both palms out. A blue glow pooled in her palm and crept around to the back of her hand until it painted its way to her fingertips.

"What the hell?" Shala stared past Nicole to the wall of water that was forming. It pulsed and shrunk back into the pond only to repeat the process again each time growing taller until it was three stories tall.

Nicole smiled and nodded toward the growing wave, "That's my plan."

Coughing Shala covered her mouth and nose with her shirt, "Hurry. I can't stand this much longer."

Nicole nodded. The smoke was becoming very thick but to Nicole the heat building was much worse. The air in her lungs felt hot enough to cook her insides and almost too thick to breath. She pushed for one final build of the wall of shimmering water just as another fire ball slammed into the window. Shards of glass pummeled the team but worse, Nicole lost her control on the wave and it plummeted back into the water. "Not good." She bit off the words through gritted teeth. *Scott, Rain, Jake. We need some help. Try to distract Brien so I can put out this fire.* Nicole channeled the thought to the three waiting warriors she had dropped a few hundred yards back.

We're on it, replied Scott in Nicole's mind. Instantly she felt the trio join together then dart in her direction. The air around Nicole was becoming dark and the orange glow from the fire crept through the cracks of the old floor. Time was slipping away fast and there wasn't enough left for her to pull water to help them. She aimed her hand at the wall on the side of the room that was opposite to Scarface and fired. Splinters of wood blew out into fresh air but a fire ringed hole remained. "We've got to jump."

"The fall will break our legs." Shala was hesitant but she moved toward the stream of fresh air that was taunting her just outside the room.

Nicole tackled her sending both of them out the hole, "Trust me." Nicole grunted as they began to fall. Just as they cleared the building Nicole called wind to them and it pressed against her feet slowing the fall. They hit the ground smoothly in a cloud of dust and smoke without a sound.

Though they made a silent escape the place sounded like a war zone. The roar of the burning building, the blast of fireballs as they collided with stone and wood, and the shouts of Claude all rumbled into one, loud inferno of chaos. Black smoke was blotting out the sun allowing them to see only nondescript shapes and dark shadows a few feet ahead of them as they blurred forward.

We have to circle around.

Why? He's trying to kill us. We should just keep going until one of the others takes him out.

No, he's trying to kill me, not you. You can go on but I'm heading back to finish this. Nicole started to veer left but was pulled to a stop by Shala.

Do you really think I would let you go back in there alone?

"This isn't a training game anymore, Shala." Nicole blurted out loud. "You don't like me so I wouldn't expect you to fight by my side." Nicole was honest. The game was great training for war but she never was delusional enough to believe any of these warriors would obey her let alone be loyal. She was sure the first clear shot any of them had they would make her a bad memory.

Shala leaned in close with a hard look in her eyes. She spoke with just her mind, *I don't have to like you or what you are but I do care about what you're trying to do. Not right now, not in this stupid standoff with Brien—I'm talking about you uniting the races again and putting an end to this ridiculous feud.*

Nicole studied Shala suspiciously. *Why?*

Shala laughed, *You really don't have a clue what this bitterness has done to everyone do you? I lived in the kingdom too. I grew up there with my family. I had friends that were fae—best friends. Then everything fell apart. I was forced to go or risk looking like a traitor to my people but I never wanted a war. I only longed for my life back.*

Genuine pain clouded Shala's face. Nicole could tell the memories of her past hurt her as she replayed them. She patted her on the shoulder, *Glad to know I've got one person on my side here.*

The edge of Shala's lips turned up slightly, *You have a lot more than you know. Scott, Rain and even—* The hiss of a fireball streaking through the air above them cut her short. They moved forward again to where the battle was playing out.

Nicole threw out an arm, "Stay behind me," she yelled as she called wind to her. With a whip of her hands she sent the wind rushing forward clearing away all the thick, choking smoke. Once the world around them was clear again Nicole's eyes locked onto Scarface as he deflected Scott's blast with his own orb. Nicole and Shala ducked as the rogue blast streaked over their heads. The time to end this was now, while Brien was on the defensive. *Is the other twin still alive?* She could feel his presence on the edge of the field but he wasn't moving in on the action.

No, he's out of the game. All of the blue team is out except for Brien, replied Scott telepathically.

Okay. Wait for my signal to fire again. Nicole took off running but only at a human speed. She dodged around a burning pile of wood and several mounds of dirt until she was in front of Brien. "You tried to kill me," she yelled.

He smiled smugly, "It's all just a game, doll. But sometimes there are accidents." He threw flames in a blur of movements but Nicole was faster. She deflected the fire with a whip of wind then sent the gust out to wrap around him like a cocoon.

Once she was sure she had him completely under control she allowed the wind to open just over his face. The hard lines of his forehead and snarl of his lips made Nicole smile, "Accidents are very unfortunate but when it's at the expense of one of your own people," Nicole pointed to Shala, "It becomes cold and pointless don't you think? You were willing to sacrifice a fellow warrior just to kill me," Nicole commanded the cocoon to tighten around him until she could see the panic building in the tightness of his face. The fight went out of him and fear replaced the hate as he struggled for breath. "Lucky for you I am just playing a game." She commanded the wind to open up at his chest then nodded at Scott. He sent a small fireball into the target that quickly burned away the outer layer of Brien's jumpsuit exposing blood red material. "Game over."

Chapter 23

The day replayed over and over in Nicole's head as she stared at the white wall. So much had played out on that field but one fact was keeping her heart drumming in her chest—she wasn't alone here. There were warriors within Loch's ranks that are rebels. And, more importantly, these warriors didn't want a war.

A knock at her bedroom door didn't pull her from sorting her thoughts. It was time for dinner so it would be someone bringing a tray of food on a silver cart. "Are you hungry?"

Nicole spun around on the couch, "Shala, my new servant girl. Has a nice ring to it," Nicole teased.

"Very funny. You don't know what I had to go through to get in here." She groaned and motioned back toward the hall. "I now have a date with your very nice smelling guard."

Nicole snickered at the image of Shala being forced to walk hand and hand with the man standing outside the door. She had been going out of her way not to be near the man with a wild growing beard who had the scent of dead dog following him around. Any woman agreeing to a date with him was desperate. "Whatever the reason you agreed, you have my permission to fake being sick." Nicole wrinkled her nose and shook her head.

Shala smiled weakly glancing around the room. She locked eyes with the guard on the balcony. She smoothed out her uniform pants before sitting next to Nicole. "I hate that you're locked up here alone so I came to visit." She cut her eyes toward the balcony then back to Nicole.

Nicole had gotten accustomed to being watched all the time but she was guessing by Shala's reaction that now was a time for a private chat. "I'm actually very content inside my own mind tonight but if you like we could put a movie on." The movie would give them reason to be quiet and not speak and at the same time giving them the perfect cover to link minds.

"Sounds great. Here," Shala went to the shelves of stacked with movies, "I'll pick."

Nicole glanced back at the guard. He was still watching them but seemed more interested in the television being turned on for the first time since Nicole arrived then the actual actions of the women. Satisfied that the cover was working Nicole pushed her mind out to Shala's, *What's happening?*

Loch has given the go ahead for the attack.

"Attack?" Nicole whipped her head around to study Shala. Her mouth gaped trying to cover her blurted word.

"I've heard that's a good movie but how about this one?" Shala held up a movie with a forced smile.

"Fine with me." Nicole was a horrible actress but she leaned back into the couch trying to pretend she cared about whatever flick was about to play on the screen. *I thought there would be an agreed battle, not a secret attack. Isn't there some rules of engagement that everyone has to play by?*

Shala's eyes saddened as she took her spot next to Nicole, *Normally there would be but we know Loch doesn't play by the rules. He wants to burn the town down. Step one in the purifying stage.*

When? Nicole fought the rigidness of her body trying to seem like she was relaxing but rage was winning.

At midnight.

Everyone will be asleep! They won't have a chance of surviving, Nicole chewed on her lip to keep from screaming. *There are innocent children in that town.* Shala nodded but didn't say a word. Nicole knew she was thinking of the people from her past, maybe her best friend from childhood that might be killed. All Nicole could think of was Zeva's sweet smile when she handed her that beautiful flower. How could anyone disregard the life of a child without a thought?

Nicole....Nicole, Shala grabbed her hand. *You're going to give us away with your glowing eyes.*

Nicole hadn't realized that she had a death grip on the couch with both fists. She released her hold and closed her eyes to hide the fire burning in them, *Sorry.*

I'll go before we raise suspicion. You need to rest.

Wait. I need to know something before you go. Who all is on our side?

As in our side do you mean the dark one? Nicole cut her eyes at Shala. A smirk turned up her lips, *Okay, sorry. Just trying to ease the tension before you fry us both. Strangely enough the team you led in training today is on your side.*

Have you all been teaming up like that a lot?

For a few months.

Don't you think people will notice? Or more importantly that Loch will catch on?

Shala thought about the question for a moment, *I don't think anyone has noticed. Cliques form all the time without much talk. It's normal even in the warrior's world.*

Nicole rubbed her hand across her forehead. Her temples were beginning to pound. The moment she had been preparing for was just hours away and it wasn't going to play out on a battlefield like she thought. Innocent people could die if she didn't act fast.

"You look exhausted. I'll go so you can get some rest." Shala clicked the remote turning the screen black. "Oh, and by the way, great job today. That was the first time a team has walked off the field without a single injury."

Nicole smiled weakly. She managed to save a team of ten but just barely. How would she save thousands tonight? "You don't have to go. I won't be sleeping anytime soon. I think my adrenalin is still too high from today."

Shala stood and nodded toward the bed, "I can help you with that. Go get in bed."

Nicole's brows knitted together, "What are you going to do? Knock me out?"

"Kind of," she laughed. "I'm one of a hand full of warriors who can control emotions. I'll have you asleep in seconds."

Nicole's mind instantly jumped to Luke. He had that gift too though it always seemed to unleash her hormonal teenager side when he used it. But he never told her that the gift was rare.

"Hey, are you okay?"

"Yeah...sorry. I was just thinking that I know another warrior who can control emotions."

"Luke?" Shala smiled as Nicole nodded. "Yes, he and I are the only two that I know of. He always was better at it than me but I'm sure I can help you sleep." She turned back Nicole's covers and motioned for her to get in.

Nicole reluctantly obeyed. She really wanted to be left with her thoughts now that she knew what the night would bring but her body was tired. She laid her head back on the pillow. Shala took her hand and within seconds she felt the darkness of sleep tugging her under. But just before she slipped away she thought of the royal blue flower Zeva had given her. The creation of a precious child sat wilting away in a tower high above the fae town while the little girl was being tucked into her bed.

~**~**

A hard shove to Nicole's shoulder had her jumping from her bed. Three men stood in her moon-lit room staring at her. They were all dressed in their black uniforms but tonight they wore ski mask covering their faces. "Get dressed."

Nicole could feel the warriors' unique prints in her mind so she knew the one speaking to her was Kade. She nodded and started for her closet determined to seem like she knew nothing. "Is this some kind of special training?"

"We'll get our orders when we are assembled."

"What's that supposed to mean?" she snapped as she pulled her uniform from the closet.

"It means at this point you know as much as I do. My orders were to retrieve you." The sharpness of his voice didn't cover the unease Nicole could see in his eyes. He knew what was going on but the rest of the group wasn't part of the rebels so he had to remain the perfect solder, always following orders without questioning them.

Nicole closed the bathroom door behind her and quickly changed. When she returned to the group Kade held out a small, black cloth bag with a drawstring closure. "What's this for?"

"Orders were to blindfold you so put this on. You're not allowed to see where we are going until we are there."

Nicole bit on the inside of her cheek to keep from calling him an idiot. Instead she quickly braided her hair then allowed Kade to place the bag on her head and tie it closed. She had to take a few calming breaths to fight off the claustrophobic feeling that was trying to overtake her.

Soon she was sitting on the back of an ATV and listening to the shuffle of bodies around her. There was no chatter as everyone prepared to leave. Nicole imagined they were under orders to not speak around her to keep her in the dark but it didn't matter. She could feel everything she needed to tell her what she wanted to know. The group around her was the same one she had trained with. Everyone was there from Shala to Scarface. The real surprise was when Nicole stretched her senses farther out. The lights that represented warriors in her mind lit up like a night sky full of stars. There were hundreds of warriors being kept out of her sight and hearing range. A real army had been assembled and was going to war.

All too soon Nicole could feel the magical power of the gateway getting stronger as the ATV traveled through the woods. Just as she started to feel the power reaching its peak in her skin the caravan stopped. A tug came at her arm as she was guided off the machine to the ground. Kade removed her hood, "Wait here." He didn't give her a chance to answer before he strode away.

Nicole couldn't help but admire the magical gateway in the dark of night. The electric blue orbs that were beautiful and mysterious during the day were even more enchanting as they danced in the glow of moon light. She noticed a few eyes kept glancing in her direction then remembered how her own skin reacted to this ancient place. Being the only person with fae blood in a group of warriors had never made much of a noticeable difference until this moment. Not only did it make her glow but it filled her with a burning desire to open the gateway to return home as if the realm itself was her mother calling her home from a long day of play.

Unaware of her actions she found her feet taking her toward the spirit tree. She shook her head and took a step back grabbing onto the rack of the ATV to ground herself. The urge to cross over was so overwhelming. Unable to resist any longer she started to move forward again, this time crossing under the heavy, thick limbs of the willow to where she could see the thick trunk that held the gateway hidden inside. She wanted to enter so bad but why? The pull wasn't like this the first time she came here. Why would she want to open the gateway that would allow pain and destruction to enter the place she loved? Fighting past the craving to run to the tree she spun on her heels and strode away. The desire to run back was eating at her, making her struggle to keep moving, each step like an addict trying to walk away from her drug of choice cold turkey, but why? Then everything snapped into place. Warriors could control people, convince them to do things by playing with their minds and someone was playing with hers. She scanned the group of people. No one seemed to be noticing her as they talked among themselves. But then she saw it...the bright red glow of eyes. Loch's eyes.

Loch was suddenly standing toe to toe with Nicole. "You are very strong but I should have known that."

"I won't be your puppet."

"Yes you will only you will do it on your own. Open the gateway," he demanded.

This was why he brought her here. Only a fae could open the gateway and she was the only one with that magic blood running through her veins. She was Loch's only hope at getting to his war. "I will not."

"Have you forgotten our deal, my dear?" The sweetness of his voice didn't cover the danger dancing on the edge.

"Our deal was I would lead your warriors into battle not slaughter innocent people while they slept."

Lochs eyes glowed brightly and a sickening grin stretched his lips, "You will obey me." The burning desire to open the gateway was back only this time her body was on fire with invisible flames. If she didn't move toward the gateway she would die. Her mind screamed for her to go, to quench the need, to put out the fire that was torturing her. Without thought her feet moved forward taking her closer to the tree. Within seconds her hand was outstretched, reaching to touch the bark that would send the fire away. She needed the relief, she prayed for the burning to stop. She placed her hands on the warm bark. The blue electric glow that lived inside the willow danced all around her hands and along the crevices of the bark as the power pooled waiting for her command but instead she called wind to her and wrapped herself inside of it. It didn't completely chase away the craving but it did weaken it enough that she could think. "Luke," she whispered. She had to warn him. Dropping the shield she sent a wave of fire out from her causing the warriors who were following her to jump back outside the limbs. She didn't hesitate. Opening the gateway just slightly she reached with her mind to the fae kingdom and for Luke. Instantly she found him. *Luke, Loch's warriors are trying to break through the gateway. I don't know how long I can keep them away.* No response came. Confusion and worry seeped in. She had to close the gateway fast before Loch sent the warriors back in but she needed to know that Luke had heard her. He felt so close so why wasn't he answering? *Luke, can you hear me?* Desperately she tried again but she could hear the warriors breaking past the ring of fire. Time was up. She pulled her hand away from the tree so the small opening would go away but it stayed. "No, No, No." she patted around the tree trying to urge it to close but the hole was still there and getting bigger.

A dark laugh echoed around Nicole. She turned her back on the tree and stood preparing to defend the gateway at all cost. She had somehow opened a rift that wouldn't close but she wasn't going to stand by and let her mistake be the end of the Fae. "You're such a brave warrior," crooned Loch. "Now step aside and let destiny take its course."

A tingle in Nicole's mind caused her to step to the side. The tides were changing....good or bad she didn't know...but it was now. "You forget, I'm also a brave fairy." She swept her hand around her head and twisted in a complete circle sending a gust of wind out from her in all directions. Warriors tumbled to the ground but a few remained covering their eyes from the sand and leaves that pelted them but that was all Nicole needed. The gateway ripped to full size and blurs of fae and warriors came pouring out.

Chaos consumed the area in seconds. The stream from the gateway seemed endless but no one hesitated to jump right in. Swords clinked together, bodies rolled and tumbled, and the night sky lit up with balls of fire. Just as Nicole lunged forward a strong arm caught her around the waist, "You're safe?" Nicole spun in Luke's hold slinging her arms around his neck and not wasting a second to press her lips against his until she pulled away breathless. "I'll take that as a yes. Come on. I've got to get you out of here."

"Not a chance. I'm fighting. Not all of Loch's warriors are against us."

"That's good to hear," Slade had slipped up behind Nicole. She smile widely and hugged him tightly. "I'm so glad you're both alright."

"What? No kiss for me?" he teased.

Nicole rolled her eyes, "Come on, we've got a war to stop."

Chapter 24

Nicole darted out from under the willow and across the small stream temporally bolstered by the fact that she had stopped Loch from crossing into the fae realm. About a hundred yards out Loch was surrounded by warriors. They were creating a shield around him giving him room to retreat back toward the road as fire rained down on them from all directions. All attention was on him because, like her, everyone knew he was the one to take out. You chop off the head of the snake then the body lies there confused and rolling in circles until all life is gone. She locked eyes with him for only a moment but she could see the smile on his face. He was up to something—something big.

Nicole then remembered the army of troops that he had lagging well behind them. She whipped her powers out farther but it was too late. They were pouring out of the woods behind her. "Protect the gateway," she commanded. Instantly the rebel warriors joined with the warriors and fae from the kingdom and charged the fast moving army. "Shala, Kade, Rain, stay in front of that door."

The night sky was lit up by all the fires burning as the two sides collided. Wave after wave of Loch's warriors kept flowing into the area but they weren't getting close to the gateway. Nicole turned her cold eyes back onto Loch who was watching her closely as she quickly closed the distance between them, "Seems you made a few friends while you were at my home but it doesn't matter. They will fall and so will you." His whole body was instantly covered in flames. The warriors that surrounded him stumbled away from the scorching heat. The waves of power and flame rolled around him like the incoming tides of a stormy ocean. "And to think, you've sacrificed your father, your best friend and that whole pathetic country town that raised you all so you could pretend to be a hero." His voice roared with the lick of the flames, crackling and popping as it ate away her confidence.

"You have to survive for that to happen and I'm not going to let that happen." A scream turned her head just in time to see Brien driving a sword into the stomach of Shala. He yanked the blade from her in one smooth motion letting her fall to the ground at his feet. "Luke, stop him." Nicole commanded but before anyone could move a wave of power slung them through the air. Nicole slammed into the willow. The limbs of the tree were split by her body causing the tips of the broken stems to bleed blue magic. When her eyes cleared from the impact she crawled to Shala who was gasping for air. "Will your body heal this?" Shala nodded. Her brow was covered in sweat as the pain riddled her body. Nicole knew she had to move, to get back on her feet, but she couldn't leave Shala like this. She was an easy target while she tried to heal. "Hold still." Nicole placed her hand over the wound. The white flame she had used only once before poured from her fingertips covering the crimson stained area. Nicole could feel her own energy leaking out of her and into Shala as it healed.

"Stop it," Shala shouted slinging Nicole's hand away. "You have to fight. Don't use all your energy on me." She pushed herself up against the tree keeping a tight hold on her stomach, "I will heal. Now go end this."

Nicole jumped to her feet then gave Shala a quick nod. She couldn't help but see Sage's face staring back at her from the strong woman in front of her. Turning on her heels she darted from under the tree. She spotted Luke battling with Scarface. Each read the others move before blood could be drawn but everywhere else there were the casualties of war. Bodies were being trampled, wounded were looking for a safe place to hide and blood painted everything. The rocks, the ground, the dead leaves—all dripped crimson as the battle raged on.

"No," Nicole gasped. This is what she wanted to stop. The death, the hate, and the fear all poured out as everyone fought to survive. With each slash of silver a new trail of red appeared causing Nicole's heart to pound harder. With each familiar face she found lying on the ground her body became numb with anger...no, not anger—hate for Loch.

A guttural roar from Nicole's left spun her just as Scarface swung his sword down catching the sleeve of Nicole's black shirt leaving a long cut in her skin. She gave a quick glance past him to see Luke struggling to fight off three men but that's all she had time for before Brien swung again. Nicole darted to the side and slung a ball of fire at his face. He blocked it with the blade, "You and I have a score to settle."

Nicole spun around sending a gust of wind toward him. He staggered backwards but regained his footing. "I have bigger fish to fry so you'll have to take a number." Nicole aimed for his chest and fired. A large fire ball hit him in the face before Nicole's hit its target. Luke gave her a quick wink then ran back into the fighting. Just as he reached his first target he was lifted from the ground like he was being grabbed by an invisible hand and slung through the air. His body cut through a large pine tree then he fell with a lifeless thump to the ground.

Running with all her might she crossed the distance to Luke. She dropped to her knees beside him but before she could touch his sweat covered skin she was lifted into the air and slammed to the ground at Loch's feet. All the breath was knocked from her lungs but instead of collapsing she stood up facing the roaring inferno that was Loch. "You have failed," his voiced rumbled over the roar of the war. Nicole could feel the lights disappearing in her mind as warriors crossed the gateway into the fae realm.

Closing her eyes she shut everything else out. There was no war, no lifeless bodies littering the ground or screams of pain echoing in the night sky. In her mind there was only Loch. She could see him inside her head. He was the brightest of all the lights. He pulsed in red and blue as his power grew into something she had never felt before. Nicole took a deep breath refilling her battered lungs then began to pull her power to the surface of her body. This war would end here. Failing was not an option. Sage died to bring about change and she would have it.

Just as she had reached her body's limit she noticed the life around her offering strength too so she pulled from everywhere. Earth, water and even the great willow filled her soul with a power so deep she thought she might burst. When she opened her eyes the world was bathed in indigo flames. The hottest of all fires was hers to command as it danced across her skin from the soles of her feet to the tips of her hair. Her gaze locked with Lochs and she smirked. "Are you sure you want to play this game?"

His face twisted with hate as he lunged forward sending a red flame like the breath of a mighty dragon down on her. Nicole pressed forward sending blue flame into his with a thunderous crash. The world around them glowed bright as everything burned. With each push her fire gained a little more strength and shoved Loch's flame back but it also became hotter. The trees turned orange with embers and the rocks between them became lava as the battle raged on. *Nicole,* it was Slade inside her head, f*ighting fire with fire is only going to burn everyone. You have to be smarter.*

I'm way ahead of you. Watch for my signal then do what you do best."

Nicole trained her eyes on a large Elm tree behind Loch. It was already damaged and burning so she just had to wait until the right moment. Suddenly Loch slung a massive wave of power out from him knocking Nicole off her feet. Her head slammed into a rock leaving her dazed and stunned. She couldn't pull herself together before the blue flame she held slipped out of her grasp leaving her panting powerless on the ground. She reached up swiping at the blood that dripped down into her eye. Her hand blurred as she tried to gauge the amount of blood on her fingers.

Loch stood towering over her laughing darkly. "Game over, princess." He held his hand out inches away from her face and she watched it fill with a red orb. The orb would take her life if she couldn't pull herself together.

"Not yet." She slung wind like a saw blade but Loch dodged out of its way with ease. He smiled at her failed attempt to save her own life. "Now," Nicole shouted to

Slade as she sent another gust of wind into Loch hitting him hard and flinging him onto his back. He lay there just long enough to realize two things: his powers were gone and so was his life. The great flaming Elm crashed onto his powerless body with a sickening crunch. The shot Loch had thought was meant for him was actually the final cut that sent the tree falling.

The fighting stopped. Both warrior and fae stood confused. "Game over." Nicole whispered as she stood. "Enough of this grudge between you. Too many friends have lost their lives because of this pointless hate. My body bleeds fae and warrior blood because I am both. I cannot be divided or be loyal to only one race." She held her hands wide as she took in all the battered faces that surrounded her, "I am proud of my heritage and would never want to be only one because they are both great races. Today is your chance to have the life you really want—to be united again but this time as equals. I will take the crown and we will share the kingdom once more."

Silent stares met her. Nicole was preparing herself for the fighting to start again. The atmosphere was tense and heated as glances were exchanged but then Shala stepped forward tossing her sword to the ground with a loud clang. "About damn time we had a real leader." The crowd erupted with cheers as everyone tossed their weapons to the ground. Shevea, the warrior who commanded water during her training at the Fae Kingdom, pulled a large, blue orb from the stream and sent it high up in the air to rain down on the burning embers that remained from the battle.

Strong arms pulled Nicole tight, "You did it, love." Slade hugged her then kissed her cheek. She smiled up at him then her face turned somber. "Where's Luke?" She couldn't feel him. His light was gone from her mind. There was only an empty hole where he was moments ago. Pushing past Slade she ran to the spot where she a left him. Nothing. No sign of him at all. He was gone.

Chapter 25

Nicole dove through the gateway with Slade following close behind. Luke had to be in the fae realm. She wasn't ready to accept that he could be dead. She hadn't come this far just to lose him now. Digging her toes in she barreled forward. As soon as she passed the limbs of the willow she could see the orange glow below them. The town was burning.

"How many warriors are down there?" Slade yelled over the roar of wind as they rushed forward.

"I don't know for sure. I can't tell who's friend or foe but I can feel close to twenty warriors." Just as she reached out her powers searching for Luke a large arm caught her around the throat stopping her in her tracks and slamming her to the ground. They had reached the edge of the town and the smoke was thick and choking but it didn't stop Nicole from seeing who was holding her. "Brien, you can stop fighting. Loch is dead." Nicole fought for air as he tightened his grip on her neck. "I killed him," she wheezed.

"Good, then I can take his place." Brien laughed dryly as he drew his fist back. Just as he swung Slade knocked him into the dirt. Within seconds Scarface was back on his feet staring coldly at Slade, "Do you think just because you suck my powers away you'll win? I'm not helpless like your little princess without my warrior gifts." In the blink of an eye he tackled Slade and they both went rolling in a cloud of smoke and dust.

Nicole couldn't stand by and let Slade fight her battle. Brien had wanted this fight since the day they met and he was about to get it. As soon as the two men rolled apart Nicole slammed her fist into Brien's face sending him stumbling backwards and, to Nicole's surprise, a jolt of pain had her shaking her hand. "Damn it, Slade. Pull your power back."

"You're too close to him. If I pull my power back he will have—"

Brien slammed his fist into Nicole's face knocking her into the dirt. The world spun on its axis as she tried to keep conscious. She was back to being human and Brien knew it. As her vision danced she saw Slade and Brien grappling for the upper hand. They swung fists, exchanging blow after blow until they moved out of her sight. Black dots covered her eyes and she knew was about to pass out just as a figure moved across her vision. She prayed that it was Slade but the man reached down and grabbed a fist full of her curls and pulled her to her feet. "Ahhh..." he breathed into her ear. "I've been waiting for this day for so long." Brien spun her so she was facing him and pulled her tight against his body. "Maybe I'll keep you instead of killing you. I'll make you my whore."

The edge of Nicole's lips tilted up just slightly as memories flooded her mind. She had been in this exact position before on a deserted stretch of highway with a drug dealer who thought he had the upper hand. She didn't have powers that day either—just the know-how of a police officer and the seductive body of a woman. "Do you think you're man enough for me?" she laughed dryly in his face. "A weak warrior like you couldn't satisfy me. You're nothing without your power and you know it" she taunted him.

The anger building in Brien's eyes was dark as he yanked Nicole's head back exposing her neck. He stared down at her body greedily, "Shall I prove you wrong right now, sweetheart?" His breath was putrid as it rolled across Nicole's face.

He yanked at her black shirt popping the buttons off with one move. The shirt fell open exposing her thin, white t-shirt that was damp with sweat making it easy to see the lace material of her bra underneath. "Men," Nicole whispered smugly. Using the exact motion she had used that day on patrol she took advantage of Brien's distracted state and drove her elbow into his stomach then spun driving the same elbow into his nose with a sickening crunch.

"You forgot one thing." She spoke as she swung her foot planting it between his legs. "I'm twice as strong as you." She held out her hand in front of his face to be sure he saw the power pooling into her palms. "I'm not so easy to control." Without another thought she sent flames out of her hand in one powerful burst then she turned away. She didn't want to see. She knew he was dead just like he deserved but she couldn't stand to see any more death. She rushed over to find Slade who was pulling himself from the bottom of a ditch.

"So much for you needing my protection," Slade said dryly as he knocked the dirt from his shirt.

"No time for ego petting. There are houses on fire in the town."

Slade nodded and they ran toward the town. Nicole could feel warriors all around but it wasn't the pattern of fighting. There were no grunts or roars like people at war. The yells and screams were commands, "More water before it spreads. You, take these people to the castle until it's safe."

"Luke!" Nicole ran in the direction of his voice. She could see the silhouette of a man through the smoke but the pulling in her mind told her it was him. She blurred forward and without a seconds hesitation wrapped her arms around his neck hugging him tight. "Damn you, you could have let me know you were okay. I thought you were dead," she whispered into his chest.

"I saw you kill Loch at the same moment the warriors started crossing over. I knew you were safe so the town needed my help more." Luke kissed the top of her head. "The town needs you now too. Do you think you could make it rain?"

Nicole nodded. The flames were fading as the warriors and fae people ran about but she knew how to finish this off and put out the fire completely. Closing her eyes she focused on the sea. The smell of salt water filled her lungs and the damp spray of the waves danced in the air around her as the water awaited her command. She held her hands up and imagined a large ball of water pulling together on the surface then, with a whip of her hands, she pulled it up into the sky. Large droplets like a sudden summer shower rained down on the town causing the embers to hiss and smolder as they were extinguished.

As soon as the fires were dowsed Luke retrieved Teya and stood her in the center of the town for all to see. Nicole ripped the necklace from around the woman's neck so she would be fully aware of the world that now surrounded her. "Tell these people why you locked the gateway to the burial grounds."

At first Teya was confused and timid but as reality became clear her face hardened. "To keep control. You all are sheep who need a shepherd. Without it you would all fall to those warriors. Even now you prove your stupidity by following this...child."

"This child understands that these people need their powers. It's what makes them fae. You will unlock the gateway." Nicole demanded.

Teya cackled throwing back her head, "Such a fool. You cannot command me." She whipped her dark powers out lightning fast. People screamed and started to run but Nicole stood strong in front of the black power. "Such a brave little princess in the face of a queen. You can't open the gateway because you aren't the leader these people think you are."

"That's where you're wrong." Nicole leaned her head back taking in a deep breath, "I can feel all the gateways just as sure as I feel the wind on my cheeks." She smiled then called the blue flame to cover her body in a rush of power that forced Teya to cower back covering her face. "I just need the people to see the truth about you and what better way than to let you show them." Nicole turned to Luke, "I believe she would be a great maid, don't you?"

"I think you're right, my Queen." Luke smiled.

Slade stepped up just as Teya slung a web of black from her fingers. The dark ooze evaporated before it reached Nicole. "Kill me," she shrieked running at Nicole but two warriors pinned her to the ground.

"There will not be another death by my hand." Nicole turned her back on Teya as she was pulled away screaming. Nicole couldn't stand to have more blood on her hands but Teya had to be punished for the lives she took. Wiping her mind would be a much kinder way to eliminate the threat that Teya held.

<u>**Chapter 26**</u>

"Dad, do you really have to go back? You could stay here." Nicole begged.

James hugged his daughter tight kissing the top of her head, "I can't be living under your feet. Plus the guys back home would miss me."

"You can go back and visit them any time you want," Nicole pressed the issue. She didn't want him to leave the fae realm. Life was easy here for him. He didn't have to worry about anything other than enjoying himself so she couldn't understand why he would want to go back to his empty house. Kat was staying with Rhys so why wouldn't he stay with her?

"You can come visit me. Plus," He stepped back taking in his daughter's long white dress with a wide smile lighting his face. "You and Luke are about to be newlyweds so you will need your space."

"Space!" she laughed. "Dad there's a whole

kingdom here for you to get lost in." Music started to play outside drifting in to them. Nicole gave a nervous glance out the open window and took a deep breath. "I need you here," she whispered trying hard to keep the tears away.

James took her hand giving it a tender squeeze. "Don't worry, baby. I'll always be here for you." With a smile he helped her place her shimmering crown on her head then led her out of the castle doors. Rows and rows of people sat in white chairs with red ribbons laced into the back of each seat. The garden was mesmerizing and the air was soft with the beautiful fragrance of enchanted flowers but Nicole's eyes were drawn past the gorgeous scenery to the end of the path covered in red rose petals. Luke stood smiling at her in a white suit. The happiness radiating from him filled her heart to the point of bursting and chased away the nervous knot in her stomach. "Are you ready for this?" James whispered as they stood at the end of the path.

Nicole nodded not taking her eyes off of Luke, "He's all I've ever wanted."

"Marriage can be hard."

"I've fought a war and won so I think I can handle one warrior," Nicole whispered back as they started forward.

James chuckled under his breath, "I know you can handle it...I was worried about Luke."

Nicole fought to keep the giggle under control as they closed the distance, "Me too." James handed his daughter to her future husband then took his seat. She did a quick wave to Kat who was her glowing bride's maid then turned to smile up into Luke's face, "Did you miss me?" She whispered.

"More than you would believe. Slade's bachelor's

party was more of a punishment."

Nicole smiled as she glanced over Luke's shoulder to where Slade stood next to Rhys as Luke's best man. A few weeks ago she never would have dreamed Slade would agree to be part of their wedding but since the war was finished he seemed happy to just be close to her. She thought of the lump in her throat as she tried to tell Slade that she was marrying Luke.

"Why?"

"Because I love him. Why else?" Nicole had snipped at his question.

"You love me too." Slade smiled. He knew she wouldn't deny loving him so he had to try to change her mind or at the very least make damn sure she knew he wasn't going away silently.

"It's a different kind of love, Slade." Nicole stared down at the floor afraid to meet his stare. He was right. She did love him but it wasn't the love like she had for Luke. From the day she met Slade she knew he fit into her life and she didn't want to lose him but he had to accept that she was in love with Luke.

Slade lifted her chin with a finger forcing her eyes to his. "At least you admitted it finally." One side of his lips turned up showing a dimple but she could see the sadness he was trying to hide away. "If he makes you happy then I will concede."

Nicole felt her heart lift. She didn't realize until that moment she had been holding her breath as she waited for his approval. She let it out with a smile just in time for Slade to say, "But, I will be here if you change your mind. One slip by that warrior and you will be mine."

Nicole smiled at the memory. She was sure the smirk on Slade's face as he stood next to Rhys meant that he had made Luke's bachelor's party in the Earth realm a living hell.

Epilogue

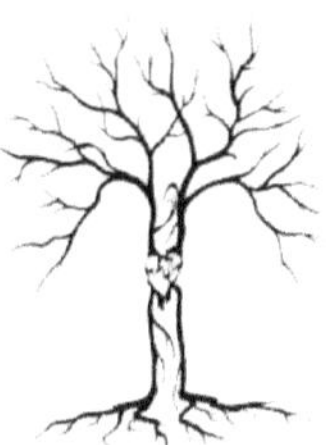

After a few weeks of trial and error Nicole finally opened the lost gateway to the fae burial grounds so power could be restored to generations to come. The magic of her dreams did not disappoint her as she physically stood in the graveyard for the first time. The brittle headstones, the wild vines, and the great willow tree towering in the center were all just as she remembered. She stepped out from under the limbs of the willow and took a deep breath filling her lungs with the salt kissed air from the sea. Walking along the path she found Titania's grave. She traced her grandmother's name in the rough stone and whispered, "Thank you for everything, grandmother. I never would have found my strength without you." Sitting in silence she listened to the birds singing in the trees. The magical feeling she felt in her dreams was just as strong now as she stood in the once hidden realm.

Following the smell of the sea she climbed the

green hill behind the resting ground and found herself standing on the edge of a cliff. The waves rolled in as the seagulls flew overhead on wide stretched wings. "I'd forgotten how beautiful the sea was." Titania spoke as she appeared beside Nicole. She was young again with long brown hair that matched Nicole's curls and skin so clear it was translucent. Nicole smiled, "So now what? Do you pass on to the next world?"

"Normally, that is how it would work but I've decided to stay a little longer."

Nicole's brows pressed together, "This has been your prison. What would make you want to stay a second longer?"

"To pass my powers on to a deserving child," she smiled widely then drifted away on the breeze.

"Nicole..." Luke spoke as he jogged up to her. He kissed her cheek then wrapped his hands around her waist pulling her back against his chest. "Everyone is here."

"Have they started the work?"

"Yes. We'll have this place back to the beautiful paradise it used to be soon."

"Wonderful." She smiled up at him kissing him gently. She let her eyes drift back out to the sea. "Do you think it's too late for Sage's soul to return to the spirit tree?" In the weeks since the war had ended Nicole had spent a lot of time thinking about Sage. She missed her so bad it hurt and she could see the same sadness in Slade's eyes. He may have made some bad choices in life but he truly loved his sister. They both agreed that when Nicole found a way to open the gateway to the sacred resting ground that they would move Sage's body there. Though they had never spoken the words she knew he hoped just as much as she did that her spirit and power would be reborn.

"I don't doubt anything anymore...especially when you're involved." He took her hand and kissed the ring on her finger then spun her in his arms, "Have faith. Everything will work out."

She giggled, "You're just happy because you tied me down with this ring." There was no doubt for Nicole that she belonged to him and he belonged to her. Life was wrong when they were apart. A piece of her heart had been missing all her life and Luke held that piece beating in his chest. Together they would rule the kingdom of warriors and fae and live out their immortal lives together.

"I'll be happy when your barefoot and—"

"Don't say it," she laughed, "There are a lot of things I want to take care of before we make that leap."

"Like what?"

"I don't know....maybe I'd like to go back to police work for a while."

"The Queen taking on a day job?" Luke snorted. "I don't see the General letting you slip that past him."

"We'll see," Nicole winked. "Come on, we've got work to do."

The following day the graveyard was filled with fae and warriors who came to say their final goodbyes to Sage. The whole kingdom knew Sage had made the ultimate sacrifice to ensure that Nicole became Queen of the Fae and Warriors. Nicole's heart ached as she ran her fingers along the engravings of Sage's coffin. The beauty of the intricate designs and the detail of the birds sitting on elaborate vines didn't ease her desire to have her friend back at her side. Nothing could ever replace the wonderful person who was enclosed inside and there would never be a way for Nicole to prove to Sage how much she loved her. At least she could give her a traditional burial in the sacred lands of her people—she deserved all of that and more.

"Are you okay?" Slade asked as he placed an arm around her shoulders and a hand on his sister's casket.

Nicole nodded taking a shaky breath before responding, "I should be asking you that question." With everything that had happened no one had been able to properly mourn the loss of Sage. Too much had happened so shortly after her death from the war, to Nicole taking the crown and then to her wedding only days after that. And they had the problem of finding and re-opening the portal so Sage could be in her final resting place. But now, as Slade and Nicole stood next to Sage's body, everything else seemed so insignificant.

Slade looked from the casket to Nicole, "I wish I would have apologized to her but I was too head-strong. I wasn't the best brother to her but she always forgave me." He gave a weak smile as he traced the lines of a dove in the wood. "I guess everyone has regrets when someone passes too soon."

Nicole nodded. Sage had passed too soon. "Well, we are going to give her a chance to be reborn in some form." She didn't say it aloud but she was praying that the chance hadn't already slipped past them as she fumbled around trying to unlock the gateway.

The sound of singing pulled Nicole from her thoughts. It started off very faint at first then, as the seconds ticked by, more voices joined in until all were singing. The melody was soft as a lullaby drifting on the wind.

Lay your head on the green moss

Rest your soul in the great tree

Though you're gone from us now

Forever it will not be

Time is no more

Bonds set free

Our love dances beside you

As you sleep beneath the tree

As the words were repeated, blurring into a spell like hum, the ground began to rumble. Just lightly at first then enough to cause Nicole to take a startled step back. Luke stepped to her side and took her hand while Slade took her other hand. "It's happening," Luke whispered with a smile.

Nicole was confused but when she glanced at Slade he was smiling too. A single tear rolled down his face as he watched his sister's casket slowly become wrapped in roots and gently tugged down into the earth. The ground closed over the hole as she watched in awe. What happened next was beyond anything Nicole had ever dreamed. The great willow lit up with a vibrant blue glow and Sage's bell like laughter played on the breeze all around them. Nicole could feel her friend's hands on her face and smell the scent of her perfume. She closed her eyes and took a deep breath as she placed her hands on her own cheeks.

Thank you, Sage's voice whispered in Nicole's mind. Before Nicole could speak she felt Sage drift away from her. She selfishly wanted to reach for her and beg Sage not to leave but instead she watched as Slade closed his eyes. Tears rolled down his face as he silently cried. She was sure he was saying farewell to his little sister because when he opened his eyes again the sadness was gone. A joy lit his face that Nicole had never seen in him before.

Slade pulled Nicole in a hug that surprised her, "Thank you." He whispered into her hair as he held her tight.

"No, it was all of us. I couldn't have done any of this without you," she turned to Luke and held his hands in hers. "Without all of us this would have never happened. Life is how it should be for everyone now." Nicole smiled when she looked down at the grave that cradled Sage. Bright yellow flowers, the same ones that had guided her path the day she found this magical place in her dreams, had covered the ground like a beautiful quilt tucking Sage in for a restful sleep. "Sleep well," Nicole whispered.

About the Author

Author Wenona Hulsey is an avid reader who writes in her spare time. She currently lives in Alabama where she grew up surrounded by family and friends who remain her greatest supporters and motivators. When she's not working you can find her enjoying the outdoors with sand between her toes, a fishing pole in her hand, or sleeping under the stars.

Connect with the Author

Website: http://www.wenonahulsey.com

Facebook:
http://www.facebook.com/wenonahulseyauthor

Twitter: @wenonahulsey

Other Works By The Author

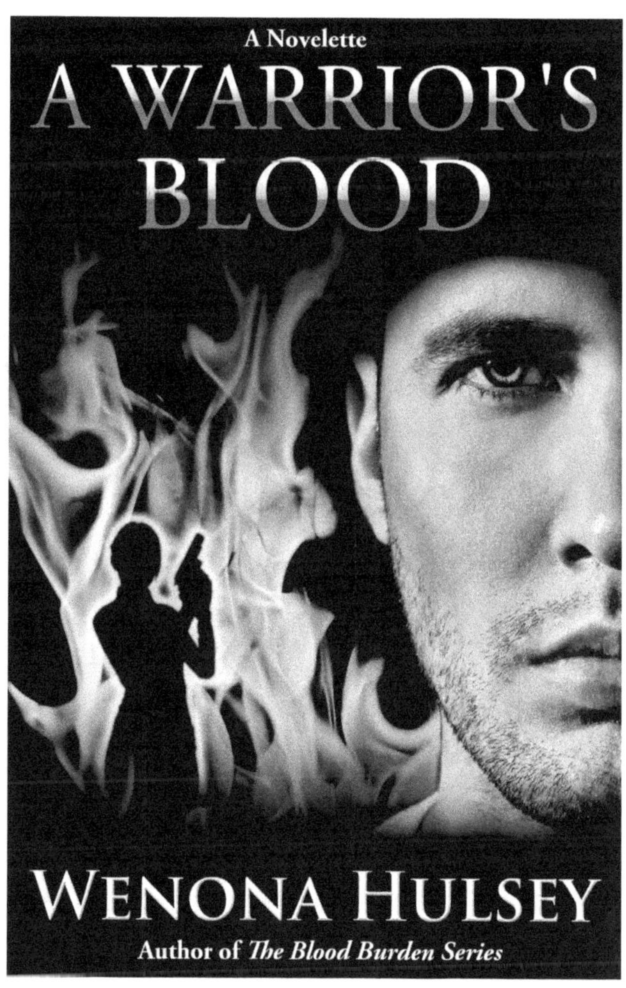
A Novelette
A WARRIOR'S
BLOOD
WENONA HULSEY
Author of The Blood Burden Series

BURDEN OF
BLOOD
Wenona Hulsey

www.ingramcontent.com/pod-product-compliance
Lightning Source LLC
LaVergne TN
LVHW020702110826
845149LV00012B/2067

* 9 7 8 0 9 8 5 7 3 0 7 1 0 *